"ABOUT THIS ... W

There was nothing she could do but wait and see what he had to say.

Sam floundered, but finally bit out, "Want to tell me why?"

"Why what?"

"Why do you want me?"

Amazingly enough, when she came to her feet Sam backed up. Silly man. "Why wouldn't any woman want you?"

"Ariel . . ."

She took two steps toward him. He took one more back, then planted his feet and refused to budge.

"You're smart and dedicated and heroic and . . ." She shrugged, inching closer, more determined than she'd ever been about anything in her life. "You really are so sexy."

She'd gotten close enough to touch him. Lifting one hand, she reached for his shoulder.

Enough was enough. She'd warned him, but he persisted in throwing her age in her face. With a smile of warning she gripped his neck with her free hand and went on tiptoe to reach his mouth.

from "My House, My Rules"

Books by Lori Foster

Too Much Temptation
Never Too Much
Unexpected
Say No to Joe?
The Secret Life of Bryan
When Bruce Met Cyn
Just a Hint—Clint
Jamie
Murphy's Law
Jude's Law
The Watson Brothers
Yule Be Mine
Give It Up

Anthologies
All Through the Night
I Brake for Bad Boys
Bad Boys on Board
I Love Bad Boys
Jingle Bell Rock
Bad Boys to Go
I'm Your Santa
A Very Merry Christmas
When Good Things Happen to Bad Boys
The Night Before Christmas
Star Quality
Perfect for the Beach
Bad Boys in Black Tie
Truth or Dare
Bad Boys of Summer
Delicious

LORI FOSTER

THE WATSON BROTHERS

ZEBRA BOOKS
KENSINGTON PUBLISHING CORP.
http://www.kensingtonbooks.com

ZEBRA BOOKS are published by

Kensington Publishing Corp.
119 West 40th Street
New York, NY 10018

All Kensington titles, imprints and distributed lines are available at
special quantity discounts for bulk purchases for sales promotion,
premiums, fund-raising, educational or institutional use.

Special book excerpts or customized printings can also be created
to fit specific needs. For details, write or phone the office of the
Kensington Sales Manager. Attn.: Sales Department. Kensington
Publishing Corp., 119 West 40th Street, New York, NY 10018.
Phone: 1-800-221-2647.

Zebra and the Z logo Reg. U.S. Pat. & TM Off.

First Brava Books Mass-Market Paperback Printing: September 2008
First Zebra Books Mass-Market Paperback Printing: May 2016
ISBN-13: 978-1-4201-3938-9
ISBN-10: 1-4201-3938-X

eISBN-13: 978-1-4201-3939-6
eISBN-10: 1-4201-3939-8

10 9 8 7 6 5 4 3

Printed in the United States of America

CONTENTS

My House, My Rules

Chapter One

He knew that damned aggravating little giggle anywhere. It was throaty and pure and never failed to set him on edge. He'd listened to it every Sunday for two long months when Pete, his baby brother, had been infatuated with her. That giddy laugh was often directed at him, instead of Pete, as it should have been.

With a heavy dose of dread and a visible grimace, Sam Watson slewed his head away from his whiskey and toward that annoying twitter. Shit. Sure enough, there sat Ariel Mathers. At the bar no less. And there were two men chatting her up.

What the hell was she doing in this dive? He glanced around but didn't see his brother anywhere. As to that, no one particular man appeared to be with her. Huh. The little twit was slumming.

So many times since first meeting her, Sam had wanted to put her over his knee. For leading his brother on at a time when he'd been vulnerable. For flirting with him, Sam, a man much too old for her. And especially for being so damned adorable, he almost couldn't stand it.

And now this.

His palm itched at the thought of it and his mind conjured the image of her over his knees, her tush bared. He started to sweat, knowing that if he had her in such a position, punishment would be the very last thing on his mind. She was so petite that her bottom would be small. And pale. And no doubt silky soft . . .

Shit, shit, shit.

His eyes burned as he stared at her slim back. She had her hair up with a few baby-fine blond curls kissing her nape. Little gold hoops in her earlobes glittered with the bar lights. The heart-shaped tush he'd so often fantasized over, now perched on a bar stool, was easily outlined beneath the clinging silk skirt of her dress.

At twenty-four she was twelve years too young for him. His mind understood that. His dick didn't care.

She paused in whatever nonsense she'd been uttering to the hapless fool beside her. As she started to look around, Sam twisted in his seat to face the window. *Do* not *let her see me,* he prayed. He waited, pretending to be drunk when he was more alert than he'd ever been in his life. He'd nursed one whiskey since coming into the bar, but he'd pretended drunkenness on his way in. Anyone who noticed him would assume he was there to top off an already inebriated night.

Fifteen seconds ticked by, then thirty, a minute—no one approached him. Sam relaxed, but kept his face averted, just in case. No way could he carry off his assignment tonight if Ariel got in the way.

He should have known better than to stare at her. People felt that sort of thing, just as he'd felt the big bruiser at the far booth watching him. He would have liked to order another drink, to call further attention to his feigned drunkenness. But with Ariel sitting there, it would be too risky.

Better to get this over with now, before he did something stupid. Like staring at her again.

Opening his wallet to show the bloated contents—two hundred dollars' worth—he pulled out a ten-dollar tip. He laid it on the table, stumbled to his feet and staggered out the door.

Once outside, he deliberately started across the street toward the abandoned, shadowed building where he would supposedly retrace his path home—and where his backup could clearly see him. Sam took his time, singing a crude bawdy tune about a woman from Nantucket, who according to the men, liked to suck it. It was a favorite limerick from his youth and he knew it by heart, but this time he missed some words, slurred a few others.

He pitched into the brick wall, laughed too loud, and started off again, only to trip over a garbage can, causing an awful racket. He gave a rank curse, stepped in something disgusting that he didn't want to identify, and dropped up against the side of a broken, collapsible fire escape.

Sam was fumbling for a more upright position when a meaty paw grabbed his upper arm, filling him with satisfaction. The perp had taken the bait.

"Give me your wallet."

Jolting around, Sam acted surprised, then spat in the big chap's face, "Fug off."

A ham-sized fist hit him in the side of the head and he saw stars for real. Jesus, he hadn't expected the fellow to get nasty so quick. Most of the thefts in the area—and there'd been plenty of late—had been done without any real personal damage.

Across a six-block area that covered three bars in Duluth, Indiana, more than twelve muggings had taken place in less than a month. It wasn't the best part of the city, so muggings weren't uncommon. But twelve? And all against men carrying substantial amounts of money. That smacked of premeditated, organized activity, and grabbed the attention of the police.

Sam twisted away, but was brought back around for another punch, this one in the gut. He bent double and almost puked.

Because he knew the guys would never let him live it down, he managed to keep his supper in his belly where it belonged. Just barely.

Where the hell were they anyway? Taking their own sweet time?

Before Sam could decide to take another punch or sneak in one of his own, a female banshee cry split the air, making his ears ring and his hair stand on end. Two seconds later his perp got hit from behind by a small tornado and the momentum drove him straight into Sam, against the side of the metal stairs. It felt like his damn ribs cracked.

Everyone started struggling at once and they went down in a heap, Sam on the bottom so that his head and back hit the hard, gravel-covered ground with jarring impact. The wind left his lungs in a whoosh.

While supine and wheezing, Sam got a good look at the familiar blond clinging tenaciously to his perp's hair with one hand while trying to use her purse like a club with the other. Sam couldn't quite tell if she was attempting to bludgeon him to death, or scream him into submission.

Wincing, the would-be robber reached back, caught her shoulder, and flipped her over his head. The next thing Sam knew, Ariel's behind was atop his face, her thighs pressed to his ears. Her dress had fluttered open and there was nothing more than a thin layer of silk keeping his nose from glory.

Damn it, why did things like this happen to him at all the wrong times?

He fought for air, breathed in her warm musk scent, and managed to shove her rump a few inches off his face. He was just in time to see the same meaty fist that had dazed him now headed straight toward her very tiny and very cute nose. Outrage exploded inside him.

He was supposed to be drunk, an easy mark.

He was undercover for the night.

But goddammit, no way could he let her get hurt.

Moving quicker than any drunk could, Sam caught the oversized fist in his own, gave one evil, toothy grin—which was somewhat smothered by Ariel's bottom cheeks—and twisted. Hard.

He heard crackling and then a loud pop.

The startled shock of pain on his target's face abruptly turned to one of sheer agony, accompanied by a guttural roar. Sam wanted to break his damn arm. Maybe a leg, too, just for good measure.

How dare he attempt to hit a woman?

Sam was still considering the possibility of doing more injury, when his backup finally charged onto the scene with a clichéd, "Hold it right there!"

Hold it? They had to be fucking kidding, right? He had a woman straddling his neck, an unethical bastard trying to strike her, and they wanted him to hold it?

He gave the fist another squeeze, then shoved, causing the man to shout and recoil on the ground in the fetal position, cradling his impaired wrist.

Sam didn't have a chance to move Ariel before Fuller Ruth, one of the cops working the undercover sting with him that night, caught her under her arms and lifted her up and away. Sam got a bird's eye view of her more womanly parts in silky panties while her high heels poked him in the abdomen, the thigh, and damn near his groin.

"You okay?" Fuller asked her, while still letting her dan-

gle in the air. Fuller was as big as the assailant, but unlike
the assailant he had a very fastidious nature. He kept his
brown hair well trimmed, his clothes wrinkle free, and he
was always clean-shaven. His blue eyes were so pale, they
reminded Sam of a Husky.

Ariel clutched at the front of her dress where it had gotten
torn. "Put me down, you oaf. I'm fine."

Fuller set her on her feet, but then had to grab for her
again when she turned in a rush, trying to get to Sam.

"Hey lady, easy now. Just come with me."

Fuller attempted to lead her away, but she turned on him,
too, thumping him on the chest. "Turn me loose! I have to
see if he's all right." In her fit, she forgot about the tear in her
dress and the whole right side drooped down, exposing the
top of one pale breast and a good bit of her beige, satin bra.

"Hey! Stop that." Fuller looked to be playing patty-cake
with her the way he swatted at her flying fists. "Damn it,
lady, you're spilling your purse. Just settle down. He'll be all
right. Let the officer check him."

The officer he meant was Isaac Star, half Native Ameri-
can, half junkyard dog. People considered Sam dark, but that
was until they saw him next to Isaac. Much leaner than
Fuller, Isaac had the blackest hair and eyes Sam had ever
seen. He was currently snapping handcuffs onto the giant,
who yelled and complained of a broken arm. The big sissy.

"Let—me—go."

It was a toss-up who made more noise, the perp or Ariel.
Since he was supposed to be a drunken slob, Sam couldn't
very well just sit up and explain to her that he was plenty
fine, other than the damage *she'd* inflicted. He did, however,
work his way to his elbows to mutter drunkenly, "Whass
goin' on?"

Isaac grinned at him, making himself look like a pleased

sultan. "I just saved your sorry ass, my man. This goon was set to roll you for your wallet."

Feigning confusion, Sam patted his chest, his front pants pockets, and finally his ass until he located the pocket holding the packed wallet. He wrested it out, held it up, and said, "S'that right? Thank you, of'ser. Got my paycheck inside."

Isaac was lean, but his size was deceptive. He was strong as an ox. He pulled the giant to his feet with no effort. "Not too smart. Stay put while I stick this guy in the car."

Not more than twelve yards away, two official police cars lit up the block with flashing red and green lights. To the spectators, it looked as though the cops had just happened onto the mugging—not like the whole thing had been planned.

As soon as Isaac had the giant out of hearing range, Sam pulled himself to his feet. For the benefit of onlookers, he stood there weaving, but he gave one barely perceptible nod to Fuller, who then let Ariel go with a shrug.

She launched herself at Sam, big tears glistening in her hazel eyes, her mouth open to blast him with questions, with mothering concern that he neither wanted nor needed.

Sam grabbed her close, squeezed her so tight she couldn't say a single word, and growled into her ear, "I'm *working*, goddammit, so you better have a good excuse for this stunt."

"Working?" she squeaked out.

Damn, it felt good to hold her so close. He shook his head and tried to ignore the way her belly pressed into his crotch, how her breasts flattened on his chest, and how her soft hair smelled so sweet.

Better than half the customers from the bar who were now out front to watch the proceedings. Sam had to keep his head, because he had to keep his cover. "That's right, and since you jumped into the middle of things, you damn well better play your part." That said, he slumped into her, forcing her to stagger under his considerable weight. She was five-two, maybe. He was six-three and outweighed her by damn near a hundred pounds.

The twit.

She grunted and nearly fell, until Fuller flattened a hand between her shoulder blades, pushing her upright again. Under normal circumstances, no cop worth his salt would let a drunk manhandle a woman. But these weren't normal circumstances, he wasn't really drunk, and his two buds had already figured out that she was an acquaintance.

Cops were notorious for trying to help each other get laid. If they thought Sam wanted her—which he did, but would never admit to anyone—they'd happily let him take advantage of the situation.

"Yer an angel," Sam said, leering at Ariel's breast with sincere interest. He'd seen more of her tonight than he had in the entire two months she'd been hanging around the family.

He rubbed his nose into her neck, making her lose her balance once more.

She tried to shove him away, but he snaked one hand down her back and grabbed her ass. *Oh, now that was nice. Real firm and plump. Not quite as generous as he liked, being he was a dedicated ass-man, but still nice.*

She gasped and struggled, but Sam didn't let go. Huh-uh. No way.

Fuller rolled his eyes. There was a limit to how much help he'd give in this particular campaign. "Here now." He dragged Ariel behind him, out of Sam's reach, then held Sam up with one outstretched arm. "You're drunk, man. I hope you weren't planning on driving home."

"Nope. Gonna walk."

"Well, you can thank the lady for being a good citizen and trying to help you."

Ariel stood there, her enormous eyes luminous in the dark night, her hair mussed in what Sam could only call a "just laid" way, and her makeup smudged. She smoothed her skirt with one hand while clutching her bodice with the other.

"That's quite all right, Officer. I did what anyone would have done under the circumstances." She looked at Sam with malice glinting in her golden eyes. "The poor drunken fool might have gotten killed otherwise."

Fuller choked on a laugh. "True, true. Now don't either of you take off, hear? I'll need statements from the both of you."

Ariel nodded. "I'll just wait over there." She pointed one manicured finger at the broken fire escape, then walked a wide berth around Sam on her way there. He noticed she was a bit wobbly on her heels, and concern struck him. Had she gotten hurt? She'd landed on his face pretty hard. He couldn't see her knees beneath the hem of her dress. Maybe she was bruised.

Playing it up, Fuller took Sam's arm and headed him in the same direction. Under his breath, he said, "Don't molest her, okay?"

"Don't be stupid."

"You're looking at her like she's the Christmas goose, but I need you to fill out paperwork, not be behind bars, resting on your lazy ass."

Sam grinned. "She won't be pressing any charges." Fuller pushed him to sit next to Ariel, causing her to scramble farther over on the rough metal step. "Ain't that right, sweetheart?"

She tucked her skirt in around her legs and smiled with false sweetness. "I won't press charges. But I might break your nose."

Fuller threw up his hands. "Young love."

He was gone too quick to hear Sam's rude snort. Ariel heard though, and she pursed her mouth, then slanted a look at Sam.

God, he hurt all over. All he needed was a boner to finish off the night.

Cautiously, every small movement enough to bring on a wince, Sam turned sideways and eased back against the brick wall, then sighed. "I'm too damn old for this shit."

Under her breath, but not under enough, Ariel muttered, "You're in your prime."

Sam stared at her, incredulous. "What was that?" Had she actually complimented him even while sending him dirty looks?

Without looking at him, she said, "Just because you're older than your brothers doesn't make you old, you know."

Sam grunted. Being six years older than Gil, his middle brother, and fourteen years older than Pete, he'd always felt old. Especially after their father had died three years ago with a heart attack.

Sam had tried to help his family cope as much as possible. He'd handled all the funeral arrangements for his mother, supported Gil in taking over the family business, and did his best to console Pete, who'd had the hardest time with the unexpected loss.

There was no denying that Pete had been a happy accident for their parents. Older and more settled when they had him, they'd doted on him in ways they hadn't been able to do with Sam and Gil. By far, Pete had been the closest with their dad.

"Does being on the downhill slide to forty make me old?"

"Hardly." Her voice was tinged with disgust. "And you're only thirty-six."

How the hell did she know that? "And here I thought all teenagers considered anyone over thirty ancient."

Apparently touchy about her age, she jerked around to face him. "Sam Watson, you know good and well I'm twenty-four, not a teenager. Wasn't that your big complaint about my friendship with Pete? That he was two years *younger* than me?"

Sam stared off toward the cruiser, wishing like hell they'd hurry up. He didn't want to sit this close to her. He didn't want to talk about her and Pete.

"Well?"

His biggest complaint? There'd been so many it was tough to pick a favorite. His baby brother *was* too young, far too immature, and entirely too unsettled to be getting serious about any one woman.

And Sam didn't exactly consider Ariel old enough either. She'd at least finished a trade school and was working as a beautician. But Pete had college to finish and he needed to do that without distractions of the female variety, which Sam knew were the very worst kind.

Worse than all that, though, Sam wanted her. It ate him up to think about Pete, who was a good kid but still a knuckle-head, fumbling around in the dark with her. Sam wouldn't fumble. Hell no. He knew exactly where he wanted to touch and taste her—not that he ever would. Nope.

He changed the subject. "What the hell are you doing in the bar by yourself?"

"None of your business."

"Yeah?" Just what he needed to clear his head: a fight with the little darling. He spoke in a growled whisper that nonetheless expressed his anger. "Well I'm making it my business seeing as you damn near blew my cover."

Her whisper was every bit as quiet and fierce as his. "How was I supposed to know you were working?"

Sam eyed her. She had a death grip on her torn dress, pulling the material so tight across her breasts that he could see the outline of her nipples. It was a hot, muggy night, but her nipples stood out like diamonds as if she were freezing. Shock maybe? Or had she liked him playing grab-ass with her?

He groaned.

Immediately concerned, she leaned over him, her small hand on his brow, her sweet breath in his face. "Ohmigod, Sam. How bad are you hurt? Do you need a doctor?"

Not unless a man could die of unfulfilled horniness. "Back off, Florence Nightingale. I'll live."

At his insulting tone, she puckered up and smacked his shoulder, making him groan again. Damn fickle woman.

She sat hunched over, her shoulders rounded, her forearms on her knees. Sam asked, "Did you see me in the bar?"

"That's a stupid question." She hugged herself, staring down at her feet. "When you're in a room, you're *in* it. Of course I saw you."

"What the hell is that supposed to mean?"

Giving him a sloe-eyed look, she said, "Even as a miserable drunk, you're sexy. I spotted you the second I stepped inside."

He tried to close his ears, doing his best to tune out her stirring comments. . . .

"Every woman in the bar noticed you."

"No shit?" Now that cheered him up. "I like that."

She went back to moping.

Sam looked around. The crowd had finally dispersed with only a few lingerers still standing around. Fuller was headed back toward him with a pen and pad, no doubt ready to take his fictitious statement just in case anyone should notice.

He stretched out his legs and bumped his big feet into her strappy, high-heeled sandals. She had her toenails painted pink. "So tell me this, Einstein. Have you ever seen me drunk before?"

A little wary, she said, "No."

"But you know I'm a cop, right?"

"Undercover. Lots of commendations. Heralded for being fearless by many, called careless by some, me included. But I know you're a good cop, Sam."

She surprised him with that string of mixed praise and censure, making him shake his head. "Yet you came charging into what could have been a very dangerous situation."

Her lips tightened; her shoulders hunched more. In a nearly imperceptible whisper, she grouched, "I thought you were getting hurt."

Sam's temper snapped. "And so you thought you, a pint-sized beautician, would dash to my rescue? Ha! Do you know what could have happened to you—what could have happened to me because you got in the way?" It took all he had not to shake her. "God save me from illogical women."

Ariel shot to her feet. "Shut up, Sam. Just . . . *shut up.*" Her entire puny body vibrated with anger, and she actually stomped one small foot. "You are so incredibly insufferable with all your endless harping."

Fuller said, "Now, now, kiddies. Let's play nice for the remaining spectators."

Pinning her with his gaze, Sam stared at her but spoke to the officer. "Ask me a question, Fuller."

"Right. Uh, how about . . ."

"Good enough. Here's my answer. Ariel, I want to know what the hell you were doing in that damn bar. And don't give me that garbage about it being none of my business because the second you blundered into things, it became my damn business."

Fuller pretended to write, nodding and smiling like a half-wit.

Mutinous, Ariel looked down her nose at him. "And if I don't tell you?"

A challenge. Sam almost rubbed his hands together. "If you don't," he said with a lot of glee, "I'll run your skinny little ass in."

Her mouth fell open and she sputtered. "For what, exactly?"

"Indecent exposure?" He dropped his gaze to her partially displayed breast so she wouldn't misunderstand.

She snatched the material higher. "Pig."

"Yeah, yeah. Real original insult for a cop. I've never heard that one before."

She turned away, came back, glared at him. "For your information, nosey, I was making sure."

His brows rose. "Making sure about what?"

As if awaiting the rest of her statement, Fuller looked at her. "Go on, Miss."

She huffed. "I was making sure there wasn't someone else who appealed to me."

Confused, Sam asked, "Someone other than Pete?"

Exasperation shown on her face. "Pete and I were never more than friends."

Sam's jaw locked. "That wasn't how Pete felt."

"And I'm responsible for that? I told him from the first day we met that I only wanted to be friends, and he agreed. When he finally admitted to me how he really felt, that he expected more, that's when I quit seeing him at all."

"And broke his damn fool heart in the process."

She swallowed. "I never meant to hurt him. He knows that. Besides, he's dating someone else now."

That was news to Sam. "He is?"

Nodding, Ariel explained, "That's why I was here. I waited until Pete found a girlfriend before . . ."

"Before?"

Her eyes narrowed. "Before making sure."

Sam threw up his hands. The woman just refused to make sense.

Fuller tilted his head. "I'm fascinated, really."

Sam turned to Fuller with a growl. "Officer, haven't you got enough there?"

"You never let me have any fun."

"Your idea of fun must be a toothache."

Ariel looked ready to spit. "If I'm such a pain—"

"You are that."

"Then I'll be on my way." Shoulders squared, her chin lifted in regal disdain, she started around Fuller.

Sam crossed his arms. "Just where the hell do you think you're going now?"

"Back into the bar."

"Like that?" He nodded at her torn dress.

"Oh." She stared down in dismay at the long rip. "Well, I suppose that might not be a good idea."

"But jumping into the middle of a brawl is?"

Her neck stiffened. "Brawl?" One slim brow arched high. "All I saw was you getting your butt kicked."

Insulted, Sam snorted, but not with much conviction this time. Surely, she didn't believe such an asinine thing. He'd been undercover, damn it, unable to fight back without messing up his cover.

But she looked serious, so he said, "You believed that act? Hey, I must be pretty good."

"Why wouldn't I believe it? I thought you were drunk."

She *was* serious. It was Sam's turn to shoot to his feet. Leaning forward in an aggressive stance, he poked a thumb into his chest. "Even drunk, I could take that guy. With one arm broken, I could flatten him. He was nothing."

She looked at her nails. "Uh-huh."

At the boiling point, Sam started to reach for her, and

Isaac hurried over to them. "Are we putting on a damn show? There's enough melodrama over here to blow the whole damn thing."

Ariel again turned away. "I'll get on my way then."

Through his teeth, Sam said, "Grab her," and Isaac automatically obeyed, catching her arm and swinging her back around.

She almost toppled off her high sandals and retaliated by clouting Isaac with that lethal purse.

"There's another offense," Sam drawled while Isaac ducked. "Assaulting an officer."

Very slowly, she lifted her head to fry him with a seething glare, and if looks could kill, he'd have been writhing on the ground at her feet.

Sam grinned. From the first day he'd met her he knew she had a temper beneath all that good-girl, innocent blond pretense. "Before you hurt yourself or someone else, you can give me a ride home."

Like a doe caught in the headlights, she went utterly still. "Why me?"

Sam sent a telling look at Isaac's hand still wrapped around her arm. "You can let her go now."

"Oops. Sorry." He grinned, unrepentant. "I think I'll take our thug on in."

"Yeah," Fuller said, "as long as you have a ride, I'll take off, too. I've got everything I need." He winked at Sam.

"Hey," Sam said, "I don't suppose you guys would—"

Fuller raised a hand. "Consider it done. But you owe us, buddy boy."

"Yeah, I assumed as much." He watched the two men saunter away, Fuller speaking into his radio, Isaac assuring the remaining people that the fanfare was over.

The second they were in their cars, Sam again leaned on

the brick wall. He realized his shoulder hurt, turned, and found out his shoulder blades were tender too. And his head . . . He didn't even want to know about his damn head. Ariel's attack had put him down hard. His brains were probably scrambled.

Truth was, he felt like he'd been run over by a Mack truck and standing on his own steam wasn't all that comfortable.

Ariel looked him over, forcing him to suck it up. "What are they going to do for you that you'll owe them?"

"Paperwork." Then, just to taunt her because he felt physically miserable and she looked as bubbly as ever, he added, "That, and they figure I might get laid if they leave me alone with you. If I did, I'll really owe them."

Rather than look offended, she blinked twice. "Laid by who?"

"You, sweets. They're assuming all your furious bluster has to do with sexual sparks, rather than honest dislike."

After a long, thoughtful moment empty of protests, Ariel nodded. "My car is this way. Should I pretend to help you or is the coast clear?"

After having her fanny on his face, he didn't want her hands anywhere near him. He had enough fodder for three wet dreams as it was. "I'll stumble my way there under my own steam, thank you very much."

Weaving this way and that, Sam trailed behind her, suspicious over her docile agreement to drive him home, and her lack of anger over his friend's crude assumptions. He was also aware of the sway in her hips and that delectable bottom he'd already manhandled.

Hell, half the things he wanted to do to that bottom were probably illegal in some states.

He forced himself to look away. He had to stop drooling over her, for crying out loud. The woman was a complete and total pain the ass, only a year or two older than a teeny-bopper, *and* his baby brother's ex-girlfriend. He had to remember all that.

Sam was none too happy when she took the liberty of opening the door for him. Worse, the car was a beat-up, banana-yellow Pinto. "I won't fit," he complained, even as he folded himself painfully inside the cramped front seat.

She slammed the door after him, went around to the driver's side and got in. After she had the key in the ignition and the engine snarled and screamed to life, she leaned back in her seat with a sigh.

Sam waited for her to put the car in gear and when she didn't, he asked, "What's wrong? Are you hurt?" She'd told Fuller she wasn't, but she was stubborn enough to lie about it. He should have checked for himself.

That thought brought a shudder of excitement. Not a good idea. Not at all.

She stared up at the ceiling. "I can't drive and hold my dress up too."

"Ah." Forcing nonchalance, Sam shrugged and said, "Hey, I've seen every female part there is, hooters included, so unless you're unique in some mind-boggling way, it's no big deal. Don't worry about it."

Appearing stunned by such an outpouring of nonsense, she said, "Fine," and dropped the torn material. It fell completely below her breast.

Oh Lord. His nonchalance obliterated, Sam swallowed hard, looked away from her bra and how her nipple poked against the silky material. He did what he could to distract himself. He tried thinking about the job he'd just done, the repeat performance he had to put in tomorrow. He considered all the endless paperwork. He even tried thinking about Pete. It didn't help.

His aching body and splitting head should have been

enough to keep him off track, but there was no suppressing those pesky sexual urges. Whenever Ariel was around, they got a stranglehold on his libido.

"Let's play some music." Sam fiddled with the radio while she pulled off the side street and into the denser flow of traffic.

"Sure. Help yourself." Irony filled her tone since he'd already located an oldie station and turned up the volume to listen to, "Ohhhh, love to love you baby . . ."

Speaking loud to be heard over Donna Summer, she asked, "Mind if I come up for a minute when we get to your place?"

The way she said that, so casually, put Sam on edge. "Why?"

"Don't look so suspicious. I just thought I could find some way to fasten my dress, maybe a safety-pin or something. I know you have a house, but I live in an apartment and who knows how many people will be around when I pull up. I don't want to flash the neighbors and I don't want to start a lot of gossip."

He didn't want her flashing the neighbors either. As long as he got her in and out of his place in a hurry, it'd be okay. He could hold off that long. Maybe. "I have a sewing kit you can use."

"You're so gracious."

"Graciousness is hard to find when my head is splitting, thanks to your tackle."

She stopped at a red light and turned toward him. "And here I thought you were so macho. Let me have a look."

Without his permission she caught his left ear and turned his head. "Ouch," she said in sympathy. "It looks like you're bleeding a little."

Reaching to the back of his head, Sam located a lump, and a spot of blood. "Damn." No wonder his head hurt so much. "It's fine," he lied. When she started to protest, he said, "Green light. Let's go."

They were cruising right along, going about forty miles an hour when she suddenly said, "They were right, you know."

He'd been so busy trying to ignore her warm, softly scented body beside him, her words caused him to start. "Who's that?"

"The other officers."

"Fuller and Isaac?"

"I suppose. You didn't introduce me so I don't know their names."

She made it an accusation, setting his teeth on edge. "It was hardly a social affair, if you'll recall."

Silence reigned until he said, "All right, I give. What were they right about?"

Without him realizing it, they'd left the main road and were now in the suburbs, close to his moderate house.

She turned down his tree-lined lane. "You getting laid. That is"—she hesitated, peeked a look at him, then forged on— "if you want to."

Several things happened to Sam at once. His stomach bottomed out, his eyes widened, and his dick gave a proud salute.

Well hell. What was she up to now?

Chapter Two

The silence was enough to squash her. Ariel didn't want to look at Sam again, not when her first glimpse had shown him to be anything but interested. Horrified, yes. Shocked, yes. But not interested.

Unfortunately, whenever he was around, she couldn't seem to *not* look at him. From the day she'd met him, he fascinated her.

It wasn't just his awesome physique that drew her, though that was pretty eye-catching. He was tall, muscular, mean, and lean. He had the attitude of a man in charge, spoke as if he expected to be obeyed, and had confidence down to a fine art.

And it wasn't just his incredible, look-into-your-soul blue eyes, so different from his brothers'. Sam had inherited his mother's eyes, while both Gil and Pete looked more like their father with chocolate brown eyes. They all had inky black hair though, and thick lashes. They were all handsome—just in different ways. Gil was sophisticated, suave. Pete was fun-loving and playful.

Sam was all basic male, rough-edged and rugged and keenly capable of handling any lethal situation.

He was also a pretty nice guy, though his gruff manner and burdening responsibility often hid that fact. Best of all, he was a bona fide hero through and through. When his family needed him, he stepped up to the plate without complaints. On the job, he did what had to be done to make things right. His brothers looked up to him, his mother depended on him, and his fellow officers respected him. He was like Superman only real. And sexier.

Finally, with an uncertain laugh, Sam said, "Come again?"

Ariel cleared her throat. His tone of disbelief didn't exactly bode well, but she'd made up her mind. "You know when I said I went to the bar to be sure?"

"Yeah, right. Sure there wasn't anyone else—whatever the hell that means."

"It means I wanted to be sure there wasn't anyone else who appealed to me. But there isn't. That's the third bar I've been in this week."

A thundercloud would appear passive next to his darkening expression. "You've been hanging out in bars?" His teeth actually clenched, fascinating her. "Do you have any idea what's been happening around the area bars lately?"

She hadn't, but judging by what he'd done tonight, she assumed some muggings were taking place. Because she didn't want a lecture, she just shrugged.

His eyes turned red.

To pacify him, she pointed out her other visits. "I've also been to two nightclubs, the grocery, the park, and three concerts. Sorry, but there is no one else who appeals to me." She drew a long breath and admitted the stark truth. "You're the only one."

At that moment, Sam looked to be choking on murderous intent.

"Say something."

He didn't, he just sat there, steam coming off his head while his face colored and his fists curled. Ariel honestly didn't know if he fought the urge to take her or strangle her. Not that she was afraid of him. Never.

Sam protected people—he didn't abuse them.

Because she and Pete had stopped by his house once, she knew where he lived. She pulled into the blacktop drive and turned off the car. She didn't at first look at him, not when it felt like he was frying her with his gaze. When she finally worked up the nerve, she turned to him.

"Well?"

Through his teeth, he snarled, "Inside."

Oh good. At least he wasn't throwing her off his property already. She considered his grudging command a positive step. Slipping out of her car, she managed to hold her dress up, drop her keys into her purse, and close the door. Sam made no gentlemanly moves toward her, but then, he was badly beaten up.

She loved his old two-story house. It had a poured front porch complete with an overhang and wooden swing. The shrubbery was original and thick and outdated, but it made a nice contrast against the red brick. Enormous oaks lined the street and during the day, squirrels scurried everywhere.

At his father's death, he'd inherited a large sum of money. She didn't doubt that Sam could have afforded a posh, upscale home in an exclusive neighborhood. She was glad he hadn't moved.

When she reached Sam's side, he took her arm in an implacable grip and started her in a trot toward the front door. Some elderly neighbors in the house to the right hailed him, forcing him to stop.

"Evening Sam."

Sam groaned, slowly turned and waved at the two people

visible by their front porch light. "Booth, Hesper. What are you doing up this late?"

Ariel giggled. It was only eleven thirty.

"The dog had business to take care of. Her old bladder just gives her fits."

Ariel's giggle got caught in her throat. She looked in the yard and saw the most hideous creature she'd ever clapped eyes on. An obese bulldog squatted by a bush, turned to sniff, and then lumbered back to her owners, who praised her as if she'd created gold.

"Who's your lady-friend?" Hesper asked with a nosiness reserved for the old or very young.

Sam leaned in close to Ariel's ear. His hot breath teased her when he growled, "Stay here." Then he moved away to the neighbor's porch railing. They spoke quietly so Ariel couldn't hear what was said.

Seconds later, both elders looked over at her with awe and horror. Ariel frowned. Just what had Sam told them? He returned, took her arm again and said, "Let's go."

"What did you say to them, Sam Watson?"

"Keep your voice down. This is a quiet neighborhood."

His walkway could use a good sweeping, she decided as her toes kicked through scattered leaves. Even the porch was littered with leaves and acorns.

As if he knew her thoughts, he said, "A recent storm blew crap everywhere. I'll get to it when I can." Using a key, he unlocked the front door and held it open for her.

She stepped into the inky darkness, then felt his hands close gently but firmly on her upper arms. With bated breath, she waited for a kiss, but got bodily moved out of his way instead, so he could turn off an alarm. "Wait here."

Left alone, Ariel tried to get her eyes to adjust to the darkness. When the lights blinked on, she squinted. "Why don't you have a wall switch by the front door?"

"The light's out and I haven't had a chance to change it yet. I've been working overtime on the bar muggings. Let's go to the kitchen. I have a feeling it might be the safest room."

"Why?" She trailed behind him.

He gave her a long look. "No place to get laid."

Refusing to let him derail her, Ariel grinned at his sarcastic wit. "There's always the countertop. Or the table. Maybe even the floor—"

His rough palm covered her mouth. "That's enough out of you." She mumbled against his palm and he lifted his hand. "What?"

"Tell me what you said to your neighbors."

His mouth curved in a sinful smile. "Sure. I told them you were a prostitute who'd ratted out her pimp, and I had to keep you close so he didn't kill you."

"Oh." He expected her to be insulted, so she asked instead, "Have you ever been with a prostitute?"

"No." He didn't bother to hide his indignation at all "Now behave for a minute so I can think."

While his back was turned, Ariel pulled out a chair, sat down and lifted her skirt to examine her scraped, bruised knees. They hurt, but Sam was in much worse shape than she so she tried not to complain.

"Now about this . . . what the hell?" He'd turned with a scowl on his face, only to pull up with a different type of anger. "You said you weren't hurt," he accused.

"Just a little. Nothing serious."

Muttering under his breath, Sam whipped off several paper towels, folded them, and doused them beneath cold water. He came to her and knelt down. "Hold still."

Despite his order, she jumped when the icy towel touched her raw scrapes. "Sorry."

"Damn." He dabbed at both knees, removing small bits of dried blood, gravel, and dirt.

Before Ariel could figure out what he intended, he flipped her skirt up higher. "Sam!"

When she tried to shove her skirt back down, he caught both her hands in one of his and held them up and against her breasts, almost shoving her out of her chair. "Shush. I want to see if you're hurt anywhere else."

She had to brace her feet apart to keep from toppling over. "This is outrageous!"

Blue eyes lit like the hottest flame, he glanced up at her. "You sitting on my face was outrageous. This is just concern."

Ariel gulped.

"Now be quiet."

Mortified, her mouth snapped shut. She *had* sat on his face. At the time, she'd been so worried about protecting him she hadn't paid much attention.

He found one large bluish bruise on her thigh. "How'd this happen?"

Ariel peered down at the mark. With both their heads bent, her blond curls brushed up against his silky black hair. "I don't know. Maybe when I jumped on that guy's back and we all crashed into the stairs."

"Anything else?"

Since he was on his knees in front of her, more caring than insulting, she showed him her elbow. It was raw and stung every time she flexed her arm. His mouth flattened in displeasure. "I ought to turn you over my knee for that damn stunt. Look at you. You're a mess."

So much for caring.

"Let me get some ice; then I'll fetch my first aid kit."

"I don't need you to doctor me."

He had his back to her, digging in his freezer. "Tough.

My house, my rules, so I'm doing it anyway." Within minutes, he had ice crushed inside a damp dish towel and he pressed the freezing compress to her thigh. Ariel almost came out of her seat. The cold prickled so badly she tried to shove it away.

"Leave it," he ordered, keeping it firmly in place until she subsided. He took her hand and put it over the compress so that she had to hold it. His commanding gaze bore into hers. "I want to see it there when I get back, you understand?"

"Yes sir."

His eyes narrowed. "A show of respect from you at this late date is beyond suspect, so stow it." Then softly, with exasperation, "I'll be right back. Sit tight."

Ariel leaned out of her seat to watch him trot from the kitchen, into the hall, and up the short flight of stairs to his bathroom. Once he was out of sight, she lifted the ice away and fell back in her chair.

None of this was what she'd expected. Not that she'd known what to expect, but worry over a few paltry bruises . . . She heard him returning and quickly replaced the ice pack, wincing at the bitter cold.

He eyed her when he reentered, his expression stern. "I hope you learned a few things tonight."

"Yeah, that you're surly when you're hurt and that you don't like women coming on to you."

He moistened a gauze pad with antiseptic and again knelt in front of her. "Wrong. I'm not all that hurt and I love when women come on to me. I just don't like little girls flirting when they don't know what they're getting into."

Seething, Ariel said, "If you don't stop accusing me of being a child, I'm going to—" She screeched when the antiseptic hit her scrapes, burning like a brand. Her legs stiffened and her hands gripped the sides of her seat.

"Sorry." For once, his voice was gentle, caring. Sam leaned forward and blew his warm breath over her knees.

A new ache filled her, one of overwhelming sexual hunger. She'd wanted him since the first time she saw him. She remembered that moment in vivid detail. Pete had taken her with him to his family's regular Sunday get-together. A storm had knocked a thick elm over in his middle brother's backyard, damaging a fence. Sam was there, shirtless, sweaty, tanned, and so sexy she'd stood dumbfounded for several moments while he swung an ax, cutting up the fallen tree alongside his brother, Gil. The muscles in his strong back had flexed with each movement. His biceps bunched and knotted. His hands were big, lean, his strength undeniable.

"Ariel? You didn't faint on me, did you?"

Taking a breath, she opened her eyes and locked gazes with him. He had one hand on her thigh, holding the ice pack there, the other gently touching her chin. The breath sighed out of her. "I want you so much."

He lurched back as if she'd kicked him, jerking to his feet in a rush. "You look besotted, damn it. Knock it off."

She couldn't reply, could only stare at him with all the love and hunger she felt plain in her eyes. *Please,* she silently pleaded, and got a wary frown from him in return.

"Here's a new rule. You have to be quiet while I finish this up. Understand?"

She stared.

"Answer me, damn it."

"Yes, all right."

He moved back to her cautiously. "Give me your elbow."

This time she bit her lip when he swabbed the remaining cuts and scrapes. She didn't want to be a wimp in front of him. She didn't want him to feel sorry for her.

He finished off by applying ointment and some bandages. Then he backed up. "All done. Now."

"Now what?"

"About this . . . wanting me business."

There was nothing she could do but wait and see what he had to say.

Sam floundered, but finally bit out, "Wanna tell me why?"

"Why what?"

"Why do you want *me?*"

Amazingly enough, when she came to her feet Sam backed up. Silly man. "Why wouldn't any woman want you?"

"Ariel . . ."

She took two steps toward him. He took one more back, then planted his feet and refused to budge.

"You're smart and dedicated and heroic and . . ." She shrugged, inching closer, more determined than she'd ever been about anything in her life. "You really are so damned sexy."

She'd gotten close enough to touch him. Lifting one hand, she reached for his shoulder.

He snagged her wrist, his warm, strong fingers wrapping around the delicate bones. "Don't curse. You're too young for that."

Enough was enough. She'd warned him, but he persisted in throwing her age in her face. With a smile of warning, she grabbed his neck with her free hand and went on tiptoe to reach his mouth.

"Ariel—" He tried to lean back, to turn his face away. But she'd backed him to the counter and there wasn't much room for him to maneuver. She knew he didn't want to hurt her and that gave her an advantage in their wrestling match.

Her mouth landed on his throat first and she licked the salty taste of his skin, groaned, and bit his chin.

"Goddammit . . ." He sounded very uncertain, pained, and he grabbed her other wrist. "You little—"

Her mouth smashed up against his. They both froze, but only for a second. Slowly, deliciously, with a purr of excitement, Ariel licked his lips. Her heart threatened to break through her ribs, it drummed so madly.

He brought her arms behind her back, but that only pressed her breasts to his chest, and since her dress hung open, she could feel his heartbeat, as wild as hers. She caught his bottom lip in her teeth and nibbled, all the while breathing hard with excitement, expectation.

And then he exploded. From one second to the next he'd been held immobile by her brazenness. But it wasn't in Sam's nature to be docile, to let anyone else take the lead.

Ariel found herself plastered against him from groin to breasts while his mouth opened over hers in ravenous demand. His tongue thrust in and he groaned low in his throat, the vibrating sound thrilling her.

He slanted his head and drew her even closer, still holding her hands behind her, straining her shoulders, almost lifting her off her feet. Her head was pressed back, leaving her mouth open and vulnerable to his. His whiskers scratched her chin, his erection pressed into her soft belly, and he tasted so good she didn't ever want him to stop.

But he did. She was limp in his arms, merely accepting the onslaught of his kiss, unable to do anything else with the controlling way he held her. With a visible effort, he raised his head a mere inch and stared down at her. An incandescent hunger burned so brightly in his eyes, it almost frightened her.

He looked at her mouth, breathed hard for a moment, then growled low in warning, "You shouldn't push me, little girl."

The way he said that, it wasn't an insult so much as an

endearment. Getting enough breath to speak wasn't easy. "You
. . . You kept ignoring me."

His hands tightened on her wrists, making her wince. He
immediately loosened his hold, but didn't release her. Every
muscle in his big body was bunched. His eyes were bright,
his cheekbones flushed, his mouth hard. "You were my baby
brother's girlfriend."

"No, just a friend," she gently reminded him.

"He still cares about you."

"Not anymore. He's seeing someone else."

"You're only twenty-four-fucking-years old."

He sounded desperate, giving her hope. "I'm a grown
woman, Sam. I know what I want. And I want you."

His head dropped forward, almost touching her shoulder.
She could feel his angry, hot breath against her throat, sending chills down her spine, building her sexual excitement to
a fever pitch.

Necessary arguments crowded her brain. She had to convince him. "Sam? Look at it this way. It's only sex, and
you're known for wanting sex."

His head jerked up. "What the hell does that mean?"

"You have a reputation."

"Several actually." His eyes narrowed. "Which reputation
are we talking about?"

She wanted to shrug, to act cavalier. It was well beyond
her. "For mind-blowing sex."

For three heartbeats he didn't move; then he gave a rough
guffaw. "I hate to break it to you babe, but I only give run-of-
the-mill sex."

"That's not what I heard."

"No? Who you been talking to? Besides me?"

That made her smile. Sam *was* prone to bragging. She'd
heard him once when she'd come to visit Pete. He and his
two brothers were in the backyard and didn't hear her ap-

proach. Sam and Gil had been teasing Pete, accusing him of being a virgin, which Pete vehemently denied with a red face. Gil offered advice, but Sam told Pete he should come to a pro if he wanted to learn how to make a lady squeal in pleasure.

The graphic details she'd heard then had held her immobile in fascination. Even Gil and Pete had looked awed.

When Pete mentioned Ariel, Sam had froze up and changed the subject.

"Your family goes on and on about what a lady's man you are."

"Yeah, well they have to sing my praises because they're family. Ask any lady, and she'll tell you I'm a pig."

"A cop."

"No, I meant in bed."

Ariel shook her head. "I'm not buying it, Sam. Especially not after that kiss." Her voice went husky. "That almost did it for me right there."

"Don't." He tightened up again, and then, slowly, a new light entered his eyes, one of challenge and determination. "So you want to get laid by the best, is that it?"

A trick question, if ever she heard one. "I want you."

He looked down at her mouth. "I think you need to learn a few lessons."

A shiver of alarm slipped up her spine. "A lesson?"

"On why you shouldn't taunt bad-ass cops with ugly attitudes."

"You do not have an ugly attitude." She couldn't really deny the bad-ass part. But she hated for him to downplay all he did for the community and his family. "You're a good man—"

"And you assume I'm a good man in bed. Is that it? You want to use me to get your jollies?"

She started to say she wouldn't care if he wasn't good, but

it'd be a lie. She wanted him, all of him, in every way, and fully expected him to be as excellent in bed as he was out of it.

He locked both her wrists in one hand and used the other to softly stroke her cheek. "You tired of twenty-something boys groping you, never quite getting you off?"

When Sam decided to be crude, he was a pro.

Those taunting fingers moved down her throat and across the top of her chest, just gliding, teasing. "Is that it, Ariel?"

She swallowed hard. What could she say other than to keep repeating the truth? "I want you."

His long, rough fingers dipped lower, nudging the edge of her exposed bra cup. "So be it. But my house, my rules."

At his agreement, her knees almost gave out. "What rules?"

So much wickedness and triumph filled his slow grin that she started to shake. "Rule number one, no one ever knows but us. I won't have Pete hurt."

Ariel was pinning all her hopes on the fact that once Sam quit denying his physical attraction to her, he'd quit denying his emotions, too. She was head-over-heels in love with the stubborn cuss, but telling him that now would blow what little progress she'd made, so she nodded. "All right."

Rather than look pleased with her acceptance, his expression hardened even more.

While he stared intently in her eyes, his fingers curled into the top of her bra cup—and then stripped it down, leaving her breast bare. Ariel gasped.

He didn't look down, but that big hot palm closed over her, kneading steadily, rasping her nipple while he continued to intimidate her with his molten stare.

The only sign he was affected by the touch was the flare of his nostrils, his increased breathing. "Rule number two. You do only what I say, when I say." She started to protest and his fingers closed around her nipple in a tantalizing grip that silenced her in an instant. "I'll make you come ten times, Ariel, but my rules stand."

She nodded dumbly, but finally found her voice. "One thing."

"You don't get one thing. You do as I say."

"It's just a . . . a question."

He considered that for far too long before nodding. "One question."

"Do you want me?"

He tugged gently on her nipple. "I won't have any problems keeping it up, if that's what you mean."

"No, it's not what I mean." She loved him. She wanted him to love her too only he had so many walls in place, so many responsibilities and he'd die before ever hurting a member of his family. She had a wealth of emotion in store for him, but she wouldn't be used. If he didn't at least want her, *her*, not just any woman, then she'd make herself walk away.

His hand was still at her breast, still teasing and taunting her nipple making it near impossible to think and speak clearly. "You . . . You've insulted me many times."

"When?" He looked genuinely puzzled.

"You've made it clear that you consider me a nuisance and not too bright."

His hand paused at her breast and his black brows pulled down. "If you're talking about that little stunt you pulled back at the bar, you're damn right—" He stopped, ground his teeth together, then admitted roughly, "You don't own an ounce of caution, but I didn't mean to say you were stupid. I don't think that at all. But I was scared shitless for you. I don't ever want to see you or any lady hurt."

Relief made her weak. "I didn't mean to scare you."

"Great. Don't ever let it happen again. Now is that it?"

"Not quite." He rolled his eyes, so she hurried through the rest. "You've insulted my body . . ."

"I *never*—"

"You said I had a skinny ass!"

He turned his face to the side and for one horrified moment, Ariel thought he was going to laugh. But when he looked at her again, tenderness filled his eyes. "You have a spectacular ass and once you quit trying to stammer out your explanation, I intend to devote about an hour to it."

"Oh."

"Enough said?"

"Yes."

He turned her around, gave her a stinging swat on the butt, and said, "Go upstairs to my bedroom and wait for me there."

"What are you . . . ?"

"No questions. My rules. Just go."

She started to recover her breast but he saw her and said, "Leave it."

She nodded and, feet dragging, made the climb up the stairs. Her belly churned in excitement and uncertainty and so much more. Finally, Sam would make love to her.

She'd give him her body and her heart, and hope he accepted them both.

The second she was out of sight, Sam turned to the sink and slumped against it. Jesus, he was only a man and not all that sterling a man to begin with. How the hell was he supposed to tell Ariel no when he'd wanted her for months?

He opened his right hand and looked at it, then curled his fingers in, reliving the feel of her young, firm breast. Fucking her would be so sweet, so hot.

And very wrong.

But Ariel was set on having her own way, so he knew he had to do this, and do it right, or she'd never leave him in peace. If he didn't take ultimate control, she'd have his balls in a ringer. Before long, he'd be on his damn knees asking her to marry him.

No. *Hell no.*

Pete would be hurt and he'd been hurt enough since their father passed away. He couldn't do that to him. And if Pete was really over her, as she'd suggested? Well, she was still too damn young and far too innocent. Where he was dark, his work and his lifestyle ugly and edgy and uncertain, she lived a carefree life of sunshine and smiles. He couldn't take that from her.

He gave himself ten minutes to get a grip on his control and to let her stew. While he kept her waiting, he took two aspirin and used an antiseptic swab to clean the cut on the back of his head. It burned like a son-of-a-bitch, making him wince in sympathy for Ariel. Her knees, her elbow . . . She could have been hurt worse, even killed if the asshole trying to rob him had had a weapon.

She was a danger to herself and to him, a giddy young woman with more bravado than common sense. What the hell did she think, putting herself in danger for him? If he let her hang around, she'd be forever underfoot, forever taking risks that no woman should take.

With renewed conviction for his quickly formed plans, Sam stormed up the stairs.

He found her sitting on the side of his bed, her feet together, her hands folded in her lap, her breast still uncovered. She looked wary and uncertain and flushed with excitement and so . . . ready, he broke out in a sweat.

Sam forced himself to stop in the doorway. Watching her,

he began unbuttoning his shirt, then gave a grimace of pain as he pulled it off his wrenched shoulder.

"You're hurt!" She shot off the bed in a flash, her soft hands fluttering all over him, finding bruises and swollen muscles, her damn tender touch setting him on fire.

"Sit—back—down."

She blinked at his tone. "But you need the ice worse than I did. That ape hurt you. We should take you to the hospital. . . ."

"*Sit,* Ariel." She drew back, hurt and confused. "One of the rules," he drawled, trying to soften his command. "You don't touch me unless I tell you to. Now, don't look like that. I'm fine, really. My own brothers have put worse bruises on me just horsing around. Trust me, I'm not being macho. It's nothing that won't heal in a day or two."

She looked undecided, but fell silent when he dropped into a chair and unbuckled his ankle holster.

She stared at his small off-duty weapon, a .38 caliber five-shot revolver. He always had it on him when working undercover because his primary weapon, a .40 caliber Glock, would be too easy to detect. "You carry a gun?"

"That's a . . ." He started to say stupid question, but caught himself. He really didn't want her to think he considered her dumb. "I'm a cop. Of course I carry a gun." And then, when he retrieved the lethally sharp knife from the other leg, he added, "Among other things."

Her eyes were huge when he crossed to the nightstand and opened the bottom drawer. He lifted out a metal box, turned the key in the lock, and opened it. Once the gun and knife were safely inside, he relocked the box and pocketed the key.

Under normal circumstances, both weapons would have sat atop the box, but then, this wasn't a normal circumstance—not by a long shot. And Sam never took unnecessary chances with safety, especially with his gun.

Shirtless, in his bare feet but with his pants on as a deterrent, he went to her. She looked adorable sitting there, all mussed and nervous and he felt like a conquering hero ready to ravish the innocent. It wasn't at all an unpleasant or inadequate perception.

Using just the edge of his finger, he stroked her exposed nipple. It was puckered tight, a pale pink, and he wanted to draw her into his mouth. *Why not?* he thought. This was his show.

He caught her hand and pulled her to her feet. "Stand still." With no preliminaries, he bent and covered her with his mouth, curled his tongue around her, and sucked.

She jerked hard and stepped back, almost falling onto the mattress.

Sam looked at her. "I said to be still."

"Reaction." She blinked hard. "I . . . I didn't mean to—"

He again took her into his mouth and this time she moaned, stiffened her arms and her back and held as still as a statue. He suckled at her, loving her taste, the way she trembled, the desperate little sounds she made. Using his tongue he stroked her, teased, then sucked hard.

"Sam!"

"Shh." He straightened to look at his handy work. Her nipple was now ripe, reddened, and wet. "This is cute," he managed to say, his voice little more than a rumble as he flipped the material of her ruined dress, "but I think I'd prefer you naked."

Her chest rose and fell, both from what he'd been doing and what he would do.

"I'm going to undress you, stretch you out on the bed, and taste you like that all over."

Her lips parted. "All . . . ?"

"Over. Don't move." He reached behind her for the zipper to her dress.

Disregarding his orders, she leaned into him and breathed deep. "You smell so good, Sam."

He grunted at that, but didn't push her away. It felt nice having her lean into him. "You find the smell of sweat and alcohol appealing, do you?"

"Your sweat, yes."

He stripped the tiny sleeves off her shoulders and let them drop down to her elbows. He reached for the back fastening of her bra. The position put his cheek over her shoulder and he could feel her silky blond curls touch his ear, his jaw. Shit, now *he* was trembling.

"You don't smell like alcohol though. Just like a man, like you. I've always thought you smelled good."

"Another rule," he said as he peeled the bra away, leaving her naked from the waist up. "No talking."

"But . . ."

"No talking. You're distracting me." *And making me crazy and I won't be able to do this if you don't quit.*

She covered her breasts with her arms, making Sam lift a brow. "Change your mind?"

She shook her head.

"Then don't hide from me." He waited, wondering if she'd call it quits, half hoping she would, half praying she wouldn't. "Make up you mind, Ariel. Anytime you want this to end, all you have to do is tell me. I'll walk you to the door."

She swallowed hard, drew a fortifying breath and let her arms hang at her sides.

He admired her courage. "It's only going to get harder you know. If you've changed your mind—"

"I haven't."

But she would. Eventually. How far would he have to go before she cried uncle? No matter, he had to carry it to the bitter end. He had to ensure she wouldn't test him again, because he wasn't at all certain of his ability to resist her.

"All right, then." He pulled the dress over her hips and let it drop. It pooled around her feet. "Step out of it."

She did, accepting the hand he offered for balance. Left only in panties and sandals, she blushed bright pink. But Sam paid little enough attention to her face when her body was all but bare. His hands at her waist, he stroked her, from her hips to her ribs and back again. She was a little too slim, her curves understated. "Damn, you're beautiful."

He didn't get a reply, but then, he didn't expect one.

He glanced up at her face. "You blond everywhere?"

Her color deepened.

"No, don't tell me. I want to find out for myself." Then, smiling into her shocked face, he whispered, "Take them off."

Chapter Three

Ariel had never felt so exposed in her entire life. She gulped and tried to find a little courage.

"I'm waiting."

He just stood there, his arms crossed over his hairy chest, his feet braced apart. His silky dark hair was mussed, hanging over his brow and beard shadow darkened his jaws and upper lip. His long black lashes hung low over his piercing eyes, direct, taunting. Watchful and expectant.

She wanted to throw him to the floor and drag his slacks off his gorgeous body and kiss him all over. But he wanted to do things his own way and she knew Sam well enough to know it was his way or not at all.

"All right." Feeling awkward and unsophisticated, she hooked her thumbs in her panties and pushed them down. Sam held her left elbow as she tried to step out, but she caught her stupid sandals on the leg bands, getting her panties twisted. She should have removed the shoes first but she wasn't exactly an expert at stripping with an audience.

When she finally got them free, she dropped the panties

on the floor with the rest of her clothes and started to sit down to take off her sandals.

Sam had other ideas. "I like the look." His voice was gruff, raw. "Leave them on."

She peeked at him, but he stared at her belly, or more specifically, below her belly. She nearly jumped out of her skin when he reached out and stroked his fingers through her pubic hair.

"Part your legs a little."

This test of his was a killer. If he'd only kiss her again, hold her . . . but he wasn't going to. She knew he wanted her to shy away, to run home scared. To prove she wasn't a mature, experienced woman.

The experience part . . . well, hopefully he'd forgive her for that. But she was a woman, *his woman,* if he'd only stop being so pigheaded. She forced her chin up and set one foot several inches from the other.

"You're not as blond here," he said while still fingering her curls. "But then your brows and lashes are a few shades darker too. It's pretty."

Never in her twenty-four years had she expected such a conversation to take place. He was complimenting her on her . . . well, on something very private. This wasn't at all as she'd assumed lovemaking would be. She thought there'd be a lot of reciprocal touching, breathless loss of control, and a simultaneous agreement to move forward in intimacy.

At the same time, being here with him like this was so wildly exciting, she knew she was wet and she feared he'd know it too in just a moment.

He stepped away from her. "Turn around."

Her mind went blank. What in the world did he have planned now? Breath rushed in and out of her lungs. Feeling wooden and clumsy in the stupid shoes, she forced herself to move. When her back was to him, he said, "There. I want to look at you."

She tried to stand straight and tall, but more than anything she just wanted to crawl into the bed under the covers and then convince Sam to crawl under them with her.

The touch of his breath on her nape raised her awareness another notch.

"I love your ass," he whispered, and then both his hands covered her there, squeezing and cuddling. Her eyelids grew heavier and heavier until her eyes closed. Without thinking, she reached back for him. Her fingertips just grazed his fly long enough for her to feel the straining power of his erection.

"No." He caught her hands. "No touching from you." He placed her hands alongside her thighs.

"I want to touch you," she said. "The same way you're touching me."

"Yeah? Like this?" His hands came around her and he caught her nipples in his fingertips.

Her back arched. "Sam . . ."

"You like that, don't you?" He tugged, plucked, and rolled. He opened his palms and grazed them over her, then covered her breasts, gently holding them while he kissed her shoulder, her nape. Every damp warm touch of his mouth brought her temperature up another degree.

"Answer me, Ariel."

"I like it, but . . . I'd like it more if I could touch you, too."

He laughed, the sound masculine and satisfied. "I just bet you would. But then you'd be breaking the rules and we can't have that."

He went back to tormenting her nipples and he took so long she wasn't sure she could stand it. Her every nerve ending was alive, sizzling. Stars danced in front of her closed eyes, her breasts ached and felt heavy, and between her legs she throbbed and burned.

And still he just played with her breasts and kissed her shoulders and back and neck.

In desperation, she whispered, "Sam, *please*." She honestly didn't know how much more she could take. An imminent explosion skirted through her, almost there, but not quite. Her hips moved, embarrassing her, shaming her but she couldn't seem to hold still.

"All right," he whispered. But he didn't turn her to him. Instead, those tantalizing hands coasted down her ribs, over her belly, and between her legs. "Open them more."

Trying but unable to get her legs to cooperate, she whimpered.

He helped her, putting one large foot between hers and nudging them open. "More. I want to be able to get to you."

Oh God.

"How I teased your nipples? I'll do that here, too." His fingertips brushed against her clitoris and she cried out at the electrifying sensation—then felt his smile press to her shoulder. "Yeah, right there," he said in deep triumph. "It'll make you crazy, Ariel, and if we're both lucky, you'll come for me. I want you to, you know."

Horrified by the thought of standing and performing to his demands, she stiffened. Surely he didn't expect her to do such a thing with him detached, manipulating her but uninvolved?

"Don't stiffen up on me." Gently, using only his fingertips, he opened her. "We'll get to the bed, I promise. No way in hell will this be it. Unless you tell me to stop." Carefully, holding her open with one hand, he circled her clitoris again. She felt his fingers, his rough, warm fingers, moving over her and she couldn't seem to get enough oxygen into her starved lungs. For one brief instant, she thought she might actually faint.

"Breathe, Ariel." He held still, waiting, leaning over her shoulder to watch her face. She did, gulping air and shaking from head to toe. "You're close, aren't you, baby? I wonder if you can do this standing up. Some women can't you know. That tidal wave of melting pleasure washes over you and your legs go weak and . . ." He shrugged. "I'll hold you, though. Don't worry."

Staring straight ahead at the window opposite his bed, Ariel bit her lip, fighting the urge to plead with him again.

"You'll tell me if I hurt you."

"Yes."

He opened his mouth on her neck, giving her a soft love bite—and pushed his middle finger into her.

Her head fell back, a deep, shuddering groan escaping her. He gave an answering growl of pleasure and pressed deeper and it was the most amazing thing, a little embarrassing, very arousing. Her hips moved again and this time she didn't care.

"You're small. And hot. And you feel so damn good."

Ariel was well beyond words. She hung in his arms, her legs open, all her attention on his hands and how he touched her and the expanding pleasure that would ebb and then grow stronger as it rolled through her.

With his finger pressed deep inside her, he found her clitoris with his thumb and he began an incredible slick friction that sent her right over the edge. She cried out, stunned at what she felt, at her total loss of control. She couldn't be quiet, couldn't hold still.

True to his word, Sam wrapped one muscled arm around her waist and held her upright while he continued the press and retreat of his fingers, kept the pleasure flowing until indeed, her legs gave out and she slumped into him, boneless, exhausted, replete.

His arm stayed locked around her while he lifted the other hand. Ariel roused herself enough to turn her head and look at him. She saw his eyes close, saw him suck his fingers into his mouth, taking her taste, her wetness.

Their eyes met. Looking far too serious, he pulled his fingers out and touched them to her lips. She shuddered, but was too spent to pull away.

Gently, Sam lowered her to the bed on her stomach, then stretched out beside her. He stroked her head, found the few pins that still held her hair and pulled them out to flick them across the room. With an open hand, he combed out the curls, spreading them over the pillow.

"Sam?"

"Mmm?" Propped on one elbow, he continued to pet her, down her spine, over her bottom.

"Will you make love to me now?"

He slanted glittering eyes at her and said, "You just can't be quiet, can you?"

Ariel felt hurt. He'd just done the most amazing thing to her and still he was apart from her. It wasn't easy, but she got her sluggish limbs to work and turned on her side to face him. He stared down at her body, his gaze concentrated, hot.

She stared at his chest. Among a smattering of older scars randomly dispersed over his torso, there was a fresh, dark bruise coloring his ribs, evidence of the night he'd just had. Stricken, Ariel thought of how many times he'd been hurt, how much he must have suffered in his efforts to protect. Maybe, she thought, he physically wasn't up to making love with her. Old wounds, new wounds . . . Was she being selfish?

He'd already given her pleasure without intercourse. She could do the same, sparing his sore body.

Wanting to make him feel as good as she did, Ariel leaned forward and brushed a butterfly kiss over the nearest scar, a small bullet wound that grazed his shoulder. Sam froze, not even breathing.

Encouraged, she spread her hands over his chest, tangling her fingers in his dark chest hair, stroking him as he'd stroked her.

Ariel noted a thin, light line near his collarbone, about two inches long. It looked like it might have been a deep cut, perhaps with a knife. Appalled at the awful risks he took, she kissed that, too.

This close, his scent was twice as potent. Those odd turbulent feelings roused in her again.

She kissed three bruises, one on his shoulder, his temple, another on his ribs. "Sam," she whispered, and opened her mouth on him. His skin was deliciously warm and sleek, his flesh firm. Turning her head, she moved closer to a flat nipple hidden beneath his chest hair. Her tongue touched him.

Sam grabbed her shoulders. In a heartbeat, Ariel found herself flat on her back with Sam straddling her hips. "I said no touching, Ariel."

She blinked up at him, unable to move, confused by how quickly he'd reversed their positions. He sounded so stern, looked so dangerous. "I'll try . . ."

"Too late."

Her eyes widened. Oh no. He was going to tell her to leave. He would throw her out and she hadn't had a real chance yet to make him understand how perfect they'd be together.

He stretched her arms high until they nearly touched the slatted headboard, then reached across her for the nightstand and jerked open the top drawer. Ariel twisted, trying to see what he was doing . . . He pulled out handcuffs.

"Sam."

"I haven't had much chance to use these since going under-cover." He let them dangle in front of her face, waiting, she knew, for her to protest, to insist he release her.

They stared at each other, his expression lethal, hers un-certain, but neither of them backed down. Sam leaned over her.

One metal bracelet clicked around her wrist, then clicked and clicked again when he tightened it to fit her small bones. She had room to turn her hand, but she couldn't slip it free. Her stomach fluttered in apprehension.

He glared down at her. "You ready to call a halt?"

Damn him. She wasn't a criminal he could intimidate so easily, because she knew Sam would never hurt her. No mat-ter his games, no matter his intent, she knew him, loved him, and trusted him. "No."

His mouth tightened. "Make sure, Ariel."

She would not let him scare her. She would not let him off the hook that easily, either. One way or another, she'd get through to him, even if that meant showing him her trust first by playing out these bizarre games of sexual dominance.

She stared him in the eyes. "I'm sure."

Sam wanted to howl, to curse the moon and punch a hole in the wall. Ariel had taken his control and turned it back on him, openly sharing her pleasure, then kissing his injuries—old and new—as if she wanted to heal him.

Like a few stupid marks on his body really mattered to her.

He was so damn hard his guts clenched and his brain cramped. Watching Ariel come had been something he'd never forget. She was so sweet she made him break out in a sweat just by smiling.

Would she taste as sweet as she looked?

Jesus. Before he could change his mind he caught her other wrist, aware of how tiny her bones were, how delicate. He slipped the chain connecting the handcuffs through a slat in the headboard then snapped the cold steel around her.

Breathing hard in both regret and shattering lust, he looked down at her pale, slim body stretched out beneath him, shackled in place. He didn't want to think about anything, he only wanted to devour her, to take everything she had and give her another mind-blowing orgasm.

He plumped up her breasts in his hands, thumbed her nipples roughly, watched her squirm.

"Not a word," he warned, knowing if she started telling him what she wanted again, he'd lose the fight. He moved off her, opened her legs wide and repositioned himself between them, on his knees so he could drape her legs over his. "That's better."

Those beautiful hazel eyes of hers, now more topaz than brown, watched him without blinking, conveying some silent message that he damn well didn't want to hear. Her mouth looked puffy and soft and kissable. Her small chin quivered, but not because she might cry. No, he knew Ariel wouldn't do that.

Probably it quivered with stubbornness.

"I like to see a woman, all of her, when I take her," he explained. Her legs draped his, white against his dark slacks, sleek and lightly muscled. He looked at her breasts. Earlier her nipples had been velvety soft, but once he'd touched them, they'd stayed puckered, begging for his mouth.

She lightly licked her lips, luring him. Bracing his hands on the pillow at either side of her head, Sam bent down and savaged her mouth with ruthless hunger, kissing her hard, thrusting his tongue between her teeth. She didn't fight him or pull back. No, she accepted his tongue, sucked on it, returned his kiss with equal passion.

He groaned, aware of her straining up to him, trying to get more of him. Her thighs were tensed, her belly lifting into him.

He pulled himself away and took his pleasure at her breasts. He loved suckling a woman and could be content to spend an hour on her nipples alone. But not this time. As soon as Ariel started writhing, he moved lower, nibbling on her ribs, then lower still until he could dip his tongue into her navel.

She held her breath, anticipating what he might do, he knew. Did she like oral sex? Had any man ever kissed her between her thighs? He hoped not. He wanted to be the first.

"Wider," he said as he pressed her legs farther apart and held them in place when she would have automatically brought them together again. He glanced up at her still face, flushed but uncertain. "Keep them that way."

Using his fingertips, he opened her lips, exposing her glistening pink flesh. Her clitoris was swollen from her recent climax, extra sensitive. Gently, he kissed her, heard her shocked, eager gasp, and he closed his mouth around the tender bud.

With a hoarse cry, she nearly lurched away, but he cupped her hips firmly in his big hands and held her secure. Because he knew her nerve endings were already tingling, still alive from her last orgasm, he was very careful not to push her too fast, to cause her any discomfort. He suckled softly, easily, taking his time, stroking with his tongue. When she was ready for more, her legs stiffened and her arms pulled tight against her bonds.

"Sam," she said, all breathless and low. "Sam, Sam, *Sam* . . ."

Her cries were raw, real, and he loved it, the way she responded, the pleasure he gave her so easily. She didn't hold back at all, didn't try to temper her response. He replaced his mouth with his fingers and raised his head to see her face.

Her neck was arched, her teeth clenched, her breasts heaving. "Beautiful," he breathed, ready to come just from looking at her. After endless moments, she quieted, and Sam moved up beside her, smoothed her hair from her face, placed a kiss on her open lips.

"That was nice." He waited, but she didn't open her eyes, didn't reply. Sam smiled. "For a youngin', you come with a lot of energy. I like it."

Sweat glistened on her chest, the tops of her cheekbones. A rosy flush covered her body and her heart still raced. With an obvious effort, she licked her lips, swallowed, and said, "Shut up, Sam."

He grinned, fighting off a chuckle. "You're not supposed to talk."

She cast him a wanton look that nearly did him in. "No? I've never been handcuffed before, Officer. What should I be doing?"

Sam lowered his hand to her belly and felt it hollow out when she dragged in a breath. "Rest. You're going to need your strength."

"I am?"

"Mmm. I'll give you a few minutes before we start again."

Her eyes widened, darkened. "Start . . . ? Sam, no. I . . . I can't."

He pushed his hand lower until he cupped her mound. She was slick, very wet and pulsing with heat. "Yes you can." All the teasing left him. "I'll see to it."

She squeezed her eyes shut. "Sam . . ."

"Crying uncle?"

A sob almost rose in her throat, but she managed to swallow it back. Sam watched her closely, waiting for the words he needed to hear, waiting for her to tell him to fuck off, to get out of her life once and for all.

"No. I'm not crying uncle."

They watched each other, at a stalemate, until finally Sam cursed. "Fine. Have it your way." His fingers curled against her, his middle finger sinking past her creamy wetness, into her up to his first knuckle—and someone rang his doorbell.

They both jerked to a breathless, astonished standstill. Their motions were frozen.

Ariel gasped, "You have *company?*"

Sam shoved himself off the bed and stalked to the window, barely moving the curtain aside to peer out. "Ah fuck."

A loud knock sounded.

He turned to Ariel, took in the sight of her handcuffed naked to his bed and knew he'd just screwed up royally.

"Who is it?" she whispered in a fearful voice.

Sam rubbed his face. "It's Pete."

"Ohmigod." She began jerking and twisting. "Let me loose!"

He walked past her. "No, just be quiet. I'll get rid of him and be right back. I promise." He snatched up his shirt and pulled it on.

"Sam!" Her face went white. "Don't you dare leave me here like—"

He held a finger to his lips. "Shhh. You made a deal, Ariel. Now keep it. If you're real quiet, Pete will never know you're here." He pulled the door shut, aware of her distress—and aware of his own regret. But she did fall silent, thank God.

He closed the door and trotted quickly down the stairs. His brain churned, trying to think of what to say, how to explain Ariel's car in his driveway, how to get rid of his baby brother.

Pete knocked again, growing impatient.

"All right already, give it a rest." Sam threw the door open. "What the hell is the matter with you?"

Pete, looking healthy and happy and in something of a hurry, burst in and said, "I need the keys to Gil's boat."

"What?"

His black hair was mussed, his shirt untucked and he had a hickey on his neck. "Gil's out of town, but he said I could use his boat only I don't have a spare key and you do."

"Gil's out of town?"

"Yeah. Business—don't you remember? He's been gone all week. Forget that part. Just give me the key."

Suspicious, Sam leaned around Pete to look out the door. His brother's sporty little Focus was at the curb, still running, and in the passenger seat was a cute blond. "Ah. Big plans?"

Pete bobbed his eyebrows. "Is she hot or what?"

Amazed that Pete apparently hadn't even noticed Ariel's car in the drive, Sam went to the kitchen for the spare key to Gil's houseboat. "Yeah, she's cute."

"Cute? You've gotta be kidding me. She's in my statistics class, smart as hell and sexier than that."

"And willing?"

With a sly look, Pete said, "Oh yeah."

At twenty-two, Pete was a good-looking kid with an athlete's body that had yet to finish filling out, sincere brown eyes, and a sexual drive exclusive to young male animals of the human variety. Sam loved him so much that it sometimes hurt and in the three years since their father's death, he'd felt more responsible for him than ever.

He held the key out of reach. "You got protection?"

"No, you wanna loan me a gun?" He grinned.

Sam didn't take birth control lightly. "You know what I mean, Pete."

"She's got it covered."

Scowling, Sam grabbed him by the ear and lifted him to his tiptoes. "*She* does? How many times do I have to tell you—"

Laughing and wincing at the same time, Pete pulled a condom from his pocket and waved it under Sam's nose. "Hey, I was teasing, all right! It's covered. Literally."

Sam turned him loose. "That's it? One?"

"With three more in the glove box."

"Then don't exceed four, you hear me?"

Pete snatched the keys from his hand. "Yeah, four." He held his heart and pretended to stagger. "Four."

Sam laughed and walked him back to the door. Not for a single moment was he unaware of Ariel upstairs, naked, waiting. "You like them blond, huh?"

Pete shrugged. "Or brunette or redhead or . . ."

"Well, I meant because both she and Ariel are blond."

"She," Pete emphasized, "is a lot more fun than Ariel ever tried to be."

Sam's knees locked. "Yeah? How so?"

"You kidding me? All Ariel could ever say was no, no, and no. No real dates, no kissing, and definitely no sex. Got to where I thought my name was No-Pete."

Sam's heart gave a heavy thump. "She cut ya cold, huh?" Now why the hell did that thrill him so much?

"She cut everyone cold, not just me. She told me she was waiting till she got married." Pete rolled his eyes.

Dropping back against the wall, Sam said, "No shit?" His head started to pound.

"Yeah, real old-fashioned attitude, right? I think she just liked to lead guys on. You know, like a tease."

Anger roiled up, making him want to take Pete by the ear again. He didn't, because it shouldn't matter to him what was said about Ariel. But as a big brother, he could say a few general things, and did. "I hope like hell you're not repeating that to anyone but me, because if I hear of it, I'll be royally pissed."

"I know." Pete winked. "Preserve a woman's honor no matter what. I remember."

Sam caught his arm. "I mean it, Pete."

He looked down at the hand holding him with marked confusion. "No sweat. I liked Ariel a lot, still do as a friend. But she made sure it was never more than that, end of story."

"You were really hung up on her."

"I thought I was. Gil told me I was suffering lust, not love and I have to admit he was right. But hey, I'm not bitter and I'm not out to trash her." He tipped his head toward the door. "I am out to have a good time tonight though, if this impromptu lecture is over."

Sam opened his fingers by force of will. "It's over. Just be careful."

"I'm twenty-two, Sam. Not fifteen."

"I remember. Make sure you remember it, too."

Rolling his eyes again, Pete playfully punched him in the ribs—causing Sam considerable pain, which he managed to hide—and then Pete trotted out to his car. Sam propped himself in the doorway, waved to the young lady when she laughed and lifted her hand toward him, and once the car pulled away he closed and locked the door.

Ariel had wanted to wait till she got married.

His pulse raced, causing a wild thrumming in his ears. Breath held, he looked up the stairs at that closed bedroom door. Surely to God she wasn't a virgin?

But even as he thought it, his balls tightened and his blood boiled. He could be her first. That upped the stakes even more, made the temptation nearly impossible to resist.

He had a choice to make—take her and give himself a fantasy to last a lifetime.

Or send her innocent little butt packing while he still could.

There was really no choice at all.

Chapter Four

Ariel was livid by the time Sam walked into the room. Her wrists were raw from the furious pulling she'd done when she heard Pete spewing such nonsense about her. She hadn't gotten this far with Sam only to have his youngest brother ruin it with exaggerated nonsense.

Frowning, Sam sat beside her on the bed and caught her arms to hold them still. "Stop that," he said, "you're hurting yourself."

"That miserable little cretin." She tried to jerk again, but Sam was too strong for her, keeping her immobile.

"Who?"

"Pete, that's who." Ooh, when she got hold of him, she'd box his ears. "I can't believe you let him stand there and say those awful things."

Sam leaned back, his expression guarded. "You heard?"

"Every damn word."

"And you're jealous?"

"Jealous?" Ariel sputtered at such a ridiculous notion. "I'm furious!"

Sam's scowl was black enough to straighten her hair.

"Because he's taking his new girlfriend out to Gil's boat for some privacy?"

She gasped so hard, she nearly choked herself. "Don't be an idiot. I couldn't care less who Pete sleeps with, as long as it isn't me. I'm mad that he stood down there and spoke about me like I was some ice princess or a . . . a . . ."

"Cock tease?"

Fury rolled through her. "Let me go. Right now."

Sam scrutinized her. "I don't think so. You look violent."

Digging her heels into the mattress, she pulled and tugged and thrashed—until she saw Sam holding the key in front of her face.

"You're destroying my bed."

Ariel arched her neck, looked upside down at where the chain for the cuffs had gouged the smooth wooden slats of his headboard, and she smiled in evil satisfaction. "Good," she practically spat at him. "I'll tear the whole damn thing apart if you don't unlock me."

Sounding very put upon, Sam sighed. "I give you two orgasms and all you can do is threaten me."

That was true enough, so she grudgingly muttered, "Sorry. I do appreciate what you did."

That made him laugh and shake his head. A second later the key clicked in the lock and the cuffs opened.

Sam drew her arms down, held her wrists loosely in his hard hands and gently rubbed. "Look what you did. You had enough scrapes and bruises without deliberately adding to them."

For the first time that night, he sounded calm, completely detached. Ariel got worried.

"Tell me something, will you, Ariel?"

Uh-oh. She didn't trust this new mood of his at all. In the time she'd known him, she'd become accustomed to his sarcasm, his sharp wit, his merciless teasing—but never indifference. "What?"

He snared her gaze with his and wouldn't let her look away. "Are you a virgin?"

Well damn. She started to pull her hands away but he resisted and Ariel didn't think it was worth a struggle. Silence stretched out, more uncomfortable by the moment. She felt pinned to the mattress with the way his unblinking stare penetrated her confidence. Stalling, hoping for an out, she asked, "Do you mean, like, *technically?*"

His eyes narrowed at her avoidance. "Have you ever had intercourse?"

She squirmed, chewed on her bottom lip. "Well, if you mean—"

"Sex, Ariel. I mean sex."

"There's like, sex, in the general term as in touching and—"

"Have you ever been fucked, goddammit?"

She nearly jumped out of her skin at his abrupt blast of outrage; then her own temper ignited and she jerked her arms away from him and came up on her knees to face him head on. Poking him in the chest to emphasize every word, she said, "No, all right? No, there's been *no one.*"

His eyes widened over her attack and he leaned back out of reach.

More softly and with a little desperation, Ariel explained, "I only ever wanted you."

Looking equal parts pained and provoked, Sam started to rise from the bed. He'd turned halfway from her when resolve overrode her anxiety, and Ariel hurled herself at him, tackling him hard from the side.

Unfortunately, her surprise attack sent him right over the edge of the bed. Unprepared, he had no way to stop himself.

Arms flailing, he crashed to the hard floor. Ariel landed on top of him with an "omph," forcing a loud grunt from Sam.

For five seconds, he just stared up at her, his face blank in shock at what she'd done. Ariel quickly took advantage. She grabbed his ears and kissed him.

When he tried to turn his head, she bit his mouth.

"Ow!" He wrenched back. "Damn it to hell—"

"You have a foul, but delicious mouth, Sam Watson." She kissed him again, licking her way past his teeth, rubbing her breasts against his naked chest. When he stopped fighting her, holding himself in a sort of suspended indecision, she ran her hands all over him, over his sleek hard shoulders, his wide, hairy chest, down his sides and back up again. She couldn't get enough of him and let him know with the way she touched him, how she crawled over him.

Sam groaned and in the next instant, his hands opened wide over her behind, gripping her tightly, grinding her into his erection. Thrilled, Ariel opened her legs to straddle his hips, and threw her head back with a triumphant moan. Beneath her mound, even through his slacks, she could feel the thick rise of Sam's erection. She had thought herself long done, half dead, uninspired toward anything else sexual.

But it took very little for Sam to have her wild again. A look. A touch. The two combined and she wanted to beg him to take her.

She kissed his chest and when his fingers gently laced into her hair and he said, softly and with apology, "Ariel," she bit him again, making him jump.

"Be quiet, Sam."

He half laughed, half moaned. "You're stealing my thunder, babe."

"I want you, enough for the two of us." She tenderly licked his discolored, sore ribs while inching her way down his muscled body. His fingers tightened in her hair, holding her back for only a moment before urging her lower with sublime surrender.

"Yes," Ariel whispered and she attacked the fastenings to his pants, hurrying before he could change his mind. Every time he shifted, she kissed him through the material, stroked him beneath the zipper, did her best to keep his lust at an urgent level so he couldn't concentrate long enough to reject her.

When she finally got his fly opened she snaked her hand inside, then paused with the wonder of it, the amazing way he felt, so alive and solid and yet velvety textured, flexing and pulsing in her hand.

Staring down at him, her lips parted to accommodate her fast breathing, Ariel examined her very first up-close and personal penis. What a revelation. "Sam."

"Kiss me, Ariel." The words were so guttural, she could barely understand him but she knew what he wanted.

Holding him now in both hands, she brushed a kiss up the length of him and heard his sharp intake of breath, felt the way his hands clenched in her hair, how his big body trembled.

Amazing. And exciting. She ran her tongue up to the very end, then over the glistening tip and he lurched so violently he nearly tossed her off. She quickly repositioned herself and did it again, this time lingering on the head, on that warm bead of moisture that tasted both salty and rich and not quite how she'd ever imagined.

"Oh God."

"I like this," Ariel purred, pleased with her discovery and Sam's reaction to her touch. She glanced up at him. "Do you?"

He laughed again, but it was a sound of agony, not humor.

"Will you like this?" She opened her mouth and drew

him in, not real deep because he was big and she was new to this, but taking the head all the way inside to suckle at it, to roll her tongue around him. She tasted more fluid, felt him grow even more, pulse. Sam let out a growling rumble and his whole big body jerked.

Before Ariel could fully appreciate all that splendid response, she found herself on her back, Sam firmly between her thighs, his mouth covering hers. He was ferocious, breathing hard and fast, his hands everywhere, his tongue hot in her mouth, his hips stroking her.

"Protection," he groaned and, as if by a mighty effort, pushed himself up enough to fumble in the nightstand drawer until he snagged three connected condoms. He ripped one free along the perforated line, opened it with his teeth and sat back on his heels to roll it on.

"You asked for this," he told her as he shoved his pants down and kicked them off, then wedged himself back between her thighs before she could get a good look at him completely naked. "Remember that."

For an answer, Ariel twined her arms around his neck, her legs around his waist, and hugged him tight. She loved him so much that tears sprang to her eyes. "I won't ever forget it," she promised him.

He hesitated, his chest working like a bellows. Ariel was so afraid he'd just changed his mind that she tightened her hold.

"Shh." He smoothed his hand up and down her side. "Relax."

"Don't leave me, Sam." She hated pleading, but if he turned her away now . . .

"No, I won't." And then, with sober apology: "I can't." He eased his weight onto her and carefully coaxed her arms from his neck. "I don't want to hurt you, Ariel."

"You would never hurt me."

"I might if I take you like a crazed sailor on shore leave. But you set me off, honey, you really do. I need you to help me out here."

With complete and utmost sincerity, Ariel told him, "You can take me like a crazed sailor. I won't mind."

He smiled, the most tender smile she'd ever seen from him. *"I'll* mind. Now quit talking and kiss me. No, gently. Yeah, that's right."

Ariel melted. Sam's voracious, hungry kisses were incredible, but the way he kissed her now, almost as if he cared about her, maybe loved her just a little, too, was enough to fill her up for a lifetime. And he took his time, kissing her long and slow and deep until she was the one who demanded more by pressing her belly up against him.

"Sam?"

"Yeah, baby?"

"I'm dying to feel you inside me."

He shuddered. "All right." After levering himself up on one elbow, Sam reached down with his other hand to guide himself in. Ariel saw that he was shaking, the high color in his face, how impossibly blue his eyes looked. The broad head of his penis nudged her soft opening, pushed marginally inside.

Sam locked his jaw. "You are so damn wet."

"I know." She flushed. "I can't help it."

"It's good. Damn good." He sank in a bit deeper with a groan. "Small and tight." His jaw worked as he forced himself into her. "And all mine."

Ariel's heart lurched at those possessive words. "Yes. Always."

But he didn't seem to know what she said, or even what he'd said. His eyes were glazed, burning as he stared down at her and she saw the acute pleasure in his face as her body accepted him. There was a stretching sensation, a little burning, but no real pain. She felt full, complete. Wonderfully alive.

Suddenly his shoulders bunched. He cursed, squeezed his eyes shut; then he snapped. He thrust into her, causing her to lose her breath in one startled gasp of mingled discomfort and joy.

"I'm sorry," he rasped, even as he slid back out, then stroked in deeper again, gaining a rhythm, harder and faster with each turn.

I love you, Sam. But the words were only in Ariel's mind. She held him, cradling his big body close to her heart while he thrust heavily into her, his arms locked tight around her, his face pressed into the side of her throat. He was sweaty, heat pouring off him, and then he arched his back, burying himself so deeply that Ariel cried out.

His face was beautiful, harshly masculine, etched with pleasure so sharp it mirrored pain. Ariel smiled at him, stroked his chest and shoulders until the tremors passed, his primal growls faded, and he slowly sank down onto her.

The carpet on her back prickled, her thighs ached, and Sam's weight pressed her down, making it difficult to breathe. But she didn't want to move. Not ever.

Without lifting his head, Sam said, his voice a sleepy rumble, "You probably have carpet burns on your ass now to add to your other injuries."

Ariel giggled.

Smiling, he forced his head up to see her. "That damn laugh," he said fondly. And he kissed her.

Ariel was so full of love, she couldn't imagine being any happier.

"You all right?"

Dreamily, she sighed. "I'm perfect."

"Yeah." He sat up beside her, his back against the side of

the bed, one leg bent, and he looked at her body. He shook his head in chagrin. "That you are. But you'll be more perfect after a shower and some sleep."

Oh no. Panic twisted inside her, but she tried to hide it. "Sam, are you sending me home?"

He shrugged, scooped her up as he stood, groaned at the pain in his shoulder and ribs, and then looked at her. "Unless you want to spend the night. Up to you."

Her heart raced. "You don't mind if I stay?"

Taking that as an affirmation that she wanted to, Sam headed for the bathroom. "The damage is done—but I'm not. Be forewarned though. If you stay, I plan to take you at least a few more times." He looked down at her. "In a few more ways."

Filled with relief, Ariel put her head on his shoulder. "Maybe," she said, tugging at his crisp chest hair, "I'll just take you instead."

He stopped in midstride, groaned again, then rushed her into the bathroom and stood her in the tub. "Virgins are the very devil." He turned away as he removed the spent condom.

"Ex-virgins." When he joined her in the tub, Ariel admired his body with eyes and hands and a few well-placed kisses. She liked the way his dark chest hair tapered off into a long thin line down his body. It circled his navel, then arrowed down to his groin, surrounding and framing his heavy sex.

"Right." Sam took her mouth, smothering her screech of outrage when he turned the cold water on full blast and it hit her in the back. "An ex-pushy virgin who gloats when she gets her own way."

"Sam!" The water quickly warmed, taking away her chills.

He lathered her up, somehow always managing to keep a

good hold on her soap-slick body. By the time he finished, Ariel was ready to learn about the new ways he'd mentioned. The night couldn't be long enough to suit her.

Sam awoke to a soft, damp kiss on his lower spine. His eyes snapped open but he didn't move. He was on his stomach, his legs sprawled out, his body heavy with sleep.

Deep shadows still filled the room, telling him it was early morning. His brain felt foggy, as if he'd been on a three-day drunk but with alarming clarity, he knew it was carnal gluttony that had him sluggish this morning, not booze.

Ariel was amazing. Everything he'd ever wanted in a sex partner. Everything he'd ever wanted, period.

He felt her warm fingertips tickling down his spine to the top of his ass. She hesitated, then stroked lower, until she found his testicles and could fondle him from behind. He bit back a rumbling groan.

After the excesses of the night, he should have been dead to the world, unable to rise to the occasion. But this was Ariel—and he was rising rather quickly.

"You're awake," she murmured, sounding more than a little pleased with herself.

"I am now." Sam rolled to his back and dragged her on top of him, appreciating her early morning, sleep-rumpled appeal. "Awake and ready, thanks to a certain little sexy lady who tried to molest me in my sleep."

She gave him a willing smile.

Sam sighed. "Unfortunately we're out of rubbers and I don't take chances, so quit torturing me."

Her face fell. "Bummer."

"Yeah." She sounded so forlorn, Sam almost laughed. "What time is it?"

"Six."

Aware of numerous aches and pains, he stretched beneath her. Laughing, Ariel almost slid off him. She grabbed him tight and managed to hang on.

Her giggle, which had once grated on his nerves, now seemed beyond adorable. "What time do you have to be at work?"

"Ten."

He swatted her bare behind. "Let's go get some breakfast, then. I'm famished."

He gently pushed her onto her back, gave her a smacking kiss on the mouth, and rolled out of bed. If he'd been alone, he would have limped to the dresser for his shorts because every muscle screamed in complaint as he moved. But with Ariel watching, he did his best to do the macho thing and hide his discomfort.

She came to her knees in the middle of the bed. "My dress is ripped and I never got around to fixing it last night, so can I borrow a T-shirt?"

He cast her a quick look. "Naw, I like seeing you naked."

Her face turned bright pink. "I can't cook or eat breakfast naked."

"Sure you can." He stepped into black boxer-briefs and hiked them up. "My house, my rules."

Her back stiffened. "Sam."

"Ariel." She was so damn cute, he couldn't resist teasing her. "You're such a spoilsport."

Her disheveled blond curls trembled in her agitation, forcing Sam to swallow a laugh. "All right, all right, don't start fuming. You can have a shirt." And then, just to tweak her anger, he added, "I suppose modesty in someone as young as you is to be expected."

He tossed her a white T-shirt, but it hit her in her glowering face, then fell to her lap. She didn't even attempt to catch it.

Sam leaned on the dresser and crossed his arms over his chest, surveying her. "Changed your mind?"

Her chin lifted; she flipped the shirt to the floor. "I believe I have." In lofty disdain, she slid out of the bed and strode naked to the door. "What's a little nudity among adults?"

Oh hell. Sam went after her, his gaze glued to her bare butt swishing and swaying down the stairs. He clutched his heart, thinking he was far too old to survive so much stimulation. He grinned at the thought, remembering that Ariel was the first one to fall asleep last night—and she'd had a fat smile on her face.

He'd literally worn the little darling out, and damn, that made him proud.

His grin died a quick death when, just as they reached the landing, an outraged knock sounded on his door. Ariel jumped a foot and dashed behind him, staring at the door as if it had suddenly become transparent and whoever lurked on the other side could see her. Scowling, Sam went to the peephole to look out. Ariel clutched at him, staying so close he felt her nipples on his back.

"Shit."

"Who is it?"

Dropping back against the door, he said, "Pete. And judging by the look on his face, he's finally noticed your car."

She covered her mouth with a hand. "Oh no."

"Oh no" was right. What the hell should he do now?

The door rattled again, and Pete yelled, "Open up, Sam! I know you're in there."

Sam gave Ariel the once over, then lifted a brow. "Now might be a good time to display that innate modesty, sweetheart. I somehow doubt Pete will believe anything I try to tell him if he sees you flitting around my house in your birthday suit."

Her mouth fell open and in a flash she turned around and dashed back up the stairs. What a sight, Sam thought, watching the way she bounced and jiggled in all the right places. He shook his head. He was an idiot, letting himself be ruled by his gonads instead of common sense. He should have sent her home last night.

Hell, he should never have touched her in the first place. But he had. And he'd more than enjoyed himself.

Now he'd have to pay.

Pete had his fist raised, apparently ready to pound the damn door down, when Sam drew it open. He took his brother off guard, saying, "Hey Pete. What's up?"

Pete's look of surprise disappeared beneath censure. He shoved his way in, looking this way and that. "Where is she?"

"She who?"

Pete whirled around to face Sam. "Don't be an asshole. You know damn good and well I'm talking about Ariel. It didn't register last night, but that's her car in your driveway and now it's still there—"

"Yeah?" Sam leaned out the open door, looked at the car, and said, "Huh. So it is."

Pete's teeth clicked together. "Where—is—she?"

From the top of the stairs, Ariel said softly, "I'm here."

Both men turned to look up. Sam took a surprised step forward. Did she have to hit him with one emotional punch after another? He knew Pete gave him a startled glance, but Sam couldn't get his gaze off her, not even to reassure his brother.

Ariel had hastily dressed in one of Sam's extra large white T-shirts. It was so enormous on her, one shoulder hung down nearly to her elbow and the hem landed almost at her knees, more than adequately covering her. Still, she'd also borrowed a pair of his drawstring running shorts. She'd tied them so tight, the string hung to her ankles. She looked . . . comically precious.

It was a wretched situation for Sam to find himself in, and still he smiled.

Pete punched him in the arm, glowering and bristling and somehow looking protective. Toward Ariel? Well hell. He'd sworn he was over her, yet here he was with his shoulders hunched and his jaw jutting forward.

"You're in your damned underwear," Pete told Sam under his breath, as if Ariel might not have already known that.

"Yeah, and you know, Ariel just might be in my underwear, too. Are you, honey? Did you find the boxers, along with the shirt and shorts, in my third drawer?"

Not amused, Pete slugged him again.

In an odd way, Sam was proud of him. Pete was a man, and apparently he'd listened to at least a little of what Sam had told him about respecting women.

"This isn't funny," Pete said.

"No, I don't suppose it is." Sam wondered how the situation could get any worse. He found out when his neighbor, Hesper, and her bloated bulldog poked their heads through the open front door.

First family and now friends. You'd think he was throwing a party, rather than debauching one very sexy, too young, slightly ex-virgin.

Emotions ran through him, guilt, regret . . . and overwhelming tenderness. He would have liked more time with her, but it appeared his time had just run out.

Chapter Five

"Everything okay, Sam?"

Before turning, Sam closed his eyes and said a quick prayer that some brilliant explanation would come to him.

His mind remained blank. "Hello, Hesper." She was still in her housecoat and slippers, curlers in her hair. "What has you up so early— given you were also up late?"

"I saw the young lady's car was still here and then your brother was pounding on the door and . . . Is there any way we can help?"

"No." Sam edged toward the door, trying to block the stairs with his body before Hesper noted Ariel. "Everything is fine. Pete's just visiting, that's all."

His efforts were in vain. The damn bulldog barked, Hesper looked up, and she spotted Ariel. "Oh my. Are you all right, sweetie? Sam told us what happened."

Pete stepped forward, aghast at such a possibility. "Just how much did my brother tell you?"

"Why, everything. That she's a dear family friend who he cares about and that she'd been mugged and was upset so he brought her home to make her feel safe for the night."

Ariel choked, coughing and gasping. Pete just stared at Sam.

A smile locked firmly in place, Sam took Hesper's arm and nudged her back out onto the porch. "Everything's fine here, Hesper, really. I promise it is. But thank you for your concern."

"That's what neighbors are for." Regretfully, she made her way to the steps and the bulldog lumbered along in their wake. "Oh Sam?" She turned to give him a coy smile.

"Yeah, Hesper?"

"If Booth looked as good in his drawers as you do, I believe I'd burn all his breeches."

Sam grinned. "Why thank you, Hesper."

"My pleasure," she said, and then to herself as she walked away, "Indeed it is."

Still grinning, Sam shut the door and turned to find his brother breathing fire and Ariel standing nervously beside him.

"I thought you told her I was a prostitute."

She sounded disappointed, and Sam shrugged, only to have Pete grab his arm and whip him around. "What's this about a prostitute?"

"Nothing. I was only teasing Ariel."

Pete's dark eyes, so much like their father's, narrowed with contempt. "Looks to me like you did a sight more than tease her."

"Pete!" Ariel tried to step between the two men. They didn't let her so she settled on poking Pete with her finger. "This is none of your business, Pete Watson. Now knock it off."

"I presume," Pete said, looking between the two of them, "that a wedding will be planned for the near future?"

Sam almost fell on his ass. *"A wedding?"* Good God, surely Ariel didn't expect . . . He cast an appalled glance her way.

She stared back, white-faced and mute, her mouth pinched.

"You heard me." Pete crossed his arms, every line of his body filled with unwavering resolve. "I told you last night how Ariel felt about this sort of thing."

Yeah, he'd known. And rather than dissuade him, the fact of her virginity had been an impossible lure. His basic nature was such that the idea of being the first—*the only?*—had driven him well beyond common sense, gallantry, and self-survival. He'd *had* to have her.

Sam cleared his throat. "Yeah, well maybe she's changed her mind about it. Did you think of that?"

They both turned to Ariel. At that moment, she appeared so small, so lost and alone and wounded, Sam's stomach twisted into a knot of indescribable pain. He started to reach out for her, intent only on offering comfort, but she backed away from him.

Chin lifted, she whispered, "Maybe I have."

Just a few minutes ago, she'd been playing, smiling, and prancing around naked to drive him wild. She'd looked happy, and now . . . Now she'd shut down, her eyes flat, empty. Sam could have thrown his brother out for ruining the pleasant, no-pressure mood she'd enjoyed before his arrival.

They all stood frozen, uncomfortable and unsure what to say or do next; then Gil's voice intruded. "Damn, I expected to find you in bed, Sam, not holding court in the foyer."

"Gil?" Sam turned to his brother, took in his beat-down, haggard expression and stormed forward with concern. "What's going on? I thought you were out of town."

"I just got home." He handed Sam his briefcase and dropped back against the wall. His tie hung loose around his neck and his shirtsleeves were rolled up past his forearms. He looked fatigued, both mentally and physically. "I checked my messages and then . . . I dunno. I wasn't sure what to do, so I just came here."

Pete crowded closer. "What's happened? Is something wrong with the company?"

Ariel had backed up so far, Gil didn't even notice her. "No, the company is fine. But it seems I have a problem." He paused, looking much struck, then laughed hoarsely, without any real humor. "Well, no, that's probably not the best way to put it. Perhaps a surprise is more like it. A life-altering surprise."

Sam's middle brother was by far the most staid of the three, serious where Pete was playful, calm where Sam was turbulent. He had a great head for business and he wasn't prone to melodrama.

Sam was more than mildly alarmed. "What the hell is that supposed to mean, Gil?"

Gil's brown eyes—so much like Pete's, identical to their father's—were bloodshot. He rubbed the back of his neck. "I got a call from a young lady who lives in Atlanta. You remember I handled some business there right after Dad passed away? Well, it seems . . ." He swallowed, closed his eyes and leaned his head back against the wall. "It seems I'm a father."

Sam hadn't seen her for a week, though God knew it wasn't from lack of trying.

But now, *here,* was not a good time to run into her.

He'd tried calling and repeatedly got her machine. She hadn't bothered to return any of his calls. He'd even dropped by that fancy boutique where she worked, only to be told by one of her coworkers that she'd taken an impromptu vacation.

When he couldn't find her at her apartment either, no

matter how long he stood in the hallway knocking, he finally decided she really was on a vacation. Maybe she'd gone out of town. Maybe she wasn't upset. Maybe she didn't even care about how their night together had ended.

She might well be off partying it up and having a blast—while he was smothering in guilt and worry.

But that last look on her face had continued to eat at him. He wanted to talk to her, to make sure she was all right.

After Gil dropped his bomb on them, Sam had been so floored he'd almost forgotten about her. The brothers had all milled to the kitchen for seats and caffeine, which was their normal routine whenever a situation arose that had to be dealt with. Sam had assumed Ariel would follow.

Only she hadn't.

He'd turned, expecting to bump into her, and her absence struck him like a sucker punch to the gut. He'd rushed back to the front door in time to see her little yellow car disappearing past the corner stop sign. She hadn't said good-bye. She hadn't said anything after letting him off the hook with that shaky, whispered, *"Maybe I have."*

She'd just stood there, silent and hurt.

Given Gil's disclosure, Pete hadn't questioned Sam too much when he'd returned to the kitchen, fallen into a chair, and announced that Ariel had gone home. Gil had looked at him funny, but Pete had said, "We'll talk about that later."

Later hadn't arrived yet, since Sam was avoiding Pete—much like he assumed Ariel was avoiding him. Except . . . She'd just walked in, and again, she sat at the bar.

This time she wore sinfully tight dark blue jeans and a flowing white blouse with a ruffle at the neck and long sleeves. She had her curls contained in a French braid and wore white sandals.

She looked so feminine and sexy, his heart lurched at the sight of her. Other body parts followed suit.

Because she didn't so much as glance his way, Sam couldn't see her face.

"Hey, I saw you get your ass beat down at Freddie's." The laughing comment was accompanied by a gust of sour alcohol breath.

Sam looked up into the grizzled, bearded face of an older man, maybe in his fifties, reeking of booze and ready to join him at the small round table. Damn. The last thing he needed was a real drunk that he'd have to protect. Trying to sound both slurred and surly, Sam said, "Ain't been to Freddie's."

The guy laughed and flopped into the seat opposite Sam. "Sure ya have. I seen ya. Two cops came along and saved your ass, though."

When Sam ignored him, putting all his concentration on his glass of whiskey, the man snickered.

"You were prob'ly too drunk to remember."

"Maybe." Sam kicked back the whiskey, suddenly needing it, appreciating the burn as it went down. *Please,* he thought, *please don't get involved in this, Ariel.* He had a hard enough time keeping her out of his head without having her close while he tried to work.

He glanced up, so did she, but she looked through him as if not recognizing him at all, then went back to smiling and talking to the young man beside her. Sam wasn't sure whether he should be disgruntled or relieved.

He definitely wanted to escort her out, away from the men vying for her attention and those leering at her, away from where he had a job to do. Away . . . to maybe someplace private where he could touch her again.

His hands curled into fists.

Unwilling to test her patience or his possessive nature, Sam pulled out his wallet—again well fattened with bills—and put money on the table. In the two hours he'd been sitting in the bar, he'd noted several possible suspects, but there was one man in particular he thought might bite. He'd watched Sam with a type of greedy anger that made Sam edgy. With any luck, the guy would follow Sam out, and Ariel would not.

To the drunk who'd joined him at his small table, Sam tipped a nonexistent hat. "I gotta go while I still can."

"Yeah, yeah sure. You be careful, now."

Without answering, Sam stumbled toward the door, ran himself into the doorframe with a curse, then continued bumbling on until he was across the street on the opposite walk.

Even though it was midnight, the temperature hadn't dropped much and the hot night air washed over him, making him sweat with both anticipation and disgust. Anticipation because he sensed they were close to finding an end to this particular assignment, and disgust because he was sick and tired of swilling whiskey and listening to drunken fools grouse and rumble as they wasted their money on drink.

There were plenty of things he'd rather be doing—and most of them centered around Ariel, no matter how he tried to fight his feelings.

He'd be damn glad to finish the paperwork on this one. Maybe then he could get his head clear.

He was thinking of her, not paying any real attention while making his way to the designated spot where his backup would be able to see him. His mind was filled with thoughts of her stretched out on his bed, teasing him, taunting him, pushing him past his control—and then a sudden flash of movement came into his peripheral vision and Sam's reflexes took over. He ducked and took a pace to the right.

A heavy pipe crashed into the brick wall where Sam's head would have been, chipping the wall and reverberating with a loud clang. Sam dropped and rolled, barely getting out of the way of a sharp knife blade that sliced toward him. He came up on the balls of his feet, battle ready, poised to move.

Two of them! Not just the man who'd been watching him, but also the drunk who'd joined him at his table.

Shit. A set up and he'd totally missed it.

His senses went on alert and adrenaline rushed through him. He said, "You picked the wrong guy," and he laughed just to taunt them.

Outraged, the bigger man with the pipe lunged forward. His cover was already blown, leaving no purpose to his pretense of drunkenness. Sam went on the attack.

Eyes locked on the assailant, he judged his next move, feigned right to dodge the pipe and turned with his elbow raised, delivering a solid clip to the chin that sent the man to his knees. A boot to the belly finished the job, and the pipe fell from the man's hand with a clatter.

Sam heard the swooshing sound too late. He jumped, but not fast enough to get completely out of the way. The lethal edge of a knife sliced through his shirt along his shoulder and across to his side, not going deep but making him grit his teeth with the awful burn. A warm flow of blood trickled down his back.

Sam whirled, saw the bearded man had drawn back his arm to strike again, and he kicked him hard in the knee. Something broke and the man crumbled, for the moment, immobilized.

This particular night, Fuller and Isaac were on shift with Sam again and they ran onto the scene shouting orders.

"About time," Sam complained.

Isaac cuffed the biggest of the two men. Fuller radioed for an ambulance and backup. Seeing he was no longer needed, Sam slumped forward, his hands on his knees while he sucked in air.

The exhilarating rush of adrenaline faded, along with his normal strength. Sam felt shaky and pissed off and so damn weak his knees wanted to give out. Then he saw Ariel standing across the street and he slowly straightened, revived by a new emotion. She had her arms around herself, her bottom lip in her teeth, and her face was etched with fear.

They stared at each other until Fuller said, "Jesus, Sam. We got here as quick as we could, but it wasn't quick enough, was it?"

He felt Fuller's hand on his arm, dragging him down to sit on the curb. Sam's vision swam a little, making Ariel weave in and out of his sight. "Ariel?"

Fuller looked up, saw her, and yelled, "Hey, c'mere, miss. I need you." Then to Sam, "Just breathe, damn it. She's coming."

Though she'd looked as still and pale as a statue up to that point, the second Fuller called her name she dashed forward. Fuller took off his shirt and folded it. "Hang on, Sam. The paramedics are on their way."

"Yeah?" He didn't take his gaze off Ariel's rapid, wild-eyed approach. When she was near, he reached up a hand and she clutched it in both of hers. "What for? I didn't do any real damage to them. Just didn't want them creeping away."

Fuller snorted. "They'll both be fine, minus a working bone or two, but you're bleeding like a stuck pig. The bastard got you. Jesus man, I'm sorry." He pulled up Sam's shirt, cursed again and pressed his folded shirt against the wound.

Ariel was so silent, Sam couldn't stand it. "Sweetheart?"

Big tears swam in her eyes and she gulped. "What?"

"I'm amazed." He would have liked to have more conviction in his voice, but even to his own ears he sounded weak and raspy, damn it. "I didn't know you could show such considerable restraint."

Not quite so pale now, she dropped to her knees in front of him. "What are you talking about?"

"You didn't interfere."

"No, of course not." She tried to pull her hand free. "Let me see your back, Sam."

He held tight. "Fuller's taking care of it."

"But . . ." Her voice shook.

"You stood off to the side like a good civilian instead of playing my White Knight. I'm impressed, really I am."

She frowned at him, shook her hand free and crawled behind him. "Ohmigod."

"It looks worse than it is," Sam told her.

"You can't even see it," she snapped back.

Sam laughed.

An ambulance's siren sounded in the distance, nearly drowning out Ariel as she said, with renewed calm, "You're a condescending, patronizing bastard, Sam Watson. The way you fight . . . well, I didn't think you needed my help. You fight dirty."

"But despite all that, you love me anyway?" He waited, breath held, his heart aching much worse than his back did.

Fuller whistled low.

As if trying to offer comfort, Ariel kept smoothing his shoulder. She stayed so close to him, Sam could smell her sweet soft scent. Then she whispered, "Yeah, I love you."

Sam's eyes closed. "I suppose that's only fair."

"What does that mean?"

But Sam couldn't do anything other than concentrate on not passing out like a girl. The ambulance raced onto the scene. Paramedics swarmed around him, gently moving Ariel aside and working efficiently over both him and the man he'd struck in the knee.

Within moments, they helped Sam to his feet. He saw Ariel wringing her hands and he whispered, "Come to the hospital with me. We need to talk."

"Sam . . ."

"Fuller, make sure she—"

Ariel huffed. "I'll be there, all right?"

Both Sam and Fuller smiled at her worried, waspish tone. Then he was inside the ambulance and they shut the doors and Sam couldn't see her anymore. He let out a long shuddering groan of intense pain.

It had been a real bitch holding it in.

Ariel waited with a crowd of Sam's family in the emergency room. They'd been notified by Fuller, who'd stopped in to see that Sam would be all right before getting back to his shift. The family had shown up minutes later, rushing in like a small battalion.

The nurse had promised them all that it was a mere flesh wound. Yes it required numerous stitches, would indeed leave a scar, but he really, truly was fine. She'd even smiled, bobbed her eyebrows, and stressed the word *fine,* when she said it, making Ariel want to smack her. They were stitching him up and he'd be ready in no time.

And then what? Ariel wondered.

Pete continually paced, but then Pete was young enough

and energetic enough that he seldom managed to be still anyway, even when he wasn't worried.

Gil sprawled in a chair sipping a cup of coffee and staring blankly off into space. Ariel assumed his mind might be divided between thoughts of his brother and his new responsibilities as a parent.

Sam's mother, Belinda, sat beside Ariel, pretending to read a mystery novel while fretting nervously.

Ariel put her head in her hands.

"He really is okay," Belinda said to her. She patted Ariel's knee, and Ariel could hear the amusement in her tone—a tone so like Sam's. Apparently, it wasn't only his mother's bright blue eyes that Sam had inherited.

Ariel nodded, but didn't uncover her face. She felt exposed, sitting with all these people who now, thanks to Pete, knew she was in love with Sam.

Gil had amazed her, giving her a big hug and saying, "Fate is the damndest thing, isn't it?" Ariel wasn't certain if he meant her predicament in loving his brother, or his current state of fatherhood.

Pete kept grumbling, saying, "I hate that he's so bull-headed and aloof and damn it, he deserves to be settled."

Belinda patted Ariel again. "Are you really so worried? Sam's tough you know. This won't be the last time he gets hurt, so you ought to get used to it."

Ariel finally gave up the dubious privacy of her hands and lifted her face. "I probably shouldn't be here."

"And why not?"

Because I told Sam I loved him but he didn't tell me anything of the kind. Ariel shrugged. "I'm not family."

A commotion came from the room where they'd taken Sam, making Ariel's heart lurch until the nurse appeared, pushing Sam in a wheelchair.

"It's hospital rules," the nurse insisted, "so just be quiet and sit still."

"It's a stupid rule and I do not need a damn wheelchair. There's not a single thing wrong with my legs and—"

Belinda stood. "Be quiet, Sam."

He shut down in an instant, but he still looked belligerent. Until he spotted Ariel. "You waited."

Belinda didn't give her a chance to answer. "Well, of course she waited. What a stupid thing to say. Now, let's go. We'll all take you home first and make certain you're settled and then I need to get to my bed. I have church early and as it is I'm not going to get enough sleep."

Ariel would have been shocked by Belinda's tone except that she'd already seen how Belinda hid her mothering behind a gruff show that made it easier for her sons to accept.

En masse, they exited the hospital, Belinda leading the charge, followed by the nurse pushing Sam, then his two brothers talking quietly together.

Feeling like an interloper, Ariel inched along behind them.

At Belinda's minivan, Sam shoved himself awkwardly out of the chair before anyone could assist him, and stood to look around for Ariel. He looked desperate for escape. The nurse gave up and went away, grousing to herself.

Sam stared at Ariel. "Did you drive?"

She nodded, cleared her throat, and said, "Yes."

"Good." He gave his mother a fast kiss on the cheek. "I'm going with Ariel."

Pete said, full of laconic insistence, "Oh no. I'm coming with you then."

Gil shrugged. "I'll drive Mom."

Belinda wasn't having it. "I'll drive my own car, thank

you, and Pete, you're coming with me." She smiled at Ariel. "We'll meet you at his house, dear, all right?"

Ariel found herself nodding before she could give good thought to other possible responses. Sam had said he wanted to talk, but whatever he had to say . . . well, she wasn't ready to hear it yet. A week of trying to prepare herself hadn't gotten her ready.

Muttering under his breath, Sam took her arm and said, "Where the hell's your car? Never mind, I see it." And then, just to be ornery, she was sure, he added, "It's kind of hard to miss."

And Pete said from behind him, evil intent lacing every word, "Yeah, ain't it, though? Even in the dark, and even when you're in a hurry with other things on your mind." With that cryptic remark, he crawled into the backseat of the minivan and slammed the door, leaving Sam to scowl at him in confusion.

Ariel fretted and worried as Sam crossed the lot and eased himself into her car. Plenty of bandages padded his back, but he still looked mighty uncomfortable as he tried to get his seat belt fastened.

She leaned over him. "Let me."

Sam stared into her face, only inches from his, while she pulled the belt over and hooked it around him as gently as possible. She tried not to look at him, but when she started to settle back into her own seat, he caught her. They were nearly nose to nose.

Sam leaned forward and kissed her. "I missed you."

"You did?"

He searched her face and nodded. "Let's go. The sooner I deal with my family, the sooner I can have you alone."

Ariel didn't know what to make of that, but she did as he said, driving slowly and trying to avoid any bumps.

Sam watched her, his gaze unwavering, setting her on edge. "I'm sorry you had to see that," he finally said.

Ariel glanced at him, then brought her attention back to the road. "You move so fast."

"I didn't have much choice. It was move or get stabbed." She gasped and he rushed to say, "But it didn't happen because I can handle myself. And it worked out for the best. The big guy, the one with the pipe? Fuller says he started spilling his guts, looking to cut a deal, as soon as he got him alone in the cruiser. Seems the other man, the old geezer who sliced me, he's the one who ran the show. By now Isaac and Fuller should have all the info they need."

Relief washed over Ariel. "I'm glad that's done then."

Sam gave her a long look. "I'm still undercover though, babe. There'll be other jobs."

"I know."

He waited as if he expected her to say more, but what else was there to say? Sam loved his job and he excelled at it. He was a cop through and through. That wouldn't change.

When they reached his house, they found his family congregated on the front porch along with Hesper, Booth, and the elderly bulldog. Sam groaned. "Jesus, can't a man find any peace?"

"They care about you."

"Yeah, well they could care about me tomorrow instead." He gave her another searching look, and seemed annoyed when she turned away. But she just couldn't bear it.

She'd meant to leave him alone, to let him get beyond his brother's ridiculous insistence on marriage. Then she'd hoped to go to him, to see if he wanted to continue seeing her, no strings attached. Despite what she'd originally told herself, she'd rather have Sam any way she could, than not at all.

Her trip to the bar had been impromptu, one last-ditch effort to get her mind off him for a few minutes.

And fate had stuck her in the same bar where he was working.

She'd been heartsick at the first sight of him, then terrified because she knew what would happen, why he was there. In a dozen different ways, loving Sam was going to be tough.

Sam didn't say anything else as he grunted and groaned his way out of the car. His family merely stood back, watching his progress without offering help. They seemed to know how he felt about assistance—not that Ariel gave a hoot. She took his arm and led him along the walkway that had thankfully been swept clean.

After helping him up to the porch, Ariel took his keys from him and opened his front door, but Sam didn't go in. He put his arm heavily around her and turned to face his family and neighbors. To Ariel, he looked pale and pained and her worry escalated.

Until he said, "I'm fine and while I thank you all for your concern, I'd really like to speak to Ariel. Alone."

Ariel felt her face turn bright red. Now they all knew that he was going to read her the riot act for being in the wrong bar at the wrong time again. Odds were, he'd tell her she had no place in his life, too.

Pete crossed his arms. "Got wedding plans to make?"

Ariel gasped at such a ludicrous comment. "Pete Watson, that is enough."

"No, it's not," Sam told her, and his arm tightened. He looked very put out with her attitude. "I'd like to explain about the other morning . . ."

"There's nothing to explain," she assured him, unwilling to have him forced into saying things he shouldn't have to say, especially with an audience. "I told you, I'm an adult. I knew what I was doing."

"What'd she do?" Booth asked his wife in confusion, and Hesper said, "You don't remember our youth?"

"Ahh." Booth gave a toothy grin. "No wonder the boy's riled."

Belinda shook her head at Ariel. "Let him explain, dear. This might prove interesting."

Sam glared, but none of them budged. "I suppose you all want to hear it?"

Gil said, "I know I do. Hell, I need a distraction."

"Fine." He turned to Ariel and cupped her face. She couldn't look away from the earnestness in his beautiful blue eyes. "I can't bear the thought of you being hurt."

Misunderstanding his meaning, Ariel swallowed, then tried to reassure him. "I'll be fine, Sam. You don't owe me anything." And to try to prove that, she added, "I'm sorry we ended up at the same bar again, but Duluth isn't exactly a hotbed of social outlets. My choices were pretty limited and I promise it was an accident."

Very slowly, the pain seemed to leave him and he stiffened. "What were you doing there, then?"

Ariel took a step away from that gritting tone. "I wasn't trying to watch over you. I promise."

Her assurances only annoyed him more. "Then *why?*"

She glanced around at the rapt faces of their audience. No one looked ready to intervene and rescue her, so she scowled and thrust her chin up. "I was there to . . . well to be sure again."

His face went blank, then turned red and angry. "*Damn it, Ariel.* I thought you were already sure."

"Don't you dare yell at me, Sam. I've had a rough enough week as it is."

He drew a slow breath, gathering himself. "I'm sorry."

Her shoulders drooped. "It's not your fault. I was the pushy one."

"I don't mean that."

Pete laughed. "No, he definitely doesn't mean that."

"Shut up, Pete."

Still grinning, Pete said, "You should be thanking me, you know. I'm the one who got her there in the first place."

Sam and Ariel turned to stare at him. "How's that?" Sam demanded to know.

"Why, I got a new girlfriend, that's how. I finally realized she was waiting for me to do that."

Ariel's brows shot up. "You knew?"

He snorted. "Everyone saw you two ogling each other."

Gil and Belinda nodded.

"You fought it, Sam, I'll give you that. But any time I brought her around, you watched her more than I did."

"I did not."

"Yes you did, Son," Belinda told him. "The poor girl couldn't blink without you noting it."

Hesper laughed. "If it was anything like the way he looks at her now, I'm surprised she didn't go up in flames."

Exasperated, Sam rubbed his face, then suddenly stiffened. His hands dropped to his sides and he stared at Pete. "You saw her car that night. That's what you meant about it being impossible to miss, even in the dark."

"Of course I saw it." Pete snorted. "Why do you think I told you all that stuff about her? Hell, I don't gossip about women, especially women I love—as friends—so get rid of that evil look, all right? I just wanted you to know up front how she felt about you."

Humiliated beyond all reason, Ariel tried to inch away, anxious to escape. Without looking at her, Sam caught her wrist and kept her at his side. "Then you came back here the next morning and pretended outrage, reading me the riot act like . . ."

"Like a brother who loves you, yeah. I was trying to make it easy for you to give up, you know, salvage your pride and all that. I figured you could blame me or something since I pretty much figured you hadn't told her that you love her." He elbowed Gil hard. "But Gil here showed up and everything got off track."

Ariel cleared her throat. "Really, none of this is necessary. I don't expect Sam to—"

Sam cast her a look. "Get used to it, honey. They're all pushy as hell, but they're part of the package."

"They are?"

His eyes narrowed. "My house, my rules. Love me, love my family."

Her heart started a furious pounding and she couldn't get a breath. "But . . ."

Sam gave up with visible bad grace. "I didn't want to involve you in my life, all right? I didn't want you to be at risk for being around me and with me. I didn't want you always worried and afraid." He touched her cheek, and Ariel felt the gentleness, the uncertainty. "You're so soft, Ariel. And so sweet. You aren't cut out for my life."

Belinda scowled. "What am I, chopped liver? I'm your mother and I'm certainly a part of your life. You don't consider me sweet or soft?" The venomous glare she gave her son kept him silent.

Gil and Pete, however, snickered with good humor.

"And don't forget your baby brother." Pete put the back of his hand to his head in a gesture of emotional distress. "I'm traumatized nightly, thinking about all the risks you take. I believe you've stunted my growth."

Since Pete was six-two, his claims were deliberately absurd.

Booth nodded vigorously in agreement. "Poor Hesper here can't sleep at night, listening for young Sam, wanting to make sure he gets home safe and sound." He harrumphed. "Don't see him concerning himself with the likes of us though."

The bulldog barked.

Sam said, "How I feel about Ariel is different, damn it."

With the concise, no-nonsense tone he was known for, Gil said, "Then will you please tell her so? She looks to be in an agony of suspense."

Sam took one look at her, nodded, then faced his family. "I need to sit down. Will you all just leave?" And then just as quickly, "Not you, Ariel."

Pete said, "He still has to propose."

Ariel fried Pete with a look. She would definitely get him later. Couldn't he see that his brother was in pain and not up to all that teasing? "Come on, Sam. I'll help you inside."

Sam allowed her to hug into his uninjured side, attempting to offer him support; then he looked back at his family and grinned. "Bye."

His mother said, "We'll leave, but I expect to hear from you in the morning."

Sam nodded. "Ariel or I, one will give you a call." And then he stepped inside and kicked the door shut. "Peace, at last."

"Are you all right?"

"Getting better by the minute." Then: "Upstairs, babe. I need to lie down."

"Oh, Sam." Her worry was a live thing, but Sam went up the steps without too much help from her and once in his room, he lowered himself painfully to sit on the edge of the bed.

"Will you help me get my clothes off?" When she stared at him, he said, "I want to lie down."

"Oh. Yes of course."

"I'm not hurt that bad, but the loss of blood . . ."

She went pale and rushed to get him out of the shirt Gil had brought up to the hospital for him. Snowy white gauze wrapped diagonally over his dark, powerful chest, from his right shoulder to beneath his left arm, covering him front and back. Ariel touched her hand to her mouth and just knew she was going to cry.

Sam kicked out of his shoes, then stood. "My pants?"

She shook herself. The last thing Sam needed now was a whining, weepy, overly emotional woman on his hands. The way he held his right arm, it had to be hurting him. "Of course."

Going to her knees, Ariel stripped off his socks and reached for the fly to his slacks. He was hard.

Her gaze snapped up to his.

He grinned. "Hey, you're on your knees in front of me, sweetheart, ready to take off my pants. What did you expect?"

She'd missed him so much, and loved him more than that. She just couldn't take his teasing right now. "You're hurt, damn it. Be serious." Shaking now, Ariel pulled his pants down over his hips and Sam stepped out of them.

His hand touched the top of her head. "You've been avoiding me for a week, Ariel. I finally have you here, alone in my bedroom. Believe me, I'm taking this very seriously." Wearing only his underwear—and that tented—he sat in the bed and leaned carefully back against a pillow on the headboard. He let out a long sigh. "Now strip off your clothes and get into bed with me."

Her stomach flip-flopped. "Sam . . ."

"My house, my rules."

His voice was gentle, but his gaze burned and Ariel felt a

smile twitch on her mouth. "Your rules are ridiculous and you know it. There's no way you're up to . . . that."

"That?"

"Whatever it is you're thinking."

"I'm thinking that I need to hold you, and I'm thinking you're more inclined to say yes if you're naked in bed with me."

"Yes about what?"

He stared at her a long moment, then, in the softest, most uncertain tone she'd ever heard from him, he said, "About whether or not you'll marry me."

Her mouth fell open. "Sam?"

He scowled, rallying forth arguments. "Look at it this way, if you marry me you get to change some of the rules because it'll be your house, too."

Happiness bubbled up, swelled until Ariel felt ready to burst. Watching his face, her own wide smile in place, she stripped off her clothes and climbed in beside him. Sam urged her close to his left side, shifted until he was comfortable, then said, "Now, tell me you love me again. It's the truth, I need to hear it."

"I love you, Sam."

He groaned, hugged her as tightly as he could, considering he was hurt, and kissed her hair. "I love you, too, Ariel. So much that I don't think I could take it if you didn't marry me. At first . . . well, I hate to admit it, but I was as fretful as an old woman."

"If you said that to your mother, she'd bop you on the head."

He smiled. "I don't like the thought of you worrying about me when I'm at work, and I absolutely can't stand the thought of you showing up where I am, maybe interfering and putting yourself at risk."

"As long as I know where you're at and what you're doing, I won't get in your way."

"And you won't worry?"

"There's absolutely nothing I can do about the worry, Sam. I love you." She gently touched the front of his bandages. "You're a good cop—"

"A great cop."

She laughed. "And you're more than capable of taking care of yourself. But I'll still worry. You'll just have to accept that."

"I'll accept it," he growled, "if you'll agree to marry me."

"I'll marry you."

"Thank God." They fell silent for a long moment, holding each other, Ariel with her hand over his heart. She thought he might have dozed, but then he said, "About those rules? There's only one you can't tamper with, okay?"

Ariel twisted to smile up at him. He looked rugged, wounded, and horny. She laughed. "And which rule is that?"

"The one about being naked at breakfast. I've decided I like that rule, and starting every day off with a view of your sweet backside . . . well, know that you're stuck with me forever, okay?"

Ariel grinned. "As long as it goes both ways. And that, Officer, is my rule."

Bringing Up Baby

Chapter One

Gil Watson was both nervous and excited—an odd combination he hadn't experienced since his first years of college. These days he was confidence personified, commanding even, an in-charge guy perfect for the corporate world. He prided himself on his professional demeanor, his calm outlook on life. He had a business to run for his family; they relied on him and he enjoyed that.

He'd grown up—and in the process permanently buried all wild inclinations.

But today, the figures blurred on the computer screen in front of him. He wasn't getting much work done, which seemed to be the norm of late, rather than the exception. It had taken only one phone call to throw him off track, but then, it wasn't every day a man learned he had a daughter, a daughter he hadn't known of until two weeks ago.

He hadn't been the same since.

Would she look like him? At two and a half years, was a child developed enough to look like anyone? What he knew about babies wouldn't fill a thimble. At thirty-two, he concentrated on knowing business, family responsibility, and finances. And not to brag, he also knew women.

But he knew zilch about being a father.

It still boggled his mind that Shelly had never said a word. He saw her two or three times a year, whenever business took him to Atlanta. He'd been to her office, to her home, met her coworkers and friends. Right after his father's death three years ago, he'd been so sick at heart that he'd done things he wasn't proud of.

Like using Shelly.

Not that she hadn't been willing. She'd sent him one of her looks and he'd reciprocated, and within the hour they'd gone from business associates to lovers. He still remembered the wild, frenzied way she'd taken him. For two days, he kept her in his motel room burning up the sheets. She'd catered to his sexual needs, his fantasies, and even his less than orthodox demands—*the demands he'd thought well under control.* She'd been everything he'd physically wanted and needed at the time.

In truth, she'd wrung him out and left his body and mind thankfully blank for an entire weekend, relieving his sense of loss for his father, obliterating his concern about taking over the family business and the overwhelming responsibilities he'd accepted as his own.

It was when he'd awakened and saw her looming over him, smiling with too much emotion for a mere sexual coupling, that Gil had realized his mistake. Shelly wanted a husband and apparently saw him as a prime candidate. But he didn't want the burden of a wife added to the new load he already carried.

His oldest brother was a cop, his youngest brother still in school, and his mother had never involved herself with the company. Taking over the successful family novelty business and keeping them all financially solvent had naturally fallen to Gil. Outwardly, he was the most staid, the only one who'd shown an interest, his father's protégé.

No, the last thing he'd wanted was a wife to further muddy the waters, so he'd done what he considered wise and responsible. He'd gently explained his lack of interest and had never again touched Shelly sexually. Yet she'd had his baby and continued to associate with him as a close friend. Without once ever telling him.

Gil's stomach clenched over such a deception. He hadn't known, damn it, but that was no excuse. Shelly had taken care of their baby alone and now she was gone. He couldn't make things right by her—but he could raise their daughter. And he would.

Giving up, he closed out the computer program and leaned back in his chair, his mind churning with regrets and curiosity and that persistent nervousness. A baby, his baby. Jesus.

A small commotion in the outer office drew him forward again in his chair. He grew alert, his brows drawn in confusion when the door opened and his assistant stuck her head in. Her frown rivaled his own. "Gil, you have . . . company."

At fifty, Alice wasn't prone to melodrama. Her expression had Gil rising from his desk in a rush. "Who is it?"

"Well, the young lady introduced herself as Anabel Truman. And the youngest lady is Nicole Lane Tyree, as I understand it, although all she's done is suck her thumb."

Every muscle in Gil's body went rigid. His brain cramped. His daughter was here—*with Anabel*—two weeks early. He rounded his desk with a long stride.

Damn Anabel; he'd offered to come to her, to buy her airline tickets, to pay for their transportation. As contrary and outrageous as ever, she'd refused, telling him it'd be at least ten days before she could leave. Ten long days before he'd get to meet his baby.

Yet she was here, at his office, where he didn't want her to be, rather than at his home where he might keep his private business private for a little while longer. At least until he could figure out what to do, how to proceed . . .

Arms crossed and eyebrows lifted, Alice moved out of his way as Gil charged forward. If this was a deliberate ploy on Anabel's part to discredit him, he'd—well, he didn't know what he'd do yet, but he'd think of something. Because Anabel had been Shelly's roommate, he'd known her as long as he'd known Shelly. She was always there when he visited, always twitting him, picking at him. Her presence was always unnerving; she made him think things he shouldn't think, things he had tried not to think now that he had new responsibilities to consider.

As Shelly's best friend, she'd been off-limits then. But no more.

He threw the door wide and then froze, his heart shooting into his throat, his stomach dropping, his knees almost giving out. Damn it, why did Anabel have that effect on him?

She looked the same as always: seductive. He'd never really liked her. She was too outspoken and pushy. Too overtly sexual and in your face. Too . . . hot. She was one of those women you just knew would be incredible in the sack and it made him nuts.

It wasn't just her jewelry, her overdone makeup and risqué clothing that had made her far too difficult to ignore. There'd been something about the way she watched him, too, her close attention, the carnality in her gaze that made him wonder if their basic natures might mesh.

That thought had kept him on edge whenever he was around her.

Now he realized that she might have watched him for the simple reason that he was Nicole's father and didn't know it. He might have totally misread her.

When she'd called, her tone had been devoid of accusation, empty of any real emotion when usually she teemed with emotion. She'd told him of Shelly's death, of his baby girl, all with a detachment that had left him bewildered and floundering—a situation he didn't like one bit. He was used to being in charge, of knowing what he did and why and having no doubts whatsoever.

Did it matter to Anabel that he hadn't known of the baby?

She stood there now in low-slung, faded jeans, a clinging stretch top of bright pink and . . . oh God, she had a belly button ring. He fixated on that for what seemed like an inordinate amount of time before he heard her low, throaty laugh. He jerked his gaze up to her face.

The woman was beyond outrageous, and in the months since he'd last seen her she'd only grown more so. "Anabel." Thankfully, his tone was even, polite. "This is a surprise."

"I know." She grinned, and that grin was so teasing that Gil felt it like a tactile touch. Then he saw the exhaustion she tried to mask, the utter weariness in every line of her body.

Sudden worry overwhelmed every other emotion. "What's happened?"

At the sound of his voice, a pale face surrounded by dark curls peeked out from behind Anabel's knees. Until that moment, Gil hadn't noticed the tiny hands hugging around her legs, the little bare feet behind hers.

The baby, his baby, was hiding.

At his very first glimpse of her, Gil's heart turned over. He couldn't get enough oxygen into his starved lungs. She was so tiny, he hadn't expected . . .

Without really thinking about it, he went to one knee, putting himself more on her diminutive level. "Nicole?"

The little girl blinked enormous chocolate brown eyes framed by long lashes. Her rosebud mouth crumbled and she tried to climb up the back of Anabel's legs, saying, "Mommy!"

Mommy? Taken aback, Gil lifted a brow and looked to Anabel for some explanation.

Anabel pulled Nicole around to her front and playfully scooped her up, holding her to her breasts and laughing. "Hey, little rat, remember what I told you? I promise you don't need to be afraid."

Little rat? But the child had a stranglehold on Anabel that she couldn't pry loose, so it didn't appear she'd taken offense at the less than complimentary endearment.

Anabel glanced at Gil and shrugged in apology. "It's been a long trip and she's tired."

Disappointment shook him, but Gil hid it. At least he hoped he did. He rose slowly to his feet again. "Come into my office." Stepping back, he held the door open until Anabel had swept past him. He could feel her energy, detect her light flowery scent. Behind on his office floor she'd left a large colorful bag overflowing with a tattered stuffed bear, a faded print blanket, a squeeze bottle of juice, and other baby paraphernalia.

Blank-brained, at an utter loss, Gil looked at Alice.

In her typical no-nonsense manner, Alice lifted the bag and pressed it into his hands. "The child might need this."

"Of course." The damn thing weighed a ton. "Hold all my calls and cancel any appointments."

"You were meeting your mother and brother for lunch."

His brain scrambled in panic mode before settling on a course. "Call Sam. Tell him Anabel is here. He'll understand."

"You're the boss." Alice hesitated. "Gil, if you need anything else . . ."

She'd been his father's secretary, and now his. She was protective and loyal, and Gil sent her a smile of gratitude. "Thanks. I'll let you know." Then, on second thought he added, "How about some coffee, Alice?"

"I'll bring it right away."

"Thank you." Gil stepped into his office, shut the door, and tried to figure out what to do next. He silently tallied the facts at hand: Anabel was here, a woman he shouldn't have wanted, but did. His daughter was here, a child he'd only just found out about but already cherished. His life was about to undergo some drastic changes. He had to do *something*—but all he managed was to stand there, watching the two of them.

Anabel had sprawled in his black leather desk chair, the child on her lap, and she was whispering in Nicole's ear, kissing her downy cheek, and rubbing her narrow back.

Gil wanted to hold her. He wanted to cuddle his child and know her and let her know him. The feeling was so alien, yet so powerful, Gil naturally shied away from it.

"We're starving." Anabel glanced up at him. "You got anything to eat?"

Finally having a purpose, Gil strolled to his desk to perch on the edge and pushed the intercom button. "Can we order up some lunch, too, Alice?"

"Sandwiches, pizza, soup."

He turned to Anabel, leaving the choice up to her, and she said, "Pepperoni pizza. Maybe some salad for me, too. And a Mountain Dew if it's available—I could use the caffeine kick. I have juice for Toots, here."

Alice said, "Give me fifteen minutes."

With that accomplished, Gil settled back, linking his fingers and resting his hands on his thighs. The pose was relaxed when he felt anything but. He made note of so many things at once. The dark circles under Anabel's green eyes, the windblown disarray of her short, fawn-colored hair. The row of hoop earrings in her left ear, each increasing in size. Five total, he counted, the largest about as big as a quarter.

A tattoo circled her upper arm. It appeared to be a horizontal flower vine, but it was too delicate for him to be sure without leaning forward for a closer look. And he wasn't about to get that close to her.

Nicole twisted slightly to see him, but she kept her nose stuck in Anabel's neck, her arms locked around her. Her round eyes were huge and wary.

Gil tried for his gentlest smile. "Hello there."

" 'Lo."

He badly wanted to touch her, and he didn't deny himself. Slowly reaching out with only one finger, he stroked the silky soft hair over her temple. His heart threatened to punch through his chest.

She shied away, going back into hiding and gripping Anabel with new fervor.

"Give her time, Gil. She's been through a lot."

The idea of what she'd been through smote him clean through to his soul. He was her father; he should have been there for her, protecting her, making her feel safe and secure no matter what else happened. He cleared his throat. "And you, as well. I know you and Shelly were close."

She looked away. In a whisper she said, "Toward the end, I barely knew her at all."

Toward the end? The end of what? Shelly had died suddenly in a car wreck, Anabel had told him. What did she mean, then? But his questions would have to wait until Nicole wasn't listening. He didn't know how much a child her age might comprehend, and he wouldn't risk adding to her trauma.

Alice knocked before stepping in with a tray of coffee and cups. "This will get you started before the lunch arrives. The little girl has something to drink?"

Anabel shoved to her feet with Nicole still clinging like a determined monkey. "Juice—never leave home without it."

"Juice," Nicole mimicked. She stuck out one skinny arm in demand, grasping at the air with her tiny fingers.

Gil wanted to melt on the spot. She was by far the most precious thing he'd ever seen. "I'll get it for her."

"Thanks." Anabel hoisted her small burden a little higher in her arms. "Methinks naptime is closing in." She winked at Gil, then moved to the leather couch and pried Nicole loose to sit her on the cushion next to her. "You're giving him a complex, rat. Say hi again, like you mean it this time."

Nicole sat there, her pudgy bare feet sticking off the couch cushion, sizing him up with an unblinking stare. To Gil's surprise, she suddenly treated him to a beatific smile, wrinkling her little pug nose and scrunching her whole face up. "Hi."

"Good girl." Anabel accepted the coffee that Alice handed to her and took a long sip, groaning in pleasure. "Wonderful. You're an angel, thank you."

"My pleasure." Alice retreated from the room.

Cautiously, not wanting to startle her, Gil handed his daughter her juice. "Is it cold enough for you?"

"She doesn't like it cold, do you, Nicki?" Nicole didn't answer. She had the squeeze bottle tipped up, guzzling away until juice ran down her chin. Anabel quickly put her coffee aside to relieve her of the drink. Eyelids drooping, Nicole turned to her side, put her head in Anabel's lap, and just that easily, dozed off.

"She's run out of gas." Anabel smoothed the dark curls, straightened the wrinkled T-shirt. "She's been up all morning, poor little thing. Long car trips make her nauseous. We're lucky we got here with only one barfing episode."

Gil drew himself up. "You drove?"

"Wanna keep your voice down? She konks out fast, but she's a light sleeper. If she's back up after only ten minutes, she'll be a hellion. You'll boot us out before she can show you her sweeter side."

Boot out his own daughter? Never.

"Hey, can you maybe produce some music? Background noise would help her sleep, and then we can . . . chat about things."

Annoyed at both her censure and that the child had been ill, Gil went to a console and turned a switch. Doors slid open to reveal a state-of-the-art television, and CD and DVD players. He glanced through his collection, picked out a classic Beach Boys CD, and put the volume on low.

Once the music filtered into the room, he turned to face Anabel Truman, his emotions boiling too close to the surface.

She beat him to the punch, blinking green eyes in horror and whispering, "What the heck is *that?*"

"What?"

"That . . . noise." She gave a theatrical shudder.

"The Beach Boys?" He should have known she'd take exception to his choice. In the past, she'd taken exception to everything.

"I forgot that you have the most deplorable taste in music." She snorted. "You listen to crap that a fifty-year-old guy would like."

Gil drew himself up. He would not be sidetracked by her ridiculous insults. "Forget my preference in music. Let's talk about how you got here."

Shrugging, she said, "I drove."

"All the way from Atlanta?"

"Yep." Unconcerned, Anabel stretched out her long legs and slumped back in her seat, nursing her coffee like a drunk nursed a whiskey. The pose exposed more of her soft belly, making it hard for Gil to concentrate. "We left at five this morning, stopped several times, and now we're here."

Forcing himself to look away from her negligent and somehow provocative posture, Gil went back to his desk, but he didn't seat himself in the chair. Again, he chose to rest his hip against the surface. He was a mature man, calm and collected, always with a purpose. A peek at a woman's belly did not waylay him. "Why, Anabel? I offered to fly you both in."

"We New Age gals like to have our transportation with us. Who knows when you might piss me off and I'll have to leave? No way will I be dependent on you."

She said all that in such an amicable, even tone that it took a moment for the words to sink in. Once they did, anger washed away his calm façade. "We should be very clear with each other, don't you think, Anabel?"

"Sure." She rested her head back against the couch and closed her eyes.

Damn it, Gil couldn't help but notice her belly again, how cute the colored stone looked there. He also noticed her breasts and the lack of a bra. Her nipples were smooth and soft right now, but he imagined a woman like Anabel could be easily aroused with a soft, leisurely suckle. She was so open about things, so casual about her body and her thoughts . . .

It'd been too damn long since he'd had a woman.

It'd been years since he'd had the raw, uninhibited sex he preferred. Not since that night with Shelly . . .

Again, he reined himself in. "She's my daughter."

"You don't have to growl it." Looking boneless and exhausted, her eyes still closed, Anabel said, "Anyone who sees you two together will know you're her dad. In case you haven't noticed, she's the spittin' image of you."

Gil glanced at the toddler, but in her slumber, her adorable little face was smooshed up against Anabel's denim-covered thigh, making it impossible to assess her features. How could she look like him? He was a two-hundred-pound man, dark enough that he had to shave twice a day to avoid beard shadow. Nicole was petite and precious and sweet. He recalled the way her dark brown eyes had assessed him, the same color brown as his own. Her hair was as dark, too, but silky soft and curly, unlike his own. So the coloring was the same, but there the similarities ended.

As he stared at Nicole, he felt that elusive yearning again, expanding inside him, almost choking him. How long would it take before his daughter accepted him? He cleared his throat. "You brought her to me."

Anabel's eyes snapped open. "Whoa, big boy. I brought her to meet you. We'll see about anything else."

"She's mine, Anabel." He wasn't certain about everything, but he had no bones about that. "She belongs with me."

Her breasts rose on an anxious breath. Carefully, she straightened and slid the child over so that she curled on her side, forming a small adorable lump on the couch. Anabel pushed to her feet. Gil knew she wanted to look in calm control, but her eyes had darkened to a forest green and her hands were curled tight in restraint. "Nicki loves me, Gil. I'm the one who's cared for her. I'm the one who's raised her so far. I'm the one who's loved her."

Where had Shelly been if Anabel raised Nicole? Gil shook his head. "I didn't even know about her."

"That was Shelly's decision, not mine." She strode to him, her body rigid, desperation pulsing off her in waves. "If

I'd told you, she said she'd take Nicki from me. I couldn't let that happen. In every way that is most important, Nicki is mine."

Feeling as though he stood on the edge of a deep cliff, Gil waited.

Anabel drew a breath, collecting herself. She tucked in her chin, met Gil's gaze squarely. "There's only one way you can have her."

Narrowing his eyes, Gil played along, knowing damn good and well that he'd never let her go, not now, no matter what. "And that is?"

She licked her lips, but her hesitation lasted no more than a few seconds. "You can marry me."

The timely arrival of pizza saved Anabel from saying any more. Not that she'd be able to get a single word out with Gil standing there, stunned mute, his expression leaning toward incredulity. *Well, what had you expected, Anabel? Open arms and gratitude?* She twisted her mouth in a grimace, wanting to cry, to sleep, wanting to grab Nicki and run as far and as fast as she could.

Those options weren't open to her.

While Alice bustled into the office with a fragrant box of pizza and a salad, Gil turned away to the window. He looked stiff, outraged, confused. He looked . . . well, delicious.

With a fine trembling making her unsteady, Anabel re-seated herself behind his desk in his cushy chair. The fancy office hadn't thrown her. She'd known he was well off, just from the fifteen-hundred-dollar suits he wore whenever he visited Shelly. He was always well-groomed, well-spoken, polite and polished.

He hid his true nature well. But she knew, oh yeah, she

did. She knew and she understood, and hopefully that'd be her ace in the hole.

Before she bungled this more, she needed to eat and she needed to sleep. Gil didn't look ready to let her do either. Damn her big blabbermouth. The stress had taken its toll and she wasn't thinking clearly to have just blurted that out. Now she'd have to retrench, laugh it off, give him a little more time to get used to her.

Maybe seduce him.

Alice put out napkins. "Sam said he expects a full accounting tonight. He'll speak to your mother for you."

"Damn it . . ."

"No. He said he'd keep her from visiting until you invited them, but he also said not to press your luck."

"Meaning my mother isn't known for her patience."

Alice just smiled. "Let me know if you need anything else." After she'd again left them, Gil strolled to the front of the desk, facing Anabel. She sat there, mostly numb, not quite daring enough to meet his gaze, while he served her a slice of pizza and the salad she'd ordered. "You can eat while you explain that outrageous comment."

She wished he sounded more passionate and less reasonable. If she read him wrong, if Shelly had mistaken things, then she'd blow this for sure.

Reaching for calm control, which wasn't really her forte on her best day, Anabel said, "Not much to explain." She took a huge bite of pizza and groaned at the mingled delights of melted cheese, tomato sauce, and spicy pepperoni. "Oh God, that's good."

Gil stared at her mouth, making her self-conscious. "Have you eaten since this morning?"

"I packed some stuff for the rat, but no, I didn't take much time to eat." She'd been too rushed, too desperate to find an alternative to the unthinkable, and far too nervous about her improbable success.

His antagonism thickened. "Must you call her that?"

"What?" Anabel peeked at him, then indulged in another large bite. He was every bit as autocratic as she remembered, and just as contained. Gil Watson never voiced his temper, never made public mistakes, was never indecisive or uncertain.

"Rat." He said it like a dirty word. "It's insulting."

From the day she'd met him, Gil had made his disapproval of her known. Oh, he wasn't mean-spirited enough to say anything, and he was never cruel. But the way he looked at her, the rigid way he held himself in her presence, told it all.

He disliked what he assumed to be her laid-back lifestyle. He disapproved of her choices, choices he knew nothing about.

He judged her and found her lacking—but he wanted her anyway. She could tell as much, whether he admitted it or not. She wanted him, too, so she had no problem with that. Even in the face of his condemnation, she'd always liked him. A lot. By necessity, he'd never known the whole story, not about her or the basis for her choices. Would it matter? She hoped so.

He'd make a good father to Nicki, and if it all worked out as she hoped, he'd make a passable husband so that they could be a family, the type of family Nicole deserved. Gil might not ever love her, but that didn't matter at this point. He would care for his daughter. He would protect them and give Nicki everything she needed.

He deserved the truth, so she mustered her wavering courage and bared her soul. "I love her more than life. She knows that. Rat is just a pet name for her."

"I don't like it."

Anabel grinned and saluted him with her cola. "Already the protective father. Remember that when she's demanding and whiny and stubborn."

He glanced at Nicole's sweet little face with disbelief. "You're just being snide and there's no reason for it."

She laughed. Oh, was he in for a surprise if he expected Nicki to be the perfect child. She was delightful and precious, but also as cranky and contrary as any other toddler. "Sorry. Just let me have two more bites before I faint from hunger and I promise I'll magically transform into a pleasant being."

He appeared doubtful at that, but nodded. "What about Nicole? I thought you said she was hungry, too." He stopped beside the couch, his hands shoved deep into his pants pockets, his head down as he watched his daughter. Her T-shirt had ridden up, showing her pale, soft back and the top of plastic-covered training pants above the waistband of her shorts. His expression was fixed, clouded with emotions.

Watching him watch Nicole made Anabel's heart hurt. He'd missed out on so much. Anabel could almost feel his desire to pick Nicki up, to hug her. It had been wrong to keep the baby from him, but what choice had she been given?

Softly, suffering smothering regret, Anabel said, "I guess she was more tired than hungry." She cleared her throat. Getting sentimental at this point would blow everything. "She'll eat when she wakes up."

"How long does she normally nap?"

"Maybe an hour if we're lucky." Anabel stared at his broad back, visible through the perfect fit of his tailored dress shirt. "Where will we sleep tonight?"

Gil's head snapped around and he stared at her over his

shoulder. His piercing attention settled on her like a thick blanket, further unnerving her.

"I mean Nicki and me, not . . ." Damn her exhausted state. She sighed, laughed a little at herself. "Is your place big enough for us? I don't exactly have the funds to start staying in motels for an extended visit, and I assumed you'd want time with her. Where she goes, I go, so—"

"I get it." He turned away from the couch to fully face her, still holding her in that unrelenting stare. "Yes, I have room. Don't give it another thought." He went to the phone on the desk near her and dialed a number. A second later he said, "Candace, this is Gil. Prepare the guestroom please. And stock the refrigerator with juice—" He covered the mouthpiece and said to Anabel, "What type of juice does she prefer?"

Candace? Who the hell was Candace? If he had a girlfriend or, God forbid, a wife, what would she do?

"Anabel?"

Her heart pounded in dread but she forced herself to answer. "Mixed fruit. And milk. And she likes fresh vegetables and bananas and crackers of just about any kind."

Gil nodded and relayed the list to Candace. When he hung up, he crossed his arms over his chest and surveyed her. He was so close Anabel could smell his cologne. It was spicy and warm—like Gil. Of course, he didn't want most people to know just how spicy he could get.

But Shelly had talked. A lot. And so Anabel knew him better than he might imagine. "Are you married?"

It came out sounding like an accusation, and Anabel winced. But Gil didn't look offended. "No."

In for a penny . . ."Engaged? Involved? Serious about anyone?"

"No."

Her breath came out in a long sigh of relief. "So who's Candace?"

At her inquisition, his gaze sharpened the tiniest bit. "She's the housekeeper."

"No kidding? You have a maid?" She knew he was well-to-do, but that just seemed so . . . extravagant.

"A housekeeper. Part-time. She comes three days a week."

"Just to clean up after you?" Anabel raised one brow, surveying him from head to toe. "And here I thought you were a pretty fastidious fellow."

His expression didn't change. "I like a certain amount of order in my life, and I like things clean and neat. Candace sees to it."

Order, neatness? Oh boy. With a falsely bright smile, Anabel said, "And now you have a very active toddler. Imagine the fun."

Gil straightened away without replying to that. "I have a few more things to do here and then we can head to my place." His attention drifted over her face before softening with concern. "You look like you could use a nap yourself."

That little bit of sympathy about did her in. She was so physically and emotionally spent that it wouldn't take much to have her bawling. She drummed up a cheery smile. "Yeah, I'm pooped. But there's no need to interrupt your day. If you want to just give us directions . . ." She could get there and get a lay of the land before him.

"I don't think so." He crossed his arms over his chest. "Tell me what's going on, Anabel."

His stance said it all. He wouldn't be put off, not a second more. She shoved one more forkful of salad into her mouth, then pushed her plate away and propped her elbows on the desk. She hoped she looked unconcerned with everything she had to dump on him. If he knew how desperate she was, would he use it against her? She didn't think so, but couldn't take the risk.

"Shelly got strange after she had Nicole." His left eyebrow shot up, and she said, "Yeah, yeah, I know what you're thinking. Who am I to talk about strange, right?" With one finger, she fluttered her row of earrings.

He didn't comment, just gave specific notice to the narrow tattoo circling her upper arm.

Anabel resisted the urge to defend herself. "What I mean is that she wanted little to do with Nicole. She spent all her time partying, trying to prove to herself that she was sexy, that men wanted her."

"She was sexy. And I know she didn't want for dates."

"No, but you rejected her and that really took a chunk out of her self-esteem." Anabel didn't want to add to his guilt, so she said, "You might not know this, but Shelly didn't have a very happy home life." *What an understatement.*

"And that made her a less than perfect mother?"

"There is no such thing as a perfect parent. But no, I just meant that it made her very insecure. I think in her own way, she loved Nicole, but she didn't want to be tied down with her. She thought having a baby made her somehow less appealing to men. She thought they'd see her differently if they knew she'd given birth. So she kept it a secret."

"From everyone?"

"Most people." Her parents had known—and vehemently disapproved. "I work at home, so I took care of Nicole." This was the part where she had to convince him, had to make him understand. "I'm the only real mother she's ever known, Gil."

He looked her over again, and Anabel just knew he found

her lacking. Not that she blamed him. When she'd taken over the task of caring for the baby, she'd worried, too. She loved Nicole and always did her best. For a while, it had been enough.

But not anymore. Now she needed Gil.

He said only, "You took care of her all by yourself?"

"For the most part." And in more ways than he could imagine. "Nicole was covered by Shelly's medical insurance, and occasionally, when she thought of it, she contributed financially. But she spent almost no time with her. When she did, it was more like Nicole was a stranger to her, not her own daughter."

He stood silent, not looking particularly convinced or skeptical. When Gil Watson chose to keep his thoughts hidden, he did an admirable job of it.

Anabel stared down at her hands. "I wanted to tell you about Nicki." She swallowed down her guilt and her reservations to give him another truth. "I always thought you'd be a good father and things would have been so much easier with your help. But Shelly was insistent. She said you'd take Nicole away."

"From her—or from you?"

Her gaze jerked up to his. "I would have been willing to share her." Her heart raced fast and her palms were damp. "I know it sounds strange, but Shelly hoped to win you over someday and she wanted to know it was for herself, not because of Nicole. You . . . you were the only man who ever dumped her."

He ran his hand over his face and began to pace the office. "We were only friends."

"You were lovers, too."

He stared at her hard.

"Shelly told me . . . things." Anabel shrugged awkwardly,

wishing she knew his thoughts, but his look was too in-
scrutable for her to decipher. "She talked about you a lot."

"I see." He made no effort to hide his displeasure.

Leaving her chair in a rush, Anabel strode to him. "She
died in that damn car wreck because she'd been drinking. I
think she might have been high, too. She was getting worse
and worse, losing her focus." She stopped in front of Gil,
hating to remember just how bad it'd gotten, how she'd been
so afraid for Nicole. "After she died, her parents stepped in
and took her business to sell, but they said there wasn't
much money left once they'd paid her debts and taken care
of the funeral."

Gil folded his arms over his chest, his face set. "So now
you need money."

He made her sound like an opportunist. In a way, she supposed she was. She wanted Nicole, and she needed him—in
more ways than one. "Yes. On my own, I can't afford to give
Nicole everything she should have. I've always chosen to
work at home so I could be with her and now . . . well, my
income isn't something to brag about."

"You're still doing web pages?"

Her chin lifted. She remembered the time Gil had walked
in on her while she'd been working on an extensive adult
site. He'd considered it porn, while she'd only seen it as one
of her better paying jobs. "I make enough to keep up with
the rent and monthly bills, but I don't have insurance for myself or Nicole. Babies get sick a lot, they need vaccinations,
checkups." Please let him understand. "They need two parents."

Gil stepped closer, casually intimidating her with his size.
His eyes were such a deep, fathomless brown, framed by
thick lashes, awesomely direct and always serious. "So I'm
supposed to marry you so that you can keep *my* daughter."

It wasn't easy, but she nodded. Then added, her voice soft, "Yes."

He took another step closer until she thought she could almost feel his heartbeat mingling with her own. Staring at her mouth, he said, "Tell me, Anabel. What's in it for me?"

Chapter Two

Gil watched her small pink tongue come out to wet her dry lips, saw the nervous flutter of her long eyelashes, the rapid pulse in her smooth throat. After her bold declaration about marriage, he was surprised anything could discomfort her.

He did want her. Hell, the wanting burned just beneath his skin every time he looked at her. In his younger days he would have damned the consequences and jumped on the opportunity afforded him now. But he was no longer that wild, impetuous youth ruled by his dick. He was a well-respected businessman—and his last uninhibited escapade had landed him with a daughter.

And Anabel.

He'd never thought much about settling down with one woman, but if he had, he wouldn't have envisioned a wife like her. No, if he had to consider it—and he didn't, not yet—it'd be with the idea of an elegant woman, subtly feminine, very refined and polite. A woman who would fit into his new corporate life, who could attend the business parties and cultivate new connections.

It would not be with a woman whose body language

screamed sex, whose every smile had his guts twisting with raunchy thoughts of sweat and moans and wet, sliding pleasure.

It wouldn't be to a woman who threatened his self-control with every breath she took.

"You'll have your daughter living with you," Anabel said in a low, soft voice that seemed contradictory to the casually sexy clothes and mod tattoo. "I think you want that."

He tipped his head in acknowledgement. "I do." She started to relax, until he added, "But I can have that without you."

"No."

Gil didn't change expression, but he felt himself softening. With her bottom lip quivering, Anabel met his stare, and she looked so small and vulnerable and . . . her damn earrings were blinding him, the way they reflected the fluorescent office lights.

His tension grew, making it nearly impossible to disguise. "It's not up to you, Anabel. She's my daughter."

"And for all intents and purposes, I'm her mother."

"And yet," he reminded her gently, "you're not."

Stark pain stole over her features, quickly replaced with iron will. "Don't con me, Gil." Her small hand came up to rest against his dress shirt directly over his heart. Her breath came fast and shallow. "I know you too well. You won't do that to her. You won't break her heart that way."

The trembling of her lips kept snagging his attention, until he wanted to warm them with his own. "Actually, you don't know me at all." He started to turn away.

Her hand fisted, wrinkling his expensive shirt, pulling him back around. She didn't raise her voice when she said, "I've known you three years."

Three years that he'd thought of fucking her, imagining how wild she'd be, how she'd taste and feel. Three years of doing his best to ignore her and her carnal appeal. Three years of resisting her because that was the right thing to do. "We've been no more than acquaintances."

Now *she* stepped closer, staring up at him, her chest heaving, her expression resolute. "We've debated business and politics and society. We've talked about the weather and clothing and music. We've argued and teased and I've . . ."

Her breath hitched and she pinched her lips shut.

She was so close he could smell her, a subtle fragrance of perfume and the headier scent of warm woman. "You've what?"

"Nothing." She released him and stepped back, moving to his desk before turning toward him again. Seconds passed like the ticking of a bomb. "Do you know, Nicki was always there when you visited. It gave Shelly a thrill to have her that close to you, without you knowing it."

Unable to comprehend such malicious machinations, Gil shook his head. "Why?"

"I don't know." She looked as dumbfounded by it all as he felt. "I had a hard time figuring her out. I think she sometimes hoped that Nicki would wake up or make a fuss and you'd find out. The matter would be taken out of her hands, so to speak. But she didn't, and so you never knew and Shelly chose not to tell you."

She kicked off her sandals and hopped her rounded behind up onto the edge of his desk. Hands in her lap, shoulders slumped, she stared down at her bare feet and said, "I wanted to tell you, Gil. I swear. But Shelly said if I ever did, she'd run off with Nicki and no one would ever find her. I couldn't bear the thought of that. Shelly birthed Nicki, but she wasn't her mother. I kept my door open at night, always listening with half an ear, always wondering if . . ."

"If?"

She looked up, her eyes sad, hopeless. "I was so afraid

she'd take my baby, that she'd run off and I'd never find her."
Anabel rolled her shoulders, shrugging off the melancholy
to give him a small smile. "I heard her first word."

"Mama?" He couldn't mesh the image of this woman
with that of a mother. Impossible.

She laughed. "No. It was 'bird.' She loved watching the
birds out the window. From the time she was a tiny baby, it'd
make her squeal. I put a feeder outside the window so they'd
come up close and it'd keep her entertained for a long time."

Wishing he could have seen her enjoying the birds, Gil
said, "I have a wooded backyard. Lots of birds and other animals to see."

Her expression was distracted, a little sad. "I stayed up
nights with her when she cut teeth. I'd hold her, and she'd
drool on my shoulder until we were both soaked, but I could
never bear to hear her cry. I bought her clothes, mostly at
secondhand shops, but I made sure everything was clean and
cute, and she always looks adorable." She turned her face up
to his, her eyes pleading with him to understand. "I've
changed all her diapers, bathed her and fed her, and I've
loved her with all my heart. You can't take that from me. I
know you won't take that from me."

Gil rubbed the back of his neck, lost in turmoil. It was the
damndest thing, an onslaught of emotions and considera-
tions and needs. Nicki was his daughter and now that he
knew about her, he'd never let her out of his sight again.

He hadn't realized how he'd feel about a kid, so he couldn't
have prepared for the strange bombardment on his heart.
The more Anabel spoke of her, the richer his love for Nicki
seemed. It crushed him that he and his family had already
missed so much of her young life. Questions about her birth,
her personality, her preferences, seemed to be building up
inside him, demanding answers the same way his lungs demanded air. He didn't just want to know. He *had* to know.

Yet mixed with that was the undeniable urge to protect Anabel—an urge he couldn't seem to stifle no matter his anger or his common sense. Never in his life had he indulged macho displays of chest beating. He left that sort of chauvinistic behavior to his older brother, Sam. As a supercop, Sam filled the role to perfection and then some.

But in Gil's world of business, women were not delicate creatures that needed a man's protection. They were intelligent, savvy, capable—and sometimes ruthless. He'd never felt like the all-powerful, superior male with any woman. He'd never felt that a woman needed him to shelter her.

But now he did.

Anabel Truman, with her multiple earrings and tattoo and come-get-me smile was tugging at his heart in a way no other woman ever had.

Damn her; she'd kept his baby from him. She was as responsible as Shelly for deceiving him.

And he still wanted to cuddle her close and hold her and make outrageous promises that weren't at all in his best interest. If he encouraged her now, what type of example would she set when his daughter started forming her own decisions? Would she emulate Anabel? His heart skipped a beat at that awesome thought, and he swallowed hard. Would Nicki want a tattoo, too? Oh God, the very idea made him cold inside.

No two ways about it: Anabel just wasn't proper mother material. He thought of mothers as being like his own—nononsense, understated, ready with a hug and advice. His mother *looked* like a mother. Soft, a little rounded, casual and comfortable.

Anabel looked like . . . not a mother. He couldn't label her, but there was nothing comfortable about her. Exciting, yes. Hot, definitely. But not maternal.

Even while she'd been pouring her heart out to him, a part

of his mind kept thinking how sweet it'd be to push her to her back on his desk, to tug those threadbare jeans down her hips and thighs so he could . . .

Suddenly she slid off the desk and started toward him. "I know what you're thinking, Gil."

Along with the look in her eyes, that throaty tone brought him out of his reverie. "You haven't got a clue." If she did, she sure as hell wouldn't get so close to him.

"Wanna bet?" He caught his breath when she leaned into him, her hands sliding up his chest to rest on his shoulders. Her cool fingertips brushed the heated skin of his nape. Eyes direct, even challenging, she whispered, "You're thinking about sex. With me. I've seen that look on your face before."

He didn't back down. "What look?"

Her smile curled, lighting up her eyes, flushing her cheeks. "Well, the look before you just went blank. It's this sort of heated expression, very direct and interested and naughty."

He caught her shoulders to hold her away—and instead, he just held her. His heart thundered and the muscles of his abdomen and thighs pulled tight. "You're mistaken."

"Oh really?" She went on tiptoe to brush her nose against his throat. "Mmm. You smell good, Gil."

Her breath whispered over his skin with the effect of a lick. Her breasts, shielded only by a clinging shirt, brushed his chest.

"Anabel." He meant his tone to be chastising, and instead it reeked of encouragement.

Her hand left his shoulder to glide down his chest, down, down to the waistband of his slacks where she lingered, making him nuts, causing his lungs to constrict. Her lips moved nearer to his, and at close range she stared into his eyes.

"You want me, Gil. Admit it."

He wouldn't admit a damned thing. But neither could he deny it.

The darkening of her eyes should have given him warning. But when her slender fingers drifted lower, cupping his testicles through his slacks, he was taken completely off guard. To call her brazen would be an understatement. To call him unaffected would be an outright lie.

She held him, gently squeezed, expertly stroked. "You're already hard," she whispered.

Yeah, from his ears to his toes, but did she have to sound so pleased about it?

Still in that soft whisper, she purred, "Gil, I want you, too. I always have." As she said it, she moved her fingers up to his throbbing cock, teasing his length, deliberately arousing him further, pushing him. "We would be good together. I know you, know what you like and what you want. I'll do anything, Gil. Any time you want, any way you want. I'll—"

The bribe finally registered, dousing him in ice water. He felt used, repelled, and he automatically sought to distance himself by pushing her back. She was taken by surprise and would have fallen if he hadn't grabbed her shoulders to steady her. Just as quickly, he released her again.

Her eyes were wide, dark. *Aroused.* "Gil, please . . ." She started to reach for him.

"No." His lip curled, disgust at himself and her boiling up to choke him. She acted in the role as Nicole's mother, and yet she'd just offered to prostitute herself. He said again, "No."

What he felt must have been plain to see, given the lack of color in her face. Devastated, appearing somewhat lost, she faced the desk and braced her hands there. Gil could see her shaking, could hear the choppy unevenness of her gasping breaths. She was going to cry and he couldn't bear it. He had to do something, say something.

"We'll leave now." His own hands weren't that steady when he went to his desk and snatched up the phone, quickly dialing his brother's cell phone. When Sam answered, Gil could hear restaurant noise in the background. He closed his eyes. "Don't let Mom know it's me, but I need a favor."

"Shoot."

"Come by the company and get my car. I'll leave a key in the office, top desk drawer. Bring it to my house later tonight or tomorrow morning before I have to get to work. By yourself."

"You can only fend them off for so long. I speak from experience, Gil."

Gil well remembered Sam's recent relationship snafus with Ariel. No, his family was not the type to stand idly by. They liked to get involved. He glanced at Anabel and wanted to groan. Her shoulders were slumped so that she curled in on herself. Her exhaustion, her desperation, was enough to flatten him.

"I just need a few days." At least he hoped he'd be able to figure something out in a few days.

"Sure thing. See ya then."

Sam hung up, and Gil knew he'd come up with some good excuse for the phone call. Sam worked undercover—he was great with lying. With that worry now in Sam's capable hands, Gil faced Anabel.

Keeping her back to him, Anabel wrapped her arms around herself. "How will you get to your house if you don't take your car?"

"I'm going to drive yours."

She jerked around. "Mine?"

There were no tears in her eyes, thank God. In fact, that unwavering resolution still remained, contradicting the slump of her narrow shoulders.

Gil caught her wrist. She was fine-boned, soft. "You just

offered to sell yourself to me, Anabel. I'd say that makes you pretty desperate. No way in hell am I letting you out of my sight with my daughter."

A second ticked by, then two and three. She drew a shaky breath and looked at his hand on her wrist. "I offered to marry you."

"In exchange for raunchy sex."

Her gaze swept up, clashing with his. She half laughed, from surprise or disbelief, he wasn't sure. "Raunchy, sweet, hot and fast or slow and easy." She shook her head. "I've wanted you since I first met you. Something about you draws me, something dark and impossible to ignore. I go to sleep every night thinking about you inside me."

Gil closed his eyes, wishing like hell that she'd shut up, that she didn't seem so determined to turn him inside out.

Her free hand touched his jaw. "I didn't offer to have sex with you as a trade to keep Nicole. I was just trying to show you how compatible we'd be. Marriage or no marriage, I'd still want you. I'm starting to think I always will."

Sincerity rang in her tone, once again knocking Gil off kilter. "I don't fucking believe this."

She smiled. "You should know that Nicki repeats everything she hears. Good thing she's sleeping through this, huh?"

Gil let her wrist drop to tunnel both hands through his hair.

"I know it's a lot to take in, Gil. First Nicole and now me. Even if you decide against marrying me, I'd still like to have you."

Have me? Speechless, Gil could only stare at her. He couldn't imagine a woman more outrageous than her. And damn it, it made him want her more.

"But . . . before you completely reject the idea of marriage, will you at least give me a trial run?"

"A . . . ?"

"Trial run." She nodded. "I could take care of your daughter while you're at work, and then take care of you at night, in bed."

He squeezed his eyes shut. "I don't think I want to hear this." He was still hard, getting more so with every insanely sexual thing she muttered.

Her words rushed out in her attempt to convince him. "I'm sorry I have to push you like this, but we only have a few days to decide. I'm hoping that if you enjoy sex with me—"

He would. He knew it down deep in his bones. He'd known it for three years, which was why he hated being around her.

"—then maybe the idea of marriage to me won't be so re- pellent. Maybe you'll see that Nicki loves me and is happier with me around. Maybe you'll even see that you like me well enough to keep me."

With very little effort, she drove him over the edge. "You make yourself sound like a stray dog."

"I want you. I want Nicki. I'm a woman trying to have it all."

He began to feel desperate. "I don't love you, Anabel. Doesn't that matter?"

World-weary cynicism shadowed her smile. "In my posi- tion, I can't let it matter."

Something she'd said struck him, making Gil frown. "You mentioned that we only had a few days to decide. To decide what? And why the time limit?"

She chewed her bottom lip, then went to the diaper bag and dug through it until she found a small diary. "I don't ex- pect you to take my word for it. I mean, you don't even like me, so why believe anything I have to say?"

"I never said I didn't like you." It was her effect on him,

the feelings she drew from him with a mere look, that he didn't like.

"Shelly told me." She said that with far too much acceptance.

"Then she lied. We never even discussed you."

"Really?" Her brows lifted. "Why would she?"

"I have no idea." He accepted the book she handed to him. "What is this?"

She swallowed hard, leveled her shoulders and her gaze. "Shelly's parents want custody of Nicole."

His jaw locked. Over his dead body.

"They're not warm people, Gil," she added in a rush. "They've never paid any attention to Nicki. Whenever they were in the same room with her, they ignored her."

Glancing at his daughter, he found that hard to believe. Who could look at her and not fall instantly in love?

"They wanted Shelly to give her up."

"What?" Gil felt a cold sweat break out on his forehead. If that was true, then he might not ever have known about Nicki. That thought was too awful to contemplate.

"Even when Shelly brought her home from the hospital, they refused to get close to her in the hopes that one day she'd change her mind and put Nicki up for adoption. They thought of her as a . . . a blot on their good name. They talked about her like she was nothing more than a mistake."

On several occasions, he'd spoken with Shelly's parents. Not in depth, just superficial pleasantries common to business introductions. They'd seemed average enough to him. But they hadn't cared about their own grandchild?

Anabel touched his arm. "It's all in Shelly's diary."

He held the small, flat journal at his side, tapping it against his thigh. "But now, with Shelly gone, they want Nicole?"

"That's what they said. I don't understand it, but I don't

trust them. They didn't want me to tell you about Nicki. They . . . well, they offered to pay me off."

Gil's chest swelled with anger. "What the hell does that mean?"

"They're rich," she told him. "They offered me money to keep quiet. They said you didn't ever need to know, that Shelly hadn't wanted you to know and I should abide by her wishes. But I couldn't do that."

Thank God.

She licked her lips. "Gil, by tomorrow morning they'll know I left with Nicki and they'll assume I came here."

Meaning they, too, would show up on his doorstep? Gil turned to stare at his precious little dark-haired daughter. By the second, things became more complicated.

Anabel's hand tightened on his arm. "I won't let them have her, but I can't fight them on my own. You and I need each other. As a married couple, we stand a chance in the courts. Otherwise, we might both lose. And Nicole would lose more than anyone."

At least in this instance, he could reassure her. "I'm not going to let anyone hurt her, Anabel."

His confidence didn't alleviate her worry. "You don't understand." She pulled on him, forcing him back around. "Nicki is used to love, to hugs all day long and lots of kisses and playtime and . . ." She stopped to collect herself. "She wouldn't be happy with a cold, detached nanny and private schools and disdain from her grandparents. She wouldn't be happy without *me.* Just read the diary tonight, and then we'll talk."

Because she looked so upset, Gil gave his promise. "All right. In the meantime, don't worry about anything, okay?"

She breathed hard in her upset. The seconds ticked by. "And the trial run?"

He wished like hell that she'd quit talking about sex. "I'll consider it." What *was* he saying?

Tension drained from her body, making her shoulders loose, her frown even out. "Thank you."

At her relieved gratitude, Gil could only shake his head. Everything that had transpired in the past hour was too unbelievable for words, culminating with that absurd *thank you.*

"So," Anabel said with new purpose, "you want to carry the little rat down to the van? Not that I can't. She's light as a feather. But I know you're dying to hold her and now's as good a time as any. If she wakes up, though, give her to me quick. You don't want her to start screaming her head off. Nicki's got a shout that can peel paint." As Anabel spoke, she stepped back into her sandals, took the diary from him and tucked it, with Nicki's juice bottle, into the diaper bag. Her movements were fluid and efficient, practiced in that way exclusive to mothers.

She hefted the bag over her shoulder. When he just stood there, she said, "Well?"

Gil took the few steps to the couch—and hesitated again. He hadn't known about her long, but already Nicole Lane Tyree had a permanent spot in his heart.

"Scoop her up, Gil. She won't break."

Being very gentle, he lifted her, and his precious bundle gave an indelicate juice belch into his shirt. Charmed, Gil positioned her against his shoulder, felt her stretch, and patted her back until she went boneless again. Holding his daughter against his heart felt more right than anything ever had in his life.

He glanced up—and his eyes met Anabel's. Seeing the way she smiled at them both felt right, too. What the hell was he going to do?

First, he'd read the diary. He needed all the facts before making decisions based on emotions—or worse, on lust. At the moment, he was feeling an excess of both, one thanks to a tiny little daughter now snoring in his ear.

The other thanks to a very sexy little bombshell currently swishing her delectable ass in front of him, on the way to moving into his home.

Life as he knew it had just been turned upside down.

Anabel jerked awake with a start when she felt Gil's fingertips brush her cheek. For a single moment, she misconstrued that tender touch, leaving her lost in a dream world where he actually wanted her. Except that she wasn't in a bed, the sun was bright in her eyes, and Gil stood outside the van, beside her open door.

Reality hit just as Gil's big hand settled warmly on her shoulder. She watched his gaze wander from her belly to her chest and finally to her face. He didn't smile, and wow, there was an inferno of heat in his eyes.

"You awake, sleepyhead?" he asked in a low, somewhat gravelly voice.

Oh no, she hadn't. Anabel's head slewed around, taking in her surroundings. She saw that they were parked in front of a very lovely home. She had passed out on him.

In the next instant, panic hit and she turned in the seat—but there was Nicole, smiling away at her, wide awake and bubbly.

"Since she's awake," Gil explained, "I didn't want to chance invoking that scream you warned me of."

It took Anabel a second to realize that Gil meant Nicole. "Oh, yeah." She pushed her hair from her face and rubbed her tired eyes. "You never know with her."

As if his patience had suddenly ended, Gil reached into the van and unfastened her seat belt. His knuckles brushed the sensitive skin of her belly and she caught her breath, startled by his forwardness. He ignored her reaction, catching her arms above her elbows and literally hoisting her out of her seat.

She stumbled into him and was struck anew at how solid and comforting he felt. He was a big man who hid his ruggedness behind a suave exterior. But she knew the truth. She knew that down deep inside, Gil Watson was a wild, carnal man.

He let her lean on him for a moment while she collected herself, and oh my, it felt nice. Her life had gotten so complicated, so scary lately, and uncertain, that borrowing some of his solid strength was more than necessary. She could have stood there feeling his heat and heartbeat, breathing in his scent forever, but Nicole laughed and Gil set her a few inches away.

She'd kicked her sandals off almost as soon as they'd gotten in the van and now she felt how the warm sunshine had heated his concrete drive. She also felt her own awkwardness. Had she snored? She hoped not, but given how long it had been since she'd had a restful sleep, she couldn't be sure. "Sorry I nodded off."

His expression enigmatic, Gil reached inside for her sandals. "No problem. You were exhausted. I'm just glad this jalopy got us here safe and sound. You need new . . . everything on it."

"Yeah." She couldn't very well take offense when it was true. "But it gets us where we're going."

He held her arm as she stepped into her sandals. "It got you here. We'll see about more reliable transportation in the morning."

Her defensive hackles rose. She didn't want him to think he needed to buy her things. But then she noticed him smiling at Nicole and realized his thoughtfulness was for his daughter, not her. Naturally, he wanted the little rat safe during transportation. "You want to get her out of her seat?"

Anticipation brightened his expression. "You think she'd mind? I don't want to frighten her."

"With me here, she'll be fine. Go ahead."

Gil nodded, then leaned through the open back door. He moved slowly, spoke softly. "Hello, Nicki. You ready to come on inside?"

"Juice." She reached out her small arms to Gil, and Anabel thought he might very well melt on the spot. It amused her to see him so affected by such a tiny person.

He unfastened Nicki's car seat and lifted her out.

Nicki put one arm around his neck, leaned back to frown into his face, and demanded again, "Juice."

Anabel laughed. "Patience is a virtue, rat. Let's get inside first, okay?"

At that moment, Nicki noticed several squirrels scurrying from limb to limb in the big elm trees in Gil's front yard. She started hopping up and down in Gil's hold, flailing her arms and kicking her pudgy legs. "Look! Look!"

"Squirrels," Gil told her while smiling ear to ear. "And lots of birds and some deer and occasionally a skunk or possum."

Anabel started to unload the van, but Gil took the diaper bag from her and turned her toward the walkway. "Come on. I'll show you around and then unload."

Nicki was still bouncing against his chest, trying to see everything at once while Anabel studied the expansive dimensions of his sprawling ranch house. "Gee, you think there'll be room for us?"

"Don't be facetious. It's actually modest."

"Uh-huh. Like the Taj Mahal, right?"

He grinned, a beautiful, bone-melting grin that made her

want to lick his mouth. Luckily, Gil was too occupied hanging onto an energetic toddler to notice her reaction. "Candace is already gone by now, but she should have your room ready for you."

"Thank you."

"The basement's finished, with a workout room, hot tub, and home theater. I'll have to put a lock on that door so Nicole doesn't try to go down the steps."

"Good idea." He already showed a willingness to adjust, giving Anabel hope that it'd work out. "Usually she sits and scoots down on her fanny, but I worry. And since I didn't know what kind of house you'd have, I brought some baby-proofing stuff. Gates, rails for a bed, outlet covers . . . stuff like that."

Gil shifted Nicki, unlocked the front door, and pushed it open. "Does she get into a lot?"

"Only everything." Anabel took two steps inside and froze. "Holy sh—" She peered at Nicki, who watched her, wide-eyed. "Um, wow. I don't think we can baby-proof everything in here."

Gil just shrugged. "I'll move things around however you think is best."

Through the wide tile foyer, she could see into the living and dining rooms. They were huge, with eleven-foot ceilings that all but echoed her surprise. His tables were heavy marble with sharp corners and glass tops, complemented by the snowy white carpeting, drapes, and walls. *White,* Anabel thought with a sick feeling, already imagining the spills and spots and fingerprints soon to occur.

His furniture, thank heavens, was gray leather, so probably a little more resistant to two-year-old terrors. But all in all, his home looked like what she'd imagine—an expensive bachelor's pad not in the least suited to kids.

Nicki squirmed to be let down, and Gil, not knowing any

better, obliged. The second her feet touched the floor she was off like a shot, tottering this way and that, careening dangerously close to hard corners, almost but never quite losing her balance.

"Oops!" Anabel raced after her, barely managing to snatch her up just before she crashed into a pewter-fronted fireplace. "You little speed demon," she teased Nicki while squeezing her close. Smiling, she turned to face Gil—and found him immobilized with shock.

It amused her how poleaxed he looked and she started to laugh.

"It's not funny," he wheezed, color just beginning to leech back into his face. "We need a padded room. Inflatable furniture. She should be wearing a damn helmet or something."

Nicki said, "Damn helmet."

Gil blinked, horrified, while Anabel said, "Damn is not a nice word, Nicki. Only adults can say it, okay?"

Nicki scowled at Gil.

"It's uncanny," Anabel told him, "how she can pick out only the curse words."

Holding a hand to the top of his head, Gil again looked around his home, and this time he appeared sick, drawing Anabel's sympathy. "Really, Gil, it's okay." And when he just stood there, she said to Nicki, "Tell your daddy it's okay, squirt."

Gil jerked around so fast, he nearly threw himself off balance. "She knows?"

Losing her smile, Anabel nodded. "I told her we were coming to meet her daddy. I wanted her to be excited about the trip. But right now, it's just a word to her." Very gently, Anabel added, "It's up to you to make it more than that."

Nicki squirmed to get down, trotted over to Gil, and patted his knee. " 'S'okay," she said with so much exaggerated sympathy that Gil swallowed hard, dropped to his knees, and smoothed her hair with a shaking hand.

Concerned, Nicki looked back at Anabel. "Mommy?"

Anabel joined them. She crouched down next to Nicki. "Daddy looks like he could use a hug, huh?"

Nicki nodded. " 'S daddy sick?"

"No, munchkin, he's just so happy to meet you. You want to give him a hug?"

"He give me juice?"

"I'll get your juice."

" 'kay." She opened her arms and wrapped them around Gil's neck, squeezing with all her puny might before treating him to a loud smacking kiss on the cheek. She pulled back and wrinkled her nose. With her little hands holding his face, she stared into his eyes at close range and said, "You better now?"

Gil nodded. "I'm very good now." He swallowed. "Thank you."

She rubbed his cheeks experimentally then gave Anabel a wide grin. "He tickles."

Anabel put her palm to Gil's cheek, smoothing with her thumb. He had a five o'clock shadow and his jaw was rough, warm, and oh so masculine. "Yep, he's whiskery."

"Whiskery." Nicole nodded, and with an abrupt about-face, said, "I want my juice."

Gil drew a calming breath and stood. "Take a look around, make yourself at home. I'll go unload everything."

Because he still appeared to be in shock, Anabel worried. "Thanks."

"Hold onto her."

"I will."

He hesitated a second more, then turned and went outside

again, carefully closing the door behind him. If he was this shook up in the first five minutes, how would he feel after a week? Anabel said a quick prayer that the joys of little Miss Nicole Lane Tyree outweighed the inconvenience, otherwise they were both in for a lot of trouble.

Chapter Three

By suppertime, Gil's house looked very different. Bumpers covered all the sharpest corners of his furniture and gates cluttered every entryway. What used to be an open, airy space was now carefully sectioned off to contain a toddler's energy. Clean lines had disappeared, replaced with toys strewn into every conceivable corner. His once immaculate, state-of-the-art chrome kitchen now sported a variety of knee-high fingerprints.

Nicki touched everything. A lot.

Next to his ebony enamel dinette table was a colorful red and yellow highchair, looking much like a spring flower blooming on blacktop. Among his trendy black dishes, set behind clear glass cabinet doors, were several sipper cups of crayon-bright red, blue, and green. There was also a stack of equally bright bowls with hideous cartoon faces on them.

Nicole had recited her colors and counted her bites while eating. Judging by Anabel's praise, that was quite an accomplishment. She put a lemon yellow potty chair in the guest bathroom, explaining that Nicki no longer used regular diapers, but pull-ups that worked like diapers, but looked a lot like little girl panties. In a few more months, Nicki would be in regular underwear, but Anabel said she didn't want to push the issue right now with everything else going on.

Gil decided he needed to get a book or two to figure out some of this stuff. He had no idea what kids did, or when.

His daughter talked a lot about everything. Her sentences were endlessly long and he caught . . . oh, maybe every third or fourth word. The rest sounded like gibberish to him, though Anabel seemed to understand her just fine.

Nicole also hugged a lot. And kissed a lot. She was such a sweet little girl. Anabel was right about that. Nicole thrived on the love she gave and received.

There hadn't been much time to talk or discuss the issues while Anabel and Nicole settled in, but Gil enjoyed just watching her. Her expressions were priceless, the way her small face scrunched up in annoyance or anger, how she always squinted her eyes shut and lifted her chin when she smiled real big.

When she was sleepy, she sucked her thumb and tugged on a curl of hair. When she was sad or mad, her bottom lip stuck out and she crossed her arms tight over her chest. And she was a master at manipulation. She'd ask for something by punctuating the request with a hug or kiss and an innocent smile.

She delighted him, more so every minute.

Gil was busy setting up Anabel's computer in the bedroom he'd given her when Nicole came streaking through, shouting, "Daddy, Daddy, Daddy!"

His little angel was naked.

Grinning, Gil sat back on the floor and caught her as she hurled herself into his arms.

Anabel, carrying a disposable pull-up diaper and a T-shirt, rounded the corner hot on her heels. When she saw Nicki tucked close to Gil's chest, she pulled up in relief.

"Sorry. Sometimes she's like greased lightning." She flopped down next to Gil, propping her back against the wall.

"I don't mind." Just the opposite. He loved hugging her, and he especially loved being called *Daddy*.

"Nicki's a true nature child," Anabel told him while reaching out to pat the baby's butt. "Give her half a chance and she loses the clothes. She learned how to strip a few months ago, and she's been doing it ever since."

Gil rubbed Nicki's soft back and kissed her downy head. "Let's hope she outgrows that."

Anabel laughed. "At least before she hits her teens, huh?"

"Oh God." Gil squeezed her closer. "I can't think that far ahead. I'm still getting used to the idea of her being a baby. A teenager—no, it's too much to take in."

Anabel leaned into his shoulder in a show of camaraderie that felt far too intimate—and far too comfortable. She wasn't the type of woman he could ever treat like a pal, not when every cell in his body stayed on alert status whenever she was near.

But Anabel seemed unaware of his dilemma. She kept touching him, leaning into him, getting too close. She hugged his right biceps now and said, "One of the first things I bought when Nicki was born was a video camera."

Balancing Nicki against his free arm, Gil looked down at Anabel. "You have tapes of her?"

"Hours' and hours' worth. Her birthdays, Christmas, even some everyday stuff. There's a really funny one of her in a bubblebath—"

"Bath!" Nicki echoed, jumping up and down within the secure hold of Gil's arm. "Bath, bath!"

The shrill squeals of excitement almost pierced Gil's eardrums. "I take it she's fond of bath time?"

"Are you kidding? I think she was a fish in another life."

Anabel released Gil to push to her feet. "And speaking of that, I better get her ready for bed before she gets her second wind. Bath, book, and bed—that's the routine, and a smart woman doesn't mess with success."

A new complication occurred to Gil. "Damn. The connecting bath in the room I gave you only has a shower."

Nicki gave him a beatific smile and said, "Damn."

"Nicole Lane, that is a bad word."

She stuck her finger in her mouth and glared at Gil, making it difficult for him to contain his smile. "I'll learn," he promised Anabel before handing Nicole up to her. "Give me just a second to finish connecting things here and I'll take you to my bathroom."

"Your bathroom?"

"It's the only tub." He had two and a half bathrooms, but only one tub—in the private bath off his bedroom. And he wasn't altogether sure it'd work for Nicole, being that the tub was so huge.

He quickly connected the rest of the cords on Anabel's computer system and plugged everything into a surge protector. "That should do it."

Anabel switched on the computer, watched her monitor light up, and nodded. "Looks like everything's working. Thanks. I don't have anything pressing, but if I want to meet the deadlines on my new website designs, I can't take too much time off."

The second Gil stood beside her, Nicole reached for him again. "Daddy."

"So I'm to be your mule, am I?" He felt her skinny arms go around his neck, her bare butt settle on his forearm, and thought to ask, "She can . . . ah, control herself, can't she?"

"Most of the time."

When his eyes widened, Anabel burst out laughing. She was as exuberant and carefree as his daughter. He liked that about her. "You're teasing me?" he asked, watching the way her green eyes twinkled.

"Yeah, I'm teasing." In a too familiar way, all things considered, she hooked her arm in his and started him toward the hall. "Without her pull-ups, she'll tell you if she needs to go."

They went down the hall and into his room. It struck Gil just how close Anabel would be to him during the night. The spare bedroom was at the far end of the hall on the right, with Gil on the opposite side and down a bit. His room was twice as big, but then, he hadn't been selfish when choosing it because there'd been no one else to consider. The third bedroom was mostly used for storage and to house his many bookcases filled with books. He'd already considered how he could rearrange things, fitting the bookcases into his den and changing the room into a playroom for Nicole. But in the meantime . . .

"I wonder if we should switch bedrooms. It might be better for you to have my room since it has a bathtub—for Nicole, I mean."

She looked flabbergasted by the offer. "Our room is fine."

He scowled. "But you might be more comfortable in the bigger room."

"No, I'd feel lost in a room that size." She grinned, but added, "Sometimes Nicki showers with me, but I try to keep that to a minimum. There are times when I want my privacy, too. So as long as you don't mind us trooping through here every now and then, we'll keep what we've got."

The idea of Anabel naked and wet flitted through Gil's mind before he could squelch the image. Maybe during her trial run, he'd get the opportunity to shower with her.

What was he saying?

Annoyed with his wandering thoughts, Gil shook his head and realized that Anabel had stopped in the middle of his bedroom to look around. She stared pointedly at his king-size bed. Candace had made it earlier so that the plump down quilt was smooth, the matching gray pillows placed just so. Anabel cocked a brow, but refrained from comment.

When they stepped into his black and gold bathroom, though, her mouth fell open. "It's as big as your bedroom."

He shrugged. "I like my luxuries." Like the immense tiled shower with five separate showerheads that could reach every aching muscle. And the heated towel bars, the double sink, the high ceilings.

"You call that a tub?"

Gil went straight to the partially sunken square bath and turned on the water. "You don't like it?" He knew that wasn't her problem, but decided he could tease, too.

"It's . . . decadent. And it could easily pass for a swimming pool." She, too, sat on the edge of the marble ledge surrounding the tub. "Wow. This is amazing."

With the temperature adjusted, Gil turned a knob that tightened the plug and the tub began to fill. Nicki tried to squirm loose, but Gil held onto her. "Will she be okay in there? I've never bathed a baby before."

Still a little bemused, Anabel shook her head. "I don't know. Let's don't fill it up too much."

He turned the water off when it was still very shallow. Keeping his eyes on Nicki as he lifted her inside, he said to Anabel, "If you'd like to take a soak sometime, feel free. With the whirlpool jets on, it's really relaxing."

"Hmm." She trailed her fingers through the water. "There's plenty of room for two." Her eyes slanted his way. "But then, I bet you already knew that, didn't you?"

Her not so subtle digging amused him. If she only knew how long it'd been since he'd had a woman, she wouldn't worry. "Actually, this is the first time a female has been in my tub." Nicki, who remained oblivious to the undercurrents between the adults, managed to splash and thrash and soak them both. "And I'm not sure the little rat here counts." The second the words left his mouth, Gil wanted to choke himself. Damn it, now she had him calling Nicki a rat.

Anabel laughed while lathering Nicki's hair. "Oh, I dunno. I think it tells a lot about you."

Gil didn't like the speculative way she said that. "It tells you only that I'm a private man who tries to keep my relationships with women as simple as possible."

"Well, this relationship won't be simple."

He didn't know if she meant with Nicki or with her, and he decided not to ask. Anabel was so good with his daughter, so natural about the whole mother thing that he almost felt the need to reassess. If he hadn't already known her, if she looked different, he'd think she was born to be a mother.

"Get in," Nicole demanded of Anabel.

Gil raised a brow.

With a crooked smile, Anabel said, "Not this time, Toots."

Nicole aimed a calculating eye at Gil. "Get in."

Gil sputtered. "Uh, no. Thank you."

Stubborn determination brought a comical scowl to Nicki's face. "Get in, get in, *get in.*" She emphasized each demand by kicking her legs and slapping the water with her hands. Gil noticed that when she wanted something, his little angel spoke very clearly indeed.

Anabel had to scurry to support her so Nicole didn't slip in the tub. She got drenched in the bargain. The front of her T-shirt clung to her breasts and water dripped from her nose. "Bath time is over, rat." Laughing, she caught Nicole beneath the arms and lifted her out onto a thick, soft towel. "Look at what you did. You got me and your daddy both soaked."

Gil hadn't realized he was wet until Anabel said that. He'd been too busy studying the way her nipples puckered from the drenching and how clearly he could see them beneath her soaked tee.

He straightened abruptly. "If you can manage on your own, I have a few things to take care of."

Anabel looked hurt by his abrupt withdrawal. "I've been managing just fine all along. Go ahead. I don't want to interrupt your routine." She did a double take at that, and shrugged self-consciously. "Any more than we already have, I mean."

He started to tell her that she wasn't interrupting at all, but Nicole was already busy trying to play and Anabel was laughing at her—and stupidly, Gil felt left out. He shoved his hands in his pockets and walked from the bathroom, unsure what to do with himself. On a normal night, he'd have gone through some paperwork, maybe watched ESPN for a bit or worked out, then retired. But tonight wasn't normal.

He remembered the diary and fetched it from Nicole's diaper bag, then headed to the den. His desk here was smaller, but his chair was identical in size and color to the one in his downtown office. He settled in and began skimming the pages.

It didn't take him long to realize just how unhappy Shelly had been. She chronicled all the ways she'd disappointed her parents; it seemed that from an early age their expectations for Shelly had been so high that she'd never been able to please them.

Time and again, Shelly's parents let her know that she hadn't quite measured up. They even criticized her business skills, which was absurd. She ran a chain of novelty stores and was quite successful with it. Gil had met Shelly through business, and she was as professional and able as anyone. She was one of his best buyers, and she could negotiate prices like a shark.

They also berated her on her friends, namely Anabel. That

made Gil wince. Anabel had read the diary, so she knew how disparaging Shelly's parents had been. Unfortunately, many of their remarks were on a level with his own personal thoughts. Only now, he knew he was wrong. Anabel might appear free-spirited with her earrings and tattoos and laid-back manner, but she'd still managed to take care of his daughter all on her own.

Worst of all, Shelly's parents hated it that she'd "shamed them" by having Nicole without benefit of marriage.

Guilt got a stranglehold on him when he read her next scrawled words: *They'll definitely approve of Gil for a son-in-law.* She'd obviously been counting on him to come back to her and profess his love.

But Gil hadn't asked Shelly to marry him. Instead, he'd broken off any romantic ties, and so, just as Anabel claimed, Shelly's parents had pressured her to give Nicole away. Given what he'd just read in her diary, they'd continued to press her right up until the day she'd died.

They were Nicole's grandparents, but they hadn't wanted her, had never warmed to her. Not once.

Why the hell did they want her now?

Gil closed the journal, unable to read any more. He already knew how his family would react to Nicole—they'd love her as much as he did. She'd be welcomed with open arms and assured of unwavering support. She'd be doted on, cherished, and protected.

It enraged Gil to think of what Shelly had gone through, and at the same time, he was awed at the steps Anabel had taken to make things right for Nicole. Shelly hadn't known how to be a mother, but Anabel had never let Nicole feel slighted in any way. His daughter had been well loved and cared for—by Anabel.

Gil stood to pace for a few minutes, chewing over complications and procedures, deciding on a course of action.

The grandparents would have to be dealt with, and that meant he'd need to cancel all his appointments tomorrow. He wouldn't take the chance of leaving Anabel in case they arrived unannounced. She'd handled enough on her own already.

Once he'd made up his mind, Gil felt urgent need to put his plans in action. He called Alice's answering machine at work and left her instructions to clear the next couple of days for him. She'd rearrange his schedule the moment she arrived in the office.

Next, Gil called his lawyer, Ted Thorton, at home. He wanted all the legalities out of the way. He gave Ted Shelly's name and last address so he could look up her parents and inform them that Gil was claiming permanent custody of his daughter. He then requested that changes be made to all of his investments, as well as his will. He wanted Nicole noted as his beneficiary in every regard. Ted promised to get right on it, and once he had the papers in order, he'd meet with Gil to get the necessary signatures.

One decision led to another, until he could no longer put Anabel from his mind. She had a stake in everything, whether he wanted her to or not. Throughout the day, he'd watched her with Nicole and now he accepted the truth—he couldn't separate them.

Anabel would accompany him to meet the lawyer, Gil decided, so that she knew his plans. He would put her mind to rest on that score, at least. She, as well as his daughter, would be taken care of.

At that moment, Anabel stepped into the room. Her wet shirt still clung to her breasts, her light brown hair was still mussed, and she looked beyond wary. She put her hand on top of Nicole's head. "You busy?"

"Not at all." Gil slipped the diary into a drawer and slid it shut. "I was just contemplating fate." He gave her a smile he hoped would ease her.

It didn't. "I usually read Nicki a story before bed, but since I still need to shower, I thought maybe you'd do the honors."

Nicole held up a thick book with both hands. "I want dis one."

Gil strolled forward and stood staring down at this tiny person whose life would have been so different if he'd only known about her. It wouldn't, he realized, have necessarily been better. Not with Anabel Truman guarding her like a mother hen.

Nicki's freshly washed hair had dried into tight ringlets around her cherubic face. Her nightgown was a soft, pale yellow and dragged the floor, almost hiding her itty-bitty toes. She was a happy, carefree, and well-loved child, and he owed Anabel more than he could ever repay her.

"I'd be honored," Gil told them both with grave formality, and then, as naturally as if he'd been doing it forever, he scooped up his daughter and held her against his chest. Again, with a naturalness that surprised him, he slid his other arm around Anabel's waist. For only a moment, he appreciated her slenderness, her softness, before steering them all toward the hall. "Take your time. Soak in the tub if you want. We'll be fine."

Anabel shook her head. "No, not this first night. I want to make sure she's settled."

Gil knew it would do no good to argue with her. "I'm sure you know best."

She gave him a disbelieving, wide-eyed look.

They stepped into the spare bedroom. The blankets on the bed had been turned down and temporary rails, attached by sliding fold-out poles beneath the mattress, lined each side. Anabel intended to sleep with Nicole tonight, but Gil considered that a very temporary situation. How he'd remedy it, he didn't yet know.

On impulse, he kissed Anabel's forehead and left her open-mouthed and speechless at the bathroom door, then pretended to drop Nicole in the bed. She squealed and laughed, and Gil knew this was a routine—with mother and daughter—that he could quickly grow accustomed to.

Anabel stood there a moment longer, until Gil had pulled a chair over to the bed, then she turned and went into the bathroom, closing the door behind her. Gil heard the shower start, but he refused to picture her stripping, or wet, or soapy. . . .

"Daddy, read."

"Right." Shaking his head to clear it, Gil took the book and flipped through the pages, looking for a story.

Nicole scampered to the end of the bed, slid out, and came around to crawl up on Gil's lap. She poked him in the throat with a pointy elbow and stepped on his testicles twice before settling herself. Gil grunted, dodged a third stomp, but didn't chastise her. He let out a sigh of relief when she quit squirming. "Comfy now?"

She nodded, pushed on his chest, and said, "Mommy's softer."

He'd just bet she was. And then because he couldn't help himself, he asked, "Anyone ever read to you besides your mommy?" Like any other men that Anabel might have dated.

"No. Jus' Mommy." She carefully turned pages in the big book until she reached a particular story. The book had a lot of pictures and Nicole focused on one. "Dis is the mommy bear. Dis is the daddy bear. And dis is the brudder bear."

Gil gave her a squeezing hug. "Very good."

"Now you read." She curled into his shoulder, closed her eyes on an enormous yawn, and stuck her thumb in her mouth.

"All right, sweetheart. I'll read." And he did. Unlike the children's books Gil remembered, this one was more detailed. Before long, he found himself engrossed in the story.

He was still reading some fifteen minutes later when he felt Anabel's presence. He glanced up to find her in the bathroom doorway, a crooked smile on her face and fat tears in her green eyes.

He started to speak, but she put a finger to her mouth. "The rat is out for the night," she whispered.

Startled, Gil glanced down, and sure enough, Nicole was boneless against him, her head dropped back on his arm, her wet thumb now against his chest.

Gil made a wry face. "I guess this means I don't get to see how the story ends?"

Anabel sauntered away from the bathroom. "I'll tell you all about it later." She lifted Nicole from his lap. As she bent close, Gil could smell the lotion on her dewy skin, the shampoo scent in her still damp hair. She wore another T-shirt, this one of soft cotton and long enough to hang to midthigh.

She laid Nicole in the bed on her side and pulled the sheet up to her waist. Her hand lingered, smoothing Nicole's hair, stroking her small shoulder. The love that Anabel felt for Nicole was almost painful to witness.

Gil couldn't recall ever seeing a baby put to bed, and he noted how small Nicole looked among the bedclothes. "Should she be in a crib?"

"No, not anymore." Her smile was teasing. "Your daughter is like a monkey—she likes to climb. Something closer to the ground is safer." Anabel switched on a night-light, then turned out the brighter lamp.

Shadows filled the room, leaving no more than a soft glow to see by. Gil still stood there, unable to pull himself away. He hadn't seen Shelly grow big with the pregnancy, hadn't felt his daughter kick or watch her be born. Despite all that, he felt such an unbreakable bond to this child of his, he knew he'd die for her if necessary.

Anabel touched his shoulder. "I know how you feel, Gil, because I feel the same."

Startled, he stared at her. Could she read his mind?

"She's pretty incredible, isn't she?" Anabel's smile wobbled the tiniest bit. "Even when she's being a hellion, yelling because she's too tired or she doesn't get her way, I just marvel at what a miracle she is and thank God that I have her, that she *can* yell and that she feels safe and . . ."

The rest of her words got choked off. Anabel shook her head in embarrassment and slipped out of the room.

Yes, she knew how he felt. Gil bent to place a barely there kiss on Nicole's head, then went to find her mother. They had some issues to resolve, and no time seemed better than the present.

Anabel stood in the formal dining room, her arms wrapped around herself, staring out the patio doors. Gil's yard was immaculately kept, displayed by decorative lighting. It was a big yard for one person. Perfect for a swing set or playhouse—things she'd always wanted for Nicole but couldn't give her.

She knew the second that Gil stepped up behind her.

He was far too close, his warmth touching her back, when he said, "I left the door open a little."

Anabel nodded. Somehow, she'd known he would.

"She'll sleep through the night?"

"I hope. Usually yes. She's a sound sleeper. But here . . . I don't know." *Great way to give a straight answer, Anabel,* she grumbled to herself. She hated showing her nervousness and anticipation.

Gil's hands settled easily on her shoulders, making her catch her breath. "Will it frighten her," he asked very near her ear, "to wake up in a strange place?"

Anabel turned to face him. Earlier, he'd lost his tie and opened several buttons on his shirt, but he hadn't changed. He seemed very comfortable in the professional suit, whereas she smothered in anything dressier than jeans. "I won't let her be afraid. Ever."

The right side of his mouth curled up in a crooked smile, while his gaze moved over her face, lingering on her lips. "You're ferociously protective of her, aren't you?"

She couldn't get a single word out, not with him looking at her like that. She shrugged.

Cupping her face, Gil smoothed his thumbs over her cheeks and across her bottom lip. She knew what was about to happen and her heart hammered in her chest.

"About that trial run," Gil murmured.

Anabel started to say "Yes," but his mouth covered hers, warm and firm. Oh God, he tasted good. Better than good, and if he thought she could be cavalier about this, he was sadly mistaken.

She clutched at him, relishing the feel of firm muscles in his shoulders, the heat of him. She pressed closer, aligning her body with his, trying to absorb him. She opened her mouth and accepted his tongue and groaned with the pleasure of it.

Two big steps and Gil had her pressed to the patio doors, on her tiptoes, his mouth eating at hers. She tried to get the rest of his buttons undone so she could touch his bare flesh, but her hands felt clumsy and she heard one button ping against the doors.

Breathing hard, his body taut, Gil lifted his head. "Come on." He took her hand and practically raced her to his bedroom. The second they stepped inside he closed the door, quietly clicked the lock, and reached for her again.

"Wait." Anabel flattened both hands against his chest. She'd dreamed of this moment for three long years. "Just . . . wait."

Gil stared at her, breathing hard, his impatience palpable.

Slowly, Anabel backed him into the door. She took her time now, carefully sliding each button from its hole, tugging his fine shirt out of his slacks, stripping his chest bare. Gil closed his eyes and let his head drop back against the door. Anabel heard him swallow, heard the racing of his breath.

She pushed the shirt off his shoulders and down his arms. His chest was incredible, lightly covered in dark hair, hard and wide, rippling with lean muscles. She stroked the crisp hair, learning the feel of him, then found his nipples.

His breath caught, but she ignored it, toying with him a moment, then leaning forward to taste him with her tongue.

"Jesus." His muscles knotted tight.

But she didn't stop there. She dropped to her knees and went to work on his shoes.

"Anabel." His shaking hand touched the top of her head, his fingers threading into her damp hair.

"This is my fantasy, Gil. Let me have it."

He didn't say anything else, just lifted each foot as needed so she could strip off his shoes and socks. He braced his feet apart and reached for his belt buckle, but Anabel brushed his hands away. Looking up at him from her submissive position, she smiled suggestively. "*My* fantasy."

His hands dropped to his sides.

She loved the sound his belt buckle made as it clinked free, the rasp of the leather sliding through his belt loops. Beneath his fly, his erection swelled and throbbed, enticing her. She wanted him naked, but she also wanted to savor each moment. Leaning forward, she brushed her cheek against his cloth-covered crotch, inhaling deeply of his rich, aroused scent.

Gil gave a low groan and stiffened.

Pleased with that reaction, Anabel slid her hands around to hold his muscled backside and teased him with her teeth. She nipped carefully, grazing his length through the light wool material.

His hands fisted and pressed to the wall at either side of his hips.

She groaned, too, loving him so much it hurt. Quickly, before he decided to take over, she opened his pants button and drew the zipper down, allowing the metal teeth to slowly part over his swollen erection. His patience shot, Gil shoved his slacks and underwear down and off, then kicked them away.

He was naked.

Awed, overwhelmed, Anabel sat back on her heels and took in the sight of him.

He made a low growling sound. "Anabel, I want you naked, too."

"Soon."

"Now."

The smile came without her permission. He was every bit the commanding man of authority. "All right." She rose to her feet. Holding his gaze, she reached under her shirt and skimmed her shorts and panties down. "But I'm not done with you yet."

His gaze burned over her, urging her to haste. "We'll see."

She dropped her shorts to the side and reached for the hem of her shirt. "Promise me you'll let me taste you first."

As if pained, his eyes closed. "Anabel."

"You know you want me to," she taunted, and pulled the shirt free.

His eyes snapped open and he went very still as he looked

at her, taking an extra long time to study her belly and the small decorative jewel in her navel.

His jaw locked. "You like giving head?"

If he thought to disconcert her, he could forget it. "I'll like sucking on you."

In a heartbeat, he went willing, resting back against the door again, his limbs deliberately loose while his cock twitched and his chest swelled with his laboring breaths.

Feeling wicked and sexy, Anabel knelt in front of him again. She tasted the firm flesh of his abdomen first, dipped her tongue in his navel, bit his hipbone—then curled her hand around him, held him still, and swallowed him deep.

His head tipped farther back, his knees locking tight. *"Yes."*

It was better than she'd imagined, the sounds he made, the way he fought to hold still, the explosive moan when he gave up, grasping her head and moving with her mouth, thrusting in, feeling the hollows of her cheeks with his thumbs.

"I'm going to come," he whispered harshly.

Anabel drew him deeper still, letting him know what she wanted. At the same time, she cradled his balls, very gently squeezing, urging him, and with a low shout, he exploded.

Slumped against the door, his eyes closed and his chest heaving, he curled his hands around her head and drew her away. Anabel gave one last, lingering lick to the head of his penis, felt him flinch, and smiled.

For the moment, she was content to enjoy her victory, to sit there and peruse his gorgeous body and think about what was to come next. Her entire body felt alive, warm and soft in some places, ripe and swollen in others.

She licked her lips, tasting him again, salty and rich, and she wanted to start all over.

Gil was watching her. His face was flushed, his thickly

lashed eyelids partially open. "Should I come down there," he murmured, "or are you going to come up here?"

Anabel reached a hand toward him. He hauled her up, proving that he might be winded, but was far from spent. He further made that point by scooping her up as easily as he had Nicole.

"What are you doing?"

"Putting you in my bed so I can give a little payback."

"Yeah?" She could hardly wait. And in fact, she didn't have to.

The second her back touched the mattress, Gil settled on top of her. He took her mouth, stifling her moan as his hands found and kneaded her breasts. He sucked at her tongue— and tugged at her nipples.

The pleasure was so acute, Anabel arched her back. Gil slid one arm beneath her, keeping her positioned that way so he could kiss a path down her throat to her breasts.

"I always wondered if you had sensitive nipples. Do you?"

"I don't know." At the moment, she barely knew her own name.

"Let's find out." He drew her left nipple into his mouth, suckling softly, stroking easily with his tongue. He was being so gentle, it startled her when he increased the pressure, drawing hard, pressing her nipple to the roof of his mouth.

His fingers at her other breast mimicked the sensation, squeezing just so much, pulling and tugging.

Anabel twisted, fighting against the dual sensations while at the same time wanting more. It did her no good. Since he'd already come, Gil was in no particular hurry. Instead, he seemed determined to drive her crazy, spending so much time on her nipples while other parts of her body grew hot and wet.

He moved to the side of her, propped himself up on one elbow, and stared at her belly. "So?"

Anabel could barely breathe. No way could she hold still. "What?"

"Are they sensitive?"

He sounded utterly unaffected while she was going insane.

"Yes."

"Good." He bent again, licking each nipple in turn while wedging one big hand between her thighs. She caught her breath, waited, but he didn't do anything other than hold her. The warmth of his hard palm was stimulating, but she wanted his fingers inside her. She needed his fingers inside her.

"Gil?"

"Shhh." He licked his way down her body to her belly. "You are so fucking sexy."

His tongue dipped, teasing her navel, nudging the tiny belly button jewelry, tickling her so that she tried to turn away.

"Hold still." He anchored her by sinking his middle finger deep into her, drawing her to an immediate stillness. Just that, just that one finger, and she felt ready to come. Her inner muscles clamped tight around him, but other than that, she didn't move.

"That's better," Gil whispered, teasing her again with his tongue. Her nipples were wet and tight from his mouth, her belly twitching with the tickling, teasing licks and prods of his tongue, and she had to fight the urge to lift her hips, to thrust against that thick, invading finger.

He stared up her body at her face, making certain she understood. "Good girl."

"I . . . I need to come now, too."

"And you will. More than once." She started to let out her

breath when he added, "But not yet," then nibbled his way down to her hipbones.

It seemed he was determined to taste her everywhere. Her thighs, the backs of her knees. And all the while, his finger was inside her. Just when she thought she couldn't play his game anymore, Gil situated himself between her thighs. "Open your legs for me."

She did, immediately. He stared down at her sex, his expression intent, determined. His finger pressed more firmly into her, and with his other hand he smoothed her pubic hair, touched her clitoris with a light stroke of his thumb, and said, "You can come now."

And oh God, she did. The pleasure washed through her, rippling through her thighs, twisting inside her. Gil watched, his thumb brushing her very gently while his finger filled her. She could feel his breath, heard the smile in his voice when he said, "That's good . . ."

Anabel couldn't believe what had happened. She was still numb, her body heavy and sated when Gil shifted, sliding his hands under her to raise her hips.

"Gil?" She lifted her head and stared down at him. He was between her thighs, his dark hair mussed, his mouth damp, his expression hot.

"Time to come again, Anabel. Then I'll get a rubber and make love to you proper. But first . . ."

She felt the damp stroke of his tongue and dropped her head back against the pillow with a low cry. She was already sensitive from her orgasm, her vulva hot and full. Gil wasn't timid about tasting her. He licked and sucked and stroked deep with his tongue until she was crying out, twisting and shaking, and just when she knew it was too much, he closed his mouth around her clitoris and sucked.

A tidal wave of sensation rushed through her, making her thighs shiver and shake, her belly hollow out, her back arch.

He kept it going, sliding two fingers into her, back out, in again. She didn't know if it'd ever end and didn't really care.

Her mind was still blank of cognizant thought when Gil very gently kissed her cheek. "You still with me, Anabel?"

"Mmm."

His mouth smiled against her jaw. "That's good. Because I'm not done yet."

A groan erupted. She honestly didn't know if she could muster up any strength to accommodate him.

"You were awfully easy. But then, so was I." He continued to press tiny, affectionate kisses to her cheek, her ear, her temple. His big hand rested on her belly, one hairy thigh over hers. "It had been a long time for me," he admitted. "I guess too long."

Anabel forced her eyes open. "Why?"

His gaze went from her eyes to her mouth. "Who knows? I thought I'd lost interest. I said I was too busy. Maybe it's just that no one really appealed to me."

She lifted a hand to his sweaty shoulder. "It's been three years since I was with anyone else."

Beneath her hand, his muscles stiffened. "Three years?"

Anabel shrugged. "Shelly was pregnant and upset and I spent a lot of time with her. Then Nicole was born. I didn't really have a baby-sitter, and I was afraid if I left her with Shelly . . ."

"That she'd take her away." His voice was low, a little angry, somber and accepting. He cupped her cheek and turned her face toward him. He wore a frown, but as he bent his head and kissed her, she felt his grave gentleness, and his silent thank you.

Amazingly enough, the second his mouth touched hers, Anabel felt revived. She loved him. For her, loving Gil was the biggest reason that she'd been celibate so long. True, she always put Nicki first, but it hadn't been a hardship to give up men when Gil was the only man she wanted.

She turned toward him, sliding her arms around his neck and pressing her belly to his. Gil rolled to his back and pulled her atop him, adjusting her legs so that she straddled his hips.

"I want you to ride me, Anabel. I want to play with your breasts and belly while I'm inside you, and I want to watch you come."

Just hearing his intent was almost enough for her. She said, "All right. Just tell me where to find a rubber."

Chapter Four

Three years, Gil thought, unable to fathom such a thing, especially for a woman as sensual and open as Anabel.

Holding her hips with one hand, he reached past her to the nightstand and pulled open the top drawer. Anabel saw the packet of condoms and pulled one out.

She flipped it like you would a fan. "I'm out of practice, so let me know if it doesn't feel right." After tearing the silver package open with her teeth, she held his cock and teasingly rolled the rubber on.

Not feel right? Gil considered the touch of her small soft hand around him, the glint in her eyes as she concentrated on the task, wonderful, mind-blowing torture.

"On your knees."

She lifted up, bracing her hands on his chest. "Like this?"

Gil didn't answer. With two fingers, he stroked her, making sure she was wet enough, opening her, preparing her. "Now ease down."

Her smile taunted. "You like to give orders, don't you?"

He met her gaze. "Sit down, Anabel."

She laughed, and slowly sank onto him. The head of his

cock passed her delicate lips, then got hugged by the hungry clasp of her body. She paused, drawing a breath, closing her eyes.

"A little more," he urged through clenched teeth. He held her hips and pressed up while drawing her down. They both moaned with the incredible sensation of him sinking inside her, stretching her a bit, fitting snugly. Her fingers curled against his chest, leaving half moons from her nails. Her head tipped back and she thrust her breasts forward.

Gil drew her down so he could latch onto a tightly drawn nipple—then he began to thrust. He wanted to be easy but he couldn't manage it. Never mind his own long abstinence; knowing Anabel had been three years without sex drove him wild. He loved seeing her shifting expressions, how her teeth bit into her bottom lip, the way her belly drew in, how her thighs gripped him. He squeezed her soft ass, guiding her until she found his rhythm, then slipped one hand around the front of her and wedged his fingers between their bodies.

She was hot, wet, gasping and making low, sexy sounds deep in her throat. Using the tips of his fingers, Gil applied pressure where he knew she'd need it most. Far too quickly, she started to come. She dropped forward to take his mouth, and Gil rolled, putting her under him again, slowing so that her climax was suspended.

"Gil."

"Shhh. Easy now." He kissed her again, long, deep, wet kisses while slowly sliding in and out, giving her only shallow thrusts, keeping her on the edge.

She tried to lock her legs around him, probably in hopes of taking over. Gil caught her knees and pressed them forward and out, opening her completely, leaving her vulnerable. Anabel went still, a little apprehensive, he knew, but nowhere near ready to call it quits.

"Am I hurting you?"

Breathlessly, she said, "No," but she strained against him, trying to hold him back.

"Good." He eased her legs farther apart. "Then relax."

She drew two deep breaths, trying to do as he asked.

Very slowly, Gil pressed forward, deeper, deeper . . .

"Oh God."

"Relax for me, Anabel." He no sooner growled the words than he felt the start of her climax. Gil marveled at her. Her eyes had darkened with trepidation, and still she enjoyed him. She quit holding him off and instead embraced him with a soft, throaty, vibrating moan of surrender.

Gil lost it. He thrust hard, fast, aware only of the draining release, the powerful rush of scalding sensation. It was more than he had ever experienced—more than he'd known existed.

Some moments later, utterly sated, he became aware of Anabel squirming beneath him. "Gil? My thighs are killing me."

Oh hell. He realized he still had her legs caught up in his elbows. He groaned, straightened away from her, and fell to his back. His bedroom smelled of sex. It smelled of Anabel. He took a deep breath, then let it out on a sigh. "Sorry," he murmured.

"All things considered," she teased, "you're forgiven."

Gil turned his head on the pillow to look at her. "What things?"

Her eyes were closed, but she smiled. "Three orgasms?"

"Ah." Knowing he had to do the manly thing, he pushed himself from the bed and stumbled on shaky legs into the bathroom. He disposed of the condom, washed, and filled a glass with water. When he returned to the bedroom, his door was open and his bed was empty.

Frowning, he stepped out into the hall and found Anabel peeking into Nicole's room. He noted with some disappointment that she'd pulled her tee and panties back on. But with a toddler in the house, he supposed some sacrifices were necessary.

He didn't own any pajamas, but he went back and got his boxers, then joined her. "She's still asleep?"

"Snoring like a bear cub." Anabel turned to him with a smile. Her gaze skipped over him head to toe and back again. "I just wanted to make sure."

Like any good mother would. Gil took her arm and guided her back to his room. This time he left his door open but turned the lights out. Without a word, he urged her into his bed, then climbed in beside her and pulled the sheet over them.

She immediately curled into his side. That felt right. More than right. He closed his eyes and said, "Sleep."

She was silent a moment before asking, "Here?"

It was fast, but Gil didn't care. "Yeah, here."

Anabel said nothing more. She just snuggled against him and quickly drifted into deep slumber. And like his daughter, she snored.

Sometime late in the night, Gil woke to the feel of damp breath in his face. He opened his eyes, then started with surprise. Nicole was on the bed beside him, leaning on his chest, her nose almost touching his.

"I'm wet," she explained in a loud stage whisper.

"Oh." Gil's brain scrambled at such a predicament. He was in his underwear. Did two-year-olds notice or care about such things?

"I can't find Mommy."

She sounded ready to cry. Gil quickly got over his squeamishness. This was his daughter, for crying out loud, and Anabel was exhausted. "She's right next to me," Gil told her.

"Why?"

Why? "She . . . got cold."

"Oh."

"Do you want me to change you? That way we can let your mommy sleep."

No answer.

Gil carefully caught Nicki and lifted her away so he could get out of the bed. Her gown was soaked, but he still cradled her close to his chest. "Let's be real quiet and sneaky, okay? Won't your mommy be surprised?"

Nicki had no comment on that, but she rubbed her little hand on his chest. "You're whiskery."

"Not too much."

"I'm not whiskery."

"No, and neither is your mommy."

"Only daddies?"

"That's right." He slipped out of the room and quietly pulled the door shut behind him. "Do you know where your nightgowns are?"

She tugged experimentally on his chest hair. "No."

Wincing, Gil untangled her fingers and set her down in her room. Together, they rummaged around until she approved a soft shirt to sleep in. The pull-up diaper was thankfully easy. He wasn't altogether sure he could have managed the other kind, not without any practice to his credit.

After he'd changed her wet sheets and was ready to tuck her in, Nicole stuck out her bottom lip. She looked half asleep on her feet, but still she said, "I want a story."

So he'd get to hear the ending of the book after all? Gil could handle that. He settled in the chair with Nicole in his lap, and had barely finished one page before he heard her breathing even out in sleep. Feeling very paternal and proud, he slipped Nicole into her bed, stood there a moment to make sure she wouldn't awaken, and then headed back to his own room.

Anabel had slept through it all, proving just how little rest she'd gotten lately.

He, on the other hand, was now wide awake and very aware that he had a warm, sensual woman curled up in his bed. Not just any woman, but Anabel. He'd always been drawn to her, no matter how he fought it. But now he liked and respected her, too. She'd done so much. Without complaint, she'd taken on responsibilities that weren't hers, and managed them admirably.

She was not only sexy, but strong. She wasn't just outrageous, she was also bighearted. She was . . . beyond appealing. Physically and emotionally. And now she was here, in his bed.

Moonlight flooding through the windows formed a halo around her face. He could see her soft hair tangled on the pillow. She had one hand tucked beneath her cheek and one slender leg bent at the knee, drawn up in what Gil saw as an invitation. Of course, in his frame of mind, even her deep, even snores seemed inviting. He was in a very bad way.

What the hell, he decided, and again locked his door.

Moving silently so that he didn't disturb her yet, Gil pulled the blankets off the bed. Anabel shifted, but didn't awaken. She had beautiful legs, slim and sleek, but it was her fanny that caught and held his attention now.

Gil pushed his boxers off. Given it hadn't been that long since he'd come twice, he stared at his boner with some chagrin, then donned a condom before getting into bed behind Anabel. He leaned close and smelled her hair, a familiar smell now, arousing and comforting at the same time. Gently, he brushed his nose against her, over her ear, her temple, down to her nape. He wallowed in the pleasure of having her near. She slept on.

Using only one finger, Gil traced her graceful spine down to the small of her back, continuing to her bottom, and on still until he found the incredible warmth between her legs. He lightly stroked, using only the tip of that one finger, and felt her soften, swell.

She made a sound in her sleep, one that sounded of growing urgency and awareness.

Gil continued to tease, to arouse her. He wanted to take her from behind. It was nice that way, giving him easy access to her breasts and sex. He could push deep while fingering her, teasing her nipples.

Biting off a groan at those erotic images, he slid one arm under her so he could keep her close, in just the right position, at the same time kneading a soft breast. "I want you, Anabel."

She fluttered awake. "Gil?"

Roughly, he stripped her panties down far enough that he could get inside her. He positioned himself, held her still, and with one firm thrust, he was there.

"Gil."

His heart pounded with the excitement, the power of it. "Push back against me, Anabel."

And with a welcoming moan, she did.

Oh yeah, his life was different now. As far as Gil was concerned, it was infinitely better.

Anabel felt a hand on her breast and groaned. Did the man never rest? Okay, so she knew he was sexually uninhibited, but no one had said anything about insatiable. "Go away."

A husky, male laugh sounded in her ear; solid morning wood nudged her hip. Against her ear, he whispered, "How late does Nicki sleep?"

Oh, good grief. She was actually sore. Deliciously sore,

but still, she needed a little time to recoup. He'd really taken the whole trial-run thing to heart. "Um . . . what time is it?"

"No, you answer first."

Knowing he was on to her, Anabel grinned. "Gee, I expect her any minute."

"Liar." Gil turned her to her back and rose over her, smiling with sensual intent.

And Nicki shoved the door open. Vaguely, Anabel remembered Gil unlocking the door after making love to her again. "Time to get up!" Like a small whirlwind, she burst into the room and scrambled up onto the bed, bursting with morning cheer.

In a flash, Gil jerked back to his own side of the bed and pulled the covers all the way to his chin. "Nicole . . ."

"Daddy!" Nicki landed between them, liked how the mattress bounced, and began to jump.

Laughing, Anabel pushed herself to a sitting position and caught Nicki. She dragged her over her lap and gave her a resounding smooch on the cheek. "Did you sleep well, rat?"

"Daddy changed me."

"He did?" Anabel noticed then that Nicki's nightgown was gone, replaced by a tee. She glanced at Gil.

He, too, had sat up, and now he had one of the plump bed pillows over his lap. "It was a small matter of a wet nightgown. Nothing too difficult."

"He read to me."

"Twice in one night?" It sounded like they'd been up having a good time without her. "Aren't you the lucky little girl."

Nodding, Nicole confided in a loud whisper, "Daddy's whiskery *all* over."

Gil sputtered. "She commented on my chest. She also pointed out that you aren't whiskery."

"I see." But she didn't, not really. It made her feel odd to know that Gil had managed a midnight crisis without her. Why hadn't she awakened? Why hadn't *he* awakened her?

But she knew why. Gil was a very capable man. She'd been fooling herself to think he needed her. For anything.

And she trusted him. It was why she'd come to him in the first place. Not only was it the right thing to do, but in her heart she'd known that he'd be a terrific father. He wouldn't completely remove her from Nicole's life, but would he let her stay in his?

As if he'd read her mind, Gil put a hand on her shoulder. "We decided to let you sleep. You were pretty wiped out."

Anabel nodded. After all her worries, she'd finally felt safe enough to sleep soundly. She didn't doubt that if Nicki had wanted her, she'd have come awake in a rush. But Gil had handled things, proving he was not only a sensitive, astounding, *tireless* lover, he was also considerate beyond belief.

She felt lost, unsure what to do next.

Very gently, Gil smoothed her hair. "If you'll throw blinders on the little monkey there, I think I'll escape into the bathroom to shave and dress. Then we can start on breakfast."

"Stay put," Anabel told him. "We'll head out and give you your privacy."

She rose from the bed, but rather than follow, Nicki threw herself against Gil and said, "I want pancakes." She ensured obedience by giving him a sweet kiss on the cheek and a tight hug. Only after finishing that did she allow Anabel to lead her from the room. Gil, the sop, looked ready to rush off in search of his griddle.

She had just finished helping Nicki dress when a knock sounded on Gil's front door. He hadn't come out of his bedroom yet, so with Nicki racing beside her, Anabel went to the living room. Before she could reach the door, a key rasped in the lock and it opened.

In stepped two big men. One looked to be in his late thirties. He had hair as black as Gil's, but the bluest, most piercing eyes she'd ever seen. He seemed startled to see her, then in one quick sweep, he took in all the changes to Gil's home. One glossy black eyebrow shot up.

Another man, this one a younger version of Gil, pushed his way in past the first with a grin. "Hey. You must be the mystery lady, huh?"

Painfully aware of her mussed hair, slept-in clothes, and lack of makeup, Anabel cleared her throat. "I'm Anabel Truman. I take it you're Gil's brothers?"

The friendly one nodded. "That's right. I'm Pete and the thundercloud is Sam. He's thundering, by the way, because he wanted to bring Gil's car back here without me, only I was too curious to wait. Sam hates it when things don't go his way."

Sam rolled his eyes. "Is Gil around?"

"In the bathroom. I'll just go get him . . ."

Nicki, who didn't like to be ignored, stepped forward and mimicked Sam's pose by crossing her arms over her chest and bracing her feet apart.

Both men stared down at her.

Clearing her throat, Anabel said, "Nicki, these are your uncles, Pete and Sam. They're your daddy's brothers."

"Daddy's brothers," Sam repeated, somewhat poleaxed.

Pete nudged him with an elbow. "Uncle Sam. Now ain't that a kicker?"

Anabel urged Nicki forward. "You want to say hi to them, rat?"

Nicki scrunched up her face, thinking about it for some

seconds before saying, " 'kay." She marched forward—and sat on Sam's foot. "You do the horsie."

"Do the—?" Sam looked at Anabel for help.

Pete started snickering uncontrollably while Anabel rushed to explain. "She rides on my foot sometimes. It's a game we play."

Sam said, "Oh," while standing there with that one leg stuck out comically, as if he feared he might hurt her if he moved.

Gil chose that moment to appear. He was freshly shaved, smelled wonderful, and wore only jeans. He scooped Nicki up with a grin. "You're terrorizing my brother, sweetheart. Look at him."

"I want pancakes."

"All right." Gil tucked her up against his hairy chest and turned to Anabel. "Why don't you go do . . . whatever you have to do and I'll take the brood into the kitchen."

That sounded like a fine idea to Anabel. Not only was she hung over from too much sex the night before, but now she had two family members to face. "Do you think you could produce some coffee?" Caffeine would hopefully kick-start her thinking processes.

"It'll be ready when you are."

As Anabel made her escape, she heard Nicki ask, "Are you as whiskery as Daddy?" She didn't know which brother Nicki addressed, and she didn't wait around to hear the answer.

What would Gil's brothers think of her? She was an interloper, a deceiver, and now a seducer. She knew she loved Gil, that she'd been in love with him almost from the day she'd met him. But they didn't know that.

In record time, Anabel washed her face, brushed her teeth, applied her makeup, and chose clean jeans and her most conservative tee to wear. Barefoot, she hurried back to the kitchen. She'd barely been gone ten minutes.

Sam and Pete were sitting at the table and Gil was at the stove. Nicki, bless her heart, was perched on Gil's foot, getting hauled around as he prepared her pancakes. No one noticed Anabel looming in the hall outside the room.

"So she showed up, asked you to marry her, and now you're sleeping with—"

Gil cut Sam off with a pointed look at Nicki. "That's about it."

"What are you going to do?" Pete asked.

"I'm taking legal measures to make sure Nicole is financially noted as my daughter. There shouldn't be any question of custody, but I'm addressing that, too, just in case."

"I meant about the woman."

Gil shrugged while measuring out batter onto a hot griddle. "I've known Anabel for three years, and I'll admit I've thought about her in a lot of different ways."

Pete bobbed his eyebrows and Sam grinned.

"But not once did I ever consider her the type of woman to marry."

"Why not?" Pete asked.

"Did you see her earrings and that damn tattoo?"

"Damn tattoo," Nicki repeated, making Gil groan and giving both Pete and Sam a chuckle.

"Sweetheart, you can't say damn." Nicki just stared up at Gil until he sighed. "Do you want to go look out the patio doors at the birds?"

"Birds!" Like a flash, Nicki left the dubious enjoyment of Gil's foot to study the backyard. He'd have finger and nose prints on the glass, but Anabel knew he wouldn't mind.

From his position at the stove, Gil could still see Nicki,

but now that she was out of hearing range, he had more freedom to talk to his brothers—much to Anabel's discomfort.

Gil shook his head. "The thing is, I kept thinking about the influence she might have on Nicole. She's not like any mother I've ever seen before, that's for sure." And then, with a thoughtful frown: "She even has a belly button ring."

"Yeah?" Pete's interest rose. "Those are sexy."

"You think everything on a female is sexy," Sam pointed out.

"And you don't?"

Ignoring Pete, Sam said, "You don't have to marry her to keep your own child."

"I have to do something with her. But it's a complicated situation, so I'm not going to rush things."

They discussed her like an inanimate object instead of a person. Anabel had heard enough. Pasting on a smile, she stepped into the kitchen. "My *damn* tattoo is part of a business agreement."

Spatula in hand, Gil jerked around to face her. His gaze was cautious, concerned. "You were listening in?"

"Nasty habit of mine, I know. Almost as bad as wearing body jewelry."

"Anabel." He sounded very put out with her.

She turned to Pete and lifted her shirt a bit. "There it is, that offensive belly button ring. Disgraceful, isn't it?"

Pete's Adam's apple bobbed as he swallowed hard. His gaze stayed glued to her stomach. "Um, cute."

"Thanks, but don't you mean sexy?"

Chagrined, he said, "Somehow I think it's in my best interest not to answer that."

Sam crossed his arms over his chest and rested back in his chair. "And you all thought my romance was entertaining."

Gil wasn't amused. "Put your shirt down, Anabel."

"Why? Am I embarrassing you?" She dropped her shirt, but only because she saw no point not to.

"No, but Pete is bright red."

She rolled her eyes. The last thing she wanted to do was explain herself to Gil and his brothers, but her situation didn't afford her the luxury of pride. "I do web page designs. It was about the only thing I could figure out that'd pay enough and still let me work from home so I could be with Nicki. Most of my work is for small businesses, and those include some that are just starting out. I let Dixon, the guy opening the tattoo shop, practice on me. He tattooed my arm, took pictures, and we used those to put up at his shop and on the website that he hired me to do. Same thing with the jewelry. Dodger gave me the earrings and the belly button ring to advertise his business. He didn't have to hire a model, and I got paid to design his website."

"So you didn't even want the tattoo?" Sam asked.

"I had never really thought about it, but no, I wouldn't have spent the money on a tattoo because my budget was too tight." She traced a fingertip over the delicate flowering vine. "But now I kinda like it. It suits me. And we know it helped Dixon get new business because it's his most requested design."

Pete said, "Got anything else pierced?"

She shook her head at the same time Gil said, *"No,* she does not."

Sam leaned over to Pete. "Gil's going to serve you for breakfast if you don't pipe down."

Gil turned off the stove. In very precise terms, each word carefully enunciated, he said, "You're telling me that pictures of your belly are on the *Internet*?"

Anabel couldn't help but laugh. "Is that the only part you heard?"

"Are they?"

"Yep. I got body parts flashing all over the Web."

Gil fell back against the sink counter. "Dear God." He looked incapable of doing or saying more.

Sam pushed from his seat and relieved Gil of the spatula. "You're burning our breakfast." Like an expert chef, he began filling the plates that Gil had set out. "And for the record, I like her tattoo, too. It's not like she's got a giant rattlesnake or the words 'I love Killer' emblazoned on her arm. It's tasteful and feminine."

"Maybe I'll suggest that Ariel get one."

"Try it, and I'll kick your ass." Sam turned to Anabel. "Ariel is my wife, and she's dying to meet you and Nicole. In fact, I'd be surprised if she and my mother didn't finagle an invite for later today."

Pete interrupted to ask, "What's the url for the sites where you're at?"

Gil rounded on him. "Forget it, Pete."

"All right, all right. Sheesh. No reason to breathe fire on me."

Sam began serving up breakfast. "Hey, Nicki, Uncle Sam has your pancakes ready."

Gil glared at him. "Way to hog all the credit."

"Hey, I gotta make a good impression while I can."

Nicki came barreling back into the kitchen, jabbering ninety miles a minute about the birds and pancakes and uncles who cooked. *She* felt right at home with Gil's brothers, so Anabel gave up. After all, it was just her feelings that were hurt, and she had to get over that real quick because it was bound to happen a few more times. She'd known from jump how Gil felt about her. Just because he enjoyed sex with her didn't mean he'd suddenly have a personality transformation. They were as different as night and day—except in bed. And Gil could certainly find another woman to fill that role if he chose to.

She'd have liked to tell him to go to hell—but she couldn't. She couldn't even really argue with him because it might mean she'd lose Nicole. An ominous dread had skated down her spine when he said he planned to take legal action to bind Nicole to him. If she didn't make headway soon, he'd probably kick her out and she'd lose Nicole as well as Gil. She couldn't let that happen.

But what could she do?

Suddenly Gil was beside her, the consummate gentleman, holding out a seat for her with one hand and offering a cup of coffee with the other.

Anabel would never understand him. "Thank you."

He kissed her forehead, saying very softly, "You're welcome."

Nicki grinned and reached up for him. "Tank you."

Gil lifted her into her high chair, then kissed her, too, before reaching for his own seat. When he turned around, Pete puckered up as if waiting his turn, but Sam wielded the spatula like a weapon, saying, "Keep those lips on the females."

Nicki thought they were hilarious; Anabel just thought they were nuts. Breakfast, she discovered, was a circus—and quite thoroughly enjoyable. The brothers were anxious to hear all about Nicole's preferences and peccadilloes, but they asked just as many questions about Anabel. As far as she could tell, Gil's brothers had no problem with her at all. Now if only Gil would feel the same.

After his brothers had gone and the kitchen was cleaned, Gil pulled Anabel into his arms. "Hi."

She blinked at him. Gil knew she was very uncertain, that she had no idea what the future might bring. Well, she'd just have to go on wondering for a little longer. He was no dummy; he'd already decided that Anabel deserved more than a trial run, and more than a marriage of convenience. How to convince her of that was the question plaguing his mind. He didn't want her to feel like a convenience, not when she was so much more. He had a plan and he'd stick to it.

"Can I have a kiss?"

Her brows came down in suspicion. "Why?"

"Because I enjoy kissing you and you look sexy as hell this morning."

Ever the doting mother, Anabel glanced around for Nicole.

"She's busy dressing up a near bald doll with crayon marks on her face. Ugly thing."

Anabel grinned. "That's her baby."

"So she told me. It looks older than dirt."

"It's not *that* old. I gave it to her for her first birthday."

Gil wasn't surprised, but he was touched. Again. "Perhaps," he whispered, "that's why it's a favorite."

Anabel's smile faded in nostalgia. "A few months ago, the little rat decided it needed makeup, and she did a job with her crayons. Then she decided she didn't like the look after all and insisted I wash the poor thing. Most of the yarn hair fell out—but Nicki still takes that doll with her everywhere."

Without waiting for permission, Gil caught Anabel's chin and tipped her face up. Deliberately, he kept the kiss tender instead of sexual. It wasn't easy.

"Do you like my brothers?"

She dropped her forehead to his chest. "The more important question is whether or not they like me."

"They do—not that it matters. I don't have to have their approval for anything I do." He held her shoulders and bent his knees to see her face. "Besides, what's not to like?"

She snorted at that. "Body jewelry? Tattoos?"

Gil grinned. "What else have you traded on the Internet?

Nothing too risqué, I hope." He rubbed his thumb over her lips and his voice dropped. "You haven't traded this pretty mouth, have you?"

She slugged him in the stomach, but he held her so close that it was an ineffectual punch. "Nicki's old room was painted by a mural artist that I worked for. I used her room as the background for the website. She had birds and trees on all her walls. It was beautiful. I've had different hairdos to help advertise for a beautician friend." She ran a hand through her short curls. "I remember you came around once when it was red."

"Yeah. I liked it."

"You did?"

He just grinned. He wouldn't tell her yet that he liked everything about her—even her belly button ring. He needed to show her first. "Why don't we take in a movie? Would Nicki like that?"

"I don't know. I've never taken her before."

Because she couldn't afford it? Gil decided they'd spend the day out. He wanted to give Nicki everything she didn't have, to watch her experience new things with him. But he was also driven to treat Anabel to a few luxuries, as well. She'd given much of herself and it was time she got something in return.

A few hours later, at the matinee show, Gil began questioning his wisdom. With so many kids in attendance, the chattering was nonstop. "I've never been to an afternoon movie before," he remarked to Anabel over the drone of crying babies, fussing toddlers, and cajoling moms. "I'm not altogether sure I like it."

She leaned into his shoulder and laughed. "You're just disappointed that you can't make out."

"True." Then he whispered, "But there's always tonight." He felt Anabel's shiver before she could move away.

They had lunch at McDonald's, but by then Nicki was getting cranky. Her constant whining was trying, more so because Anabel looked horrified that his little angel wasn't being all that angelic.

"She's tired," Anabel explained.

"And loud," Gil agreed. "But she's also a toddler and I suppose they all get this way on occasion."

Anabel rushed to give Nicki another french fry. "Just some of the time."

Gil shook his head. "Don't sugarcoat the reality. I can take it. Besides, it doesn't matter how she fusses, I can still see that you're an excellent mother."

Wary hopefulness darkened her eyes. "You really think so?"

Gil lifted Nicki from her high chair. "Of course. And I think I'll make an adequate father once I get the hang of it."

"You're already a wonderful dad and you know it."

She sounded disgruntled about it, making him fight a smile. "Thank you." He hoisted Nicki up to his shoulders. She liked that enough that they got her out of the restaurant and into his car with nothing but cheers and squeals of happiness.

But once in the park, she fell asleep on the blanket they spread beneath a shading tree. Gil smoothed her short dark hair. "I wanted to show her the different birds."

"There'll be plenty of other days for that."

"Thanks to you." He picked up Anabel's hand and kissed her palm. Together they leaned back on the tree, still holding hands. It was peaceful. And nice.

They were a family.

Gil hadn't realized how much was missing from his life until Anabel showed up. After his father's death, he'd buried himself in his work. At the time it had been a necessary escape, a way to cope with his grief. But he was done with that. He was ready to move forward.

On the drive home from the park, Gil considered all the changes that still needed to be made. Anabel could use a minivan to replace that heap she currently owned. And he should have one of the bathrooms remodeled to include a tub that Nicki could use. Perhaps Anabel would even want to do some redecorating.

Gil was contemplating the various ways he could tie Anabel into his future when they pulled up to his house and found a black BMW in the driveway.

"Oh no." Anabel stiffened in alarm. "It's Shelly's parents."

"So I assumed." Gil noted the older couple waiting on his porch, and smiled in anticipation. "I wonder if my lawyer has spoken with them yet? No matter. I'm glad we'll be able to get this settled." He parked the car and started to get out.

Anabel reached for his arm. "What are we going to do?"

"I'm going to talk to them. You're going to wait with Nicki in her room."

"No. You can't just shut me out—"

"Yes, I can." Gil walked around the car to her door. The grandparents watched impatiently from the porch. "Leave it to me, Anabel. It has nothing to do with you."

"That's not true!"

He gave her a stern look and dropped his voice to a whisper. "You're too emotional. You came to me, now let me handle this." He reached in and lifted Nicki out. She stretched awake, immediately slipping her thumb into her mouth. "Go to your mommy, sweetheart."

Nicki was too tired to argue.

Anabel squeezed her close. "Gil . . ."

He put his hand at the small of her back and urged her forward. "Trust me. Everything will be fine."

The grandparents looked beyond rigid. With no sign of welcome, Gil said, "Mr. and Mrs. Tyree. I've been expecting you."

Mr. Tyree, tall with dark brown hair showing no signs of gray, cleared his throat. "We're here to discuss—"

Gil cut him off. "We'll talk in my den." He opened the door and ushered a miserably silent Anabel inside. Nicki, bless her heart, had her head on Anabel's shoulder, her thumb in her mouth, watching the intruders warily.

Gil kissed both mother and daughter on the forehead. "This won't take long." He left Anabel standing there and led the Tyrees down the hall.

"We're here about Nicole," Mr. Tyree said the moment the door closed.

Gil ignored his opening salvo to say, "I was very sorry to hear about Shelly. She and I were good friends."

Mrs. Tyree curled her lip. "More than friends."

"Once, yes." Gil indicated the chairs. "Would you like to sit down?"

They did so reluctantly. Gil saw the weariness, the grief, still etched in their faces. Their relationship with Shelly might not have been ideal, but it could never be easy to lose a child.

Gil decided to end things quickly, for everyone's sake. "Nicole is mine. Shelly wrote of that fact in her diary, which I have, so no blood tests are necessary. I never knew about her until after Shelly's death."

"Anabel ran to you, didn't she?"

"Yes. A wise decision on her part. She loves Nicki as much as any mother would love a child. She wanted only to do what was best for her." He looked at each of them. "This is best for her. Nicole will be well cared for."

"We're her grandparents."

"Yes, I know. Any involvement you have with her will be up to you, but you won't, under any circumstances, try to take her away."

Mr. Tyree stood. "You don't even know her."

"As I said, Shelly never told me about her. But I am her father and that's something you can't challenge."

"You intend to keep her here, with you?"

"I realize it's a long way from Atlanta, but arrangements could be made for visitation—"

"No." Mrs. Tyree joined her husband, standing at his side. "We have a reputation in the community, Mr. Watson. Losing our daughter was hard enough. I don't want to have to deal with the scandal of an illegitimate grandchild as well."

Gil's sympathy for these people went right out the window. "If you don't want a relationship with Nicole, why were you going to take her from Anabel?" But then he knew, and the hairs on the back of his neck stood on end. "You wanted to put her up for adoption?"

An aged, bejeweled hand waved the air. "Anabel Truman is a gold digger. She'd have come after us for money, possibly tried to blackmail us."

Stupid woman. "Anabel was your daughter's roommate, but you didn't get to know her at all, did you?"

"I know people, Mr. Watson. And I know it requires money to support a child. Anabel is a person with no ambition, no prospects."

"You're wrong. She has more heart, more courage and determination than anyone I've ever met."

"She's got you completely fooled, hasn't she?"

Shaking his head at such blind ignorance, Gil went to the door and opened it. He wouldn't waste his breath arguing with them. "I have money, so rest assured, I won't be contacting you for anything."

Mr. Tyree hesitated. "We had no reason to believe you'd want to take on the responsibility of—"

"Of my own daughter?" Gil's tone was flat in the face of such cynicism. "Good-bye, Mr. and Mrs. Tyree."

The older couple shared what appeared to be a look of relief, and seconds later they were gone. Gil stood there, unable to comprehend how someone could not want to take part in Nicole's life. She was a tiny, incredible, wonderful miracle.

Anabel touched his back. "I heard them leave."

Gil shook off his disgust and turned to face her with a smile. "Yes, and good riddance. I doubt we'll ever hear from them again."

Anabel's eyes widened. "They . . . they won't press for custody?"

"They would have gotten her only to give her away." He looped his arms around her waist, pulled her body into his for a hug. "But I'm the father, all right and tight and no one can challenge that. You've got nothing else to worry about, Anabel." He waited for her to ask him what her role would be in it all, but she didn't.

She was probably afraid to.

Gil sighed. He'd give her a week, two at the most, to figure things out. But he'd use that time wisely. "I don't suppose Nicki went back to sleep?"

"No. She's busy renaming all her dolls, thanks to the characters in that Disney movie we saw."

"Well, if I can't engage you in a quickie, how about just necking with me a bit?" Gil noticed that her cheeks flushed with interest and a pulse raced in her throat. She reacted so quickly to him that she took his breath away. "At least until Nicki discovers us?"

"Here?"

"Mmm." He backed her into the wall. "Bedtime seems far too many hours from now."

Anabel licked her lips. "Yeah, okay." And then she was on her tiptoes, taking his mouth, stroking his chest, and, Gil hoped, loving him just a little.

Chapter Five

As Gil moved to the side of her, each of them sweaty and breathing hard, Anabel wondered just how long the trial run would last.

It had been two weeks since he'd sent the Tyrees on their way, and it was getting harder and harder to bite her tongue, to keep her questions and her fears and, damn it, her love, hidden away. Especially since, by all appearances, Gil expected to keep her around. He'd offered to let her redecorate his home to make it more suitable for Nicole—but also to suit her, as if her preferences mattered in the long run. He'd put her name on his checking account. He'd dragged her along when he met with his lawyer to show her that he'd ensured Nicole's future, but also her own by giving her access to all his accounts.

It was like being married—only they weren't, and he hadn't mentioned anything about it. If he wanted her to stick around, but she wasn't to be his wife, then what? She'd done a lot to take care of Nicole, but she wasn't sure she could be a mistress.

With a wry twist to her mouth, Anabel wondered if she

could somehow exchange that service for website business. It didn't seem likely.

Gil's big, warm hand settled on her belly. "Jesus, I think you've killed me."

Anabel turned her head to face him. It was late in the night, and Gil had just loved her twice. "Me? I was ready to go to sleep. You're the one who doesn't know when to quit."

"Moderation is overrated." His laugh was rough and winded. In the next instant, he rolled to his side and loomed over her. His dark eyes were teasing, hot, filled with tenderness. "Maybe if you didn't look so damn good . . ."

"I'm not wearing makeup. And after your . . . enthusiasm just now, my hair is a ratty mess."

He nuzzled her throat with a rumbling growl. "Then maybe it's the way you smell."

Anabel laughed. Gil had a playful side to him that she hadn't known about before moving in with him. But over the past few weeks, he'd grown more carefree, always smiling, always teasing. She liked it. She loved him. "I'm sweating like a pig, thanks to you."

His hand slipped between her thighs, pressing warmly. "You're sticky, too. But I like it." His voice deepened. "I like everything about you."

Anabel's heart gave an unsteady thump. He said things like that a lot. What did they mean? And how serious was he?

He kissed her mouth. "Do you like blue?"

The sudden change in topic threw her and she shrugged. "Sure, why?"

Again, Gil dropped to his back. "That's the color of your new minivan. I've been meaning to pick one out, but then it seems that between work and playing with Nicki and keeping you satisfied in the sack, I kept putting it off. Today during my lunch I went to a few dealers and—"

"You bought me a minivan?" Anabel knew she should just say thank you, that the new vehicle was really for Nicki's safety. Whenever she left the house, Gil insisted she take his car. But his highhandedness was about to drive her insane.

"Yeah. We'll junk your van—if the junkyard will take it, that is. Not that I mind sharing my car with you . . ." He twisted to see her. "Would you want your own car, too? I mean, for when you get out without Nicki?"

Her jaw locked. "I don't go out without Nicki."

"You haven't up till now because you couldn't. Not that my family wouldn't be great as baby-sitters, but I can understand why you're not comfortable leaving Nicki with them yet."

He didn't understand at all. If Gil didn't need her to watch Nicki, he wouldn't need her for anything. "She's already been through so many changes, Gil. And she doesn't know them that well yet."

"She will soon. God knows, they come around often enough."

Too true. All of Gil's family was delighted with Nicole and she with them. At least twice a week Pete came to visit, and he was quickly spoiling Nicole with gifts. Sam and his wife Ariel doted on her, as well. And Belinda Watson, Gil's mother, was over the moon with her new granddaughter.

Gil reached for her hand and twined his fingers with hers. He did that a lot, she realized, held her hand, touched her face, gave her small, tender kisses.

"I'm going to interview some baby-sitters tomorrow."

Slowly, Anabel turned her head on the pillow so she could see him. "You're going to do what?"

"I want someone to come in during the day to give you a break so you can do your work or just go out, or soak in the tub. Mom recommends her beautician if you want to go get . . .

whatever it is women get at those places. A manicure or facial or something. But don't change your hair. I like it."

Anabel's temper snapped. He was trying to phase her out. Little by little, her role in Nicki's life had diminished. Lately, Gil read to her more nights than not, and he'd become a regular hand at baths and pull-ups and everything else that affected Nicki's life. He was an excellent father—but damn it, she was Nicki's mother.

She was.

With fear lodged in her throat, Anabel pulled her hand away and sat up in the bed. She kept her back to Gil so he wouldn't see her ravaged expression. "What about me, Gil?" Was she relegated to bed warmer only? And if so, how long would that last?

She felt his stillness, what she perceived as empathy in his tone. "What about you?"

Her heart burned in her chest. "When I first came here, I made you an . . . offer."

"To sleep with me, I know." One finger trailed down her spine. "I love having you in my bed, Anabel."

She squeezed her eyes shut. "That's not the offer I mean."

The bed shifted as Gil sat up. He scooted around until he was beside her, one arm braced on the mattress behind her. For long moments, he just stared at her profile. "I don't *need* to marry you to keep Nicole."

There it was, the awful truth she hadn't wanted to face. "She loves me."

"A lot." She heard the smile in his tone, felt the love he had for Nicole. "You've been an incredible mother."

"I've done my best." But maybe her best wasn't good enough. No, she couldn't think that. Gil was a good man, a considerate man. Maybe he didn't want to marry her, but he would never keep her from Nicole. She knew that.

Problem was, she wanted them both. Forever.

Gil remained silent.

"I . . . I know we're very different." Could she convince him that their differences complemented each other?

"Remarkably so."

"But we both love Nicole."

"Yes, and we both have a place in her life."

That reassurance helped, but it wasn't all that she wanted. "Wouldn't that be enough for marriage?"

Gil wrapped his hand around her nape, put his forehead to hers. "I'm afraid not."

The bottom fell out of her world.

"I want a woman who loves me, too, Anabel, not just my daughter."

Her gaze shot up to his, searching, desperate. She put her hands on his chest to move him back so she could better see him. With her breath fast and shallow, she said, *"But I do.* I have for a long time."

His smile spread, slow and easy. "Yeah? You never told me that."

Frowning, Anabel punched his shoulder. "You had to know."

Tumbling her backward into the bed, Gil pinned her down with his body and caught her wrists. He grinned like a fool, confounding her further. "So you love me, huh? Damn, I'm glad to hear that."

"Gil . . . ?"

"As you said, we're very different." He stared at her mouth until she licked her lips. "I need a wife who can accompany me to business parties."

"And you think I can't?" He insulted her with his lack of faith. "I can dress up as well as any woman, I've just never had to."

"Why, Anabel," he said with mock surprise. "You mean to say you'd wear a sedate little black cocktail dress for me?"

He was so amused, Anabel glared up at him. "I don't know if I'd go that far, but I'd find something appropriate. I'm not a complete social misfit." Grudgingly, she added, "I could even find a dress with sleeves that'd hide my tattoo."

"Now that'd be a shame."

What the hell did he mean by that? It almost sounded as though he liked her tattoo.

Gil rubbed his body against hers and said huskily, "I want a woman who's strong."

He turned her on so easily. How did he expect her to have a coherent conversation while he performed a full-body caress? Anabel pushed against him, but he couldn't be budged. "I'm strong," she promised.

"Could've fooled me." With almost no effort, he nudged her thighs apart and wedged himself against her. "The mouthy Anabel Truman I used to know was strong. She had an opinion on anything and everything, and God knows, she never hesitated to share it. But lately . . ." He shook his head with feigned regret. "Doesn't matter what I do, I can't get a rise out of her."

Suspicion rose and Anabel went still, her eyes narrowing. "Wait a minute. You know damn good and well that I've been trying to get along with you."

"No, you've been trying not to rock the boat. You had some harebrained idea that I'd kick you to the curb if you stepped out of line."

"You wanted me to step out of line?"

"No, I wanted you to be you."

Her pulse raced with hope. "You're not making any sense, Gil."

He leaned down and took her mouth. This was no sweet, gentle kiss but a tongue-thrusting, wet, hot kiss that completely stole her breath. "I've always been attracted to you, Anabel. I think you're about the most sexual woman I've ever run across. But the timing was never right, it seemed. My father passed away and things happened with Shelly that I used to regret. But not anymore."

"Because now you have Nicki."

His thumbs brushed her cheeks. "And I have you. When you brought my baby to me, when I saw how much she loves you, how could I not start to love you, too?"

Her eyes widened in disbelief. *How could he not . . .* "Now wait a minute—"

Gil's mouth smothered her protest, swallowed her questions. When she went limp, he continued. "You're a little wild and unorthodox, and I thank God for it. Not many women would take another's baby to raise. Not many would readjust their lives to do so. Not many would come to a man and make him the type of offer you gave me, just so she could go on being a wonderful mother."

Anabel decided on a full confession. "That wasn't the only reason, Gil. If it hadn't been you, I might have come up with a different plan. But I always wanted you."

"And now you have me." He said that with bright satisfaction. "But not because of Nicole, and not because it's convenient. I've tried to show you that I don't need you just to be Nicole's mother. I need you because I enjoy being with you, loving you, and laughing with you, more than any other woman I've known."

Her smile wobbled. Damn it, she would not cry like some ninny.

"You're pretty damn remarkable, Anabel soon-to-be-Mrs. Watson." He drew a slow, deep breath. "And I love you."

Anabel wrapped her arms around his neck. She felt buoyant and carefree and so happy she wanted to burst. "Gil?"

"Hmm?"

"Now that I know I can speak my mind . . ."

His smile widened with anticipation. "Yes?"

"You won't expect me to listen to your Neil Diamond CDs, will you?"

"Not if I don't have to listen to Kid Rock."

Emotions rose up, almost choking her. "I love you, Gil." Now she got the tender, melting kiss. When he lifted his head, she cleared her throat. "One more thing."

"What's that?"

"I don't want a blue minivan."

He gave a short laugh. "No? And what do you want?"

"A red SUV." She kissed his chin. "Nicole." She wrapped her legs around his waist. "And *you.*"

Gil brought her closer, hugged her tight. In a voice rough with love, he said, "We'll pick out the SUV tomorrow. The others you already have."

GOOD WITH HIS HANDS

Chapter One

Pete Watson smiled as he watched Cassidy McClannahan get out of her spotlessly clean white Ford Contour. It was a familiar thing, smiling at the sight of Cassidy. Which meant he smiled a lot these days, because he saw her every day, everywhere he went. They worked together at the Sports Therapy Center and they lived in adjoining condos, thanks to the fact that Cassidy told him when one of the units became available. They left at the same time in the morning, came home at the same time each day.

It was nice. Routine. As predictable as being married—but without the chain chafing around his neck.

And no sex.

But hey, that kept it simple and easy. Besides, he could probably have sex with Cassidy if he wanted. But he didn't. Not really.

Not bad, anyway.

The spring breeze played havoc with her super-long, too-curly brown hair, whipping it into her face until, in disgust, she dropped her grocery bag and grabbed the mass with both hands.

She was such a contradiction, so much a woman in some ways, so oblivious to her own femininity in others.

Sidling up next to her, Pete said, "You should have put it in a ponytail."

"Bite me."

He laughed. Her reaction to him fell into the oblivious category. She treated him like an asexual pal. Joking with him, putting him down sometimes. And she never, ever primped or prettied up for him. Nope, Cassidy didn't want him. Still, he could get her if he wanted to.

He just didn't want to.

Scooping up her bag, which weighed a damn ton, Pete said, "Come on, Rapunzel. I'll help you inside."

She eyed his bulging biceps as if she didn't see them every day at work. But it wasn't a look of admiration, just one of observation—the same sort of look she always gave him. Un-affected. Nonsexual.

Finally she looked away, saying, "Don't strain anything."

Yeah, right. She knew better than most that he was in great shape. "What the hell did you buy, anyway?" Part of their routine for Friday was stopping at the grocery store. Since their eating habits were like night and day, they separated in the store, but met up again in the parking lot. He'd only bought enough lunchmeat and bread to last him through the week, but it felt like Cassidy had bought bricks.

While she rolled up her driver's-side window and locked her car door, she ticked off her purchases. "Baking potatoes, steak, corn on the cob, and a six-pack of pop."

"Got a big night planned?" Pete knew she didn't. Cassidy almost never dated. In fact, he couldn't remember ever seeing her date. That made him stop and think.

"Not really."

Well. That was pretty damn vague. Frowning, Pete waited to see if she'd invite him to join her. But she didn't. She never took the initiative. If he asked, she'd smile and tell him what time to show up. But why the hell did he always have to ask? Couldn't she just once extend the invitation? Another contradiction. They always enjoyed each other's company, but she never deliberately sought him out.

He loped beside her as they went up the tidy walkway to her front stoop, which was right next door to his, a mere fifteen feet away.

Assuming he'd follow, she unlocked her door, pushed it open and strolled inside, kicking her sneakers off the moment she got in. Out of the wind, she released her long hair and Pete watched as it tumbled free down to the small of her back, swishing above her plump ass.

Pete shook his head. She stayed in great shape, was always clean and well dressed, but she paid zero attention to feminine details like her hair and nails. She didn't wear makeup or perfume—not that she needed to. She always smelled great, even when sweaty. And she had a healthy, robust complexion.

Robust? Yeah, that's how normal men should think of women. Half disgusted, half embarrassed, Pete shook his head at his odd musings.

He'd asked Cassidy once about her long hair and found out she only washed and dried it. No curlers, no trims, no highlights. He'd never known a woman who didn't spend hours on her hair. When it got humid outside, her hair drew into long, bouncy ringlets that looked adorable.

Like Cassidy, her place was clean and comfortable but not overly decorated. It overflowed with plants and posters and throw pillows. By rote, Pete trailed her into the kitchen.

"You want some coffee or something?" She didn't wait for him to reply, but began filling the carafe, proving how predictable he'd become. He should politely decline and head home, maybe throw her off a bit. But he didn't.

"I can take one cup." Pete set their groceries on the counter, pulled out a kitchen chair and sat.

With the coffee preparations complete, Cassidy set out mugs and sugar before turning away. "Be right back."

"Where're you going?"

"To change. It's warm tonight."

She disappeared around the corner into the hall leading to her bedroom. Pete knew the setup of her condo because it was the mirror image of his. Where his bedroom ran to the left of the front door, hers ran to the right. He'd never been in her bedroom, though—and she'd never been in his.

Today she'd worn loose navy blue athletic pants and sneakers with the red unisex polo shirt supplied to all employees at the Sports Therapy Center.

Pete tilted his chair onto the back legs. It dawned on him that he'd known Cassidy about eleven months now. Not that he was counting or anything, but maintaining a close platonic relationship with a woman other than his sisters-in-law for almost a year had to be some sort of personal record. Usually if he knew a woman any length of time at all, he either dated her or was merely acquainted, not friendly.

The thing he'd first noticed about Cassidy—after that abundance of super-soft, crimped hair—was her focus. They'd spoken for about an hour his first day on the job, and in that time he realized that she had it together more than anyone he knew. If you asked Cassidy where she wanted to be five years from now, she could tell you. She knew where she wanted to work, where she wanted to live. She even claimed to know the type of guy she wanted to marry one day.

In comparison, Pete didn't even know where he wanted to be next week. Not that he intended to leave his job, his home, or Cassidy's friendship. But after finishing school and working three different jobs before settling at the sports center, he often felt unsettled, as if he were somehow missing the big picture.

Not Cassidy. She set new goals daily and worked hard to reach them. Maybe that's why she didn't date—she was too busy meeting her goals. Pete frowned in thought, trying to remember if any of their male clients had ever hit on her.

No one specific came to mind, but then everyone, young and old, male and female, loved Cassidy. She laughed a lot—honest laughter, not the trumped-up, polite kind. She also had nice eyes. Sort of a wishy-washy blue-green that managed to be awesomely direct. Honest, like her laugh.

She was built well enough, of course. On the short side. A little too muscular, given all the time she spent being physical on the job, but trim and fit. She had a body guys would notice. . . .

And why the hell was he dwelling on her body, anyway?

Pete stood up and went to her patio doors. With his hands stuck in his back pockets, palms out, he contemplated the darkening sky. Looked like another spring storm on the way. Trees swayed under the wind. Heavy gray clouds raced by. He slid the glass door open so the fragrant, moist air could come in through the screen, wafting around him, stirring his senses.

Now that he'd thought of Cassidy's bod, he couldn't stop thinking of it. And that was strange, because he preferred his ladies on the prissy side. He enjoyed watching a woman fuss with her hair, fret about her nails, and reapply her lipstick. It was so intrinsically female.

Dawn, the woman he'd most recently stopped dating, had done a lot of fussing. She was a corporate exec, smart, lots of ambition, and sexy as hell in a power suit. It had teased Pete, the way she'd pair a short, snug skirt, high heels, and red lipstick with a business jacket that begged to be unbuttoned. The attire emphasized rather than diminished her femaleness. Her glasses were a bonus. The way she pulled them off whenever she meant to get intimate had really turned him on.

"Coffee's done."

Speaking of turned on . . . Pete watched as Cassidy strode back into the room. No business suits, heels, or glasses for her, but unlike Dawn, Cassidy never bored him.

Her hair was pulled up into a high, sloppy knot, haphazardly clipped into place. Long, twining hanks of hair fell loose to her shoulders, around her small ears. She'd changed into a football jersey and cutoffs. A really big jersey—and really short shorts.

Being male, and healthy, and for some reason kind of horny on this almost-rainy, quiet Friday, Pete automatically gave her the once-over. Maybe there'd be a full moon tonight, or maybe the tide was high. Something, some unknown force, was making him contemplate Cassidy naked. Eyes narrowed and mouth pursed, he watched as she filled the mugs with coffee. He'd seen her in everything from sweats to bike shorts, so he knew she had lots of soft, squeezable curves to go with the muscles.

As if she felt his gaze, Cassidy looked over her shoulder, caught him staring at her butt, and looked away again. She didn't care that he was looking. She didn't care if he didn't look.

Damn abnormal woman.

Driven by some inner perversity heretofore undeveloped, Pete leaned back against the doorframe and smiled. "Your ass looks nice in those shorts."

A slight pause, then: "Thanks. You want a cookie with your coffee?"

His jaw locked. *Thanks? That was it? No more reaction than that?* Pete folded his arms over his chest. "How about I take your ass with my coffee?"

She threw a cookie at him, then dropped that delectable behind into a chair at the table with a hearty sigh. Using her toes, she snagged the chair opposite her and pulled it out enough so she could prop up her feet. "I'm so glad it's the weekend. Thanks to that tank of a guy with low back pain, I'm beat."

All week, Cassidy had worked with the man, who tipped the scales at three-fifty, on controlled, repetitive movement rehabilitation, teaching him safe movement through progression and complex exercises. That had been on top of her regulars who came in each day to work on running faster, farther. She'd been busy, no doubt about it.

Pete took his own seat. "I had an easier week. A bunch of junior high school boys working on sports conditioning. It was fun."

"You're good with kids." She sipped her coffee. "You should work with them more."

"Thanks. You know, I used to think about being a gym teacher." Before his father passed away and his brother took over the family business and everything went sideways, including all their lives. He'd gotten off track then and hadn't found his way back yet.

Cassidy nodded thoughtfully. "I can see that. You're close to having the right credits, right? It wouldn't take much to become a teacher, then you could—"

"Whoa. I didn't say I was going to do it. Just that I used to think about it."

"So what do you want to do? Work at the sports center the rest of your life?"

"I don't know." Damn it, why did she have to press him? "I'm happy there for now, so there's no rush."

Cassidy leaned her head back and closed her eyes. "I envy you the ability to keep thinking things through. It seems like I made up my mind in my teens and I've been on the same road ever since."

"You want to own a sports center someday, right?"

"A whole chain of them." With her eyes still closed, her mouth curled in a self-deprecating smile. "I've had my entire life pictured in my mind forever. First, I'd graduate with honors—"

"Which you did."

"—then learn my trade."

"Working at the sports center."

"Yeah." She shrugged. "And sometime before I got too old, I'd marry a professional man. Some guy in a suit, like Ward Cleaver." Her eyes opened. "You remember that show? *Leave It to Beaver*? Ward was always in a suit and June was always in a dress and their kids were polite, their house spotless. It seemed like the ideal setup to me. Only I don't want to wear a dress. I want to run a business in my sweats."

Used to her honesty, Pete toasted her with his coffee cup. "You look great in sweats."

"Thanks. They suit me. You know, because I'm into comfort and all that."

"I noticed." Boy, had he noticed. Especially today. She was relaxed and easy to be with, totally natural. Very appealing.

"It makes my little sister crazy. She hates to be seen in public with me."

"No way."

Wearing a sideways grin, Cassidy admitted, "She considers me a fashion disaster. But then, you'd have to meet my sis to understand. She's always perfectly groomed, manicured, and stylish." Eyes averted, she added, "Sort of like the women you date."

That had Pete frowning. It made him sound very superficial. "So you want a guy in a suit, huh?" Since he never got within ten feet of a suit, he didn't much care for that inclination, either.

Cassidy propped her chin against her hand and stared thoughtfully at the ceiling. As if picturing it in her mind, she said, "Tall, dark, and handsome, the kind of guy who looks great at black-tie events. Very serious. Dedicated to his job and his family."

Yep, she had that all planned out, too. Pete sank lower in his seat.

Her gaze met his, her eyes twinkling with suppressed laughter. "My dad is five-ten, fair, and balding, but he's got the other qualities. When I was a little girl, I'd put on his suit coat and imagine how big a man had to be to fill it out—not just physically, but intellectually and emotionally. Dad worked long hours, then got home and rolled up his shirtsleeves to help Mom with dinner. And after dinner, he'd sit at the dining room table with my sister and me and help with our homework." She laughed at herself. "My dad is great. Mom, too."

"And your sister?"

"Holly is a charmer. Beautiful enough so things come easily to her. Especially guys."

As usual, the conversation flowed between them. Pete had never realized the significance of that before, but he was as comfortable with Cassidy as he was with his brothers and his best friends—who were all male. Huh. "Speaking of family, did I tell you Ariel is pregnant? Sam is beside himself."

Cassidy's coffee cup clicked against the tabletop as she plunked it down and leaned forward. "Sam, your oldest brother, the bad-ass cop, the scary dude who likes to put himself in the line of fire, is going to be a *daddy*?"

"Yeah, how about that?" Cassidy hadn't met Sam yet, but

she had met their middle brother, Gil, when he was dropping off his daughters for Pete to babysit. Sometimes Cassidy even helped out with that. Nicki, now seven years old, adored Cassidy, as did her two-year-old sister, Rachael. "I think our nieces softened him up."

"I wouldn't be surprised. Those little angels could soften up anyone."

She looked all gentle and sweet when she said that. Someday she'd make a good mom—*whoa!* Pete snuffed that thought out with ruthless precision. No way in hell was he going to start thinking that way. It was one thing to picture Cassidy naked, especially since he couldn't seem to help himself. He would not think of her with a kid on her hip. Therein lay trouble—as Sam had discovered.

Pete cleared his throat and concentrated on his coffee cup. "They've been married five years now and Ariel said she's ready to be a mother. She told Sam he could either be the father or not, but one way or another she was getting pregnant."

Cassidy nearly choked on her coffee. "She gave him an ultimatum?"

"I think she just hid the condoms and then got naked. Didn't take any more than that to get Sam's cooperation."

Her throaty laughter seemed to wrap around Pete, mingling with the warm, moist air, further confounding him. He pushed his chair back in a rush. "I gotta run."

Cassidy picked up another cookie. "All right. See ya later."

She didn't change her relaxed posture or even look particularly curious as to why he was rushing off. Pete snatched up his grocery bag, started out, and then heard himself say, "I'm watching a movie later if you want to come over."

"You're not going out with Dawn?"

He and Dawn had parted company three days ago when

she wanted him to leave the sports center in the middle of the day to meet her for lunch. While he appreciated the enthusiasm she gave to her job, she treated his job as nothing. Shaking his head at the memories, Pete said, "That's over."

Cassidy took another sip of her coffee before shrugging and saying, "I'll let you know."

Eyes narrowed, Pete stared at her while the perils of masculine ego shoved his temper up a few notches. When he got her naked and under him, she wouldn't be so cavalier . . .

His eyes widened and his back snapped straight. Damn it, there he went again, thinking things he shouldn't. Best to make a run for it now before he did something stupid, like jump her bones. He pivoted on his heel and stalked out. It took all his control not to slam her front door.

He would not start pining after Cassidy McClannahan. Okay, so despite her comfortable-as-an-old-shoe appearance, her femininity beamed through. It didn't matter. If he wanted a woman, he'd make a phone call and—Pete snapped his fingers—he'd have a woman.

But once in his condo, Pete put away his groceries, stripped down to his boxers, and slouched in front of the TV to watch ESPN while guzzling an icy cold Coke and munching salty chips. He didn't touch the phone. But he did zone out on the latest sport clips while his mind danced around the idea of Cassidy McClannahan stripped naked, that long hair trailing over her shoulders and breasts; Cassidy with her eyes warm and inviting instead of indifferent; Cassidy as a sexual conquest, begging for more . . .

Before long, Pete was caught up in a full-fledged fantasy with predictable results.

He did need a woman, damn it. But he only wanted one. And she didn't seem at all interested.

* * *

Cassidy resisted the urge to head to Pete's. Little by little, their friendship drove her insane with sexual frustration. Against all common sense and her own responsible nature, she wanted the knucklehead. Hell, she'd wanted him almost from jump.

At first, it had been his mouthwatering appearance that had grabbed and held her attention. Tall, dark, and most definitely handsome. But not a suit in sight. Not that it mattered. Her thinking had done a one-eighty the day Pete Watson got hired on at the sports center.

For most of her life, Cassidy had bought into the idea of an intellectual, suit-wearing, serious-thinking guy with advancement on his mind as the perfect male. Pete was none of those things, but oh, he was *so* perfect.

Tall and trim, long-boned with rangy muscles, inky black hair, and dark bedroom eyes that ate a woman's soul. Outside of work, you were more likely to find Pete in jeans than dress pants. A few times, she'd even caught him in his boxers. And wow, what that man did for underwear should be illegal.

He was so sexy, there was no way on earth he couldn't know it. But amazingly enough, Pete didn't play up his sex appeal. Instead, he laughed and joked and befriended everyone. He didn't seem overly keen on advancing, but then his family owned a private novelty business and Pete got regular deposits from the profits, so he wasn't exactly hurting for cash. Pete was one of those guys who had plenty of time to *find himself,* because he didn't need to settle down to survive.

So here he was, well-to-do, gorgeous, and still so darn nice. He respected people, their accomplishments and their limitations, which made him easy to be around, easier to like.

Pride and intelligence, her two most noticeable fortes, told her Pete wasn't a guy to fall for, not with his carefree, live-for-the-moment attitude. It had been pure idiocy on her part to tell him about the condo for sale next door to her. Dumb, dumb. He'd moved in a few months ago and now they had this ultrafamiliar relationship that kept them in constant but platonic contact. It was maddening.

They were such good friends that he even felt at ease teasing her about her butt. Cassidy covered her face and groaned. He'd invited her over to watch a movie. He wanted to pal around.

The big dope.

Okay, so no one saw her as a sexual being. That didn't mean she was without desire. Where Pete was concerned, sex was about all she had on her mind. Sitting on the couch with him, knowing he was that close, pretending to watch television when instead she breathed in his scent and wallowed in his warmth and gradually melted . . . it was the act of a masochist. It was desperate and pathetic. Enough already.

She'd go to the movies by herself instead. She'd glut herself on popcorn and cola and by the time she got home, she'd have herself back in control. She'd even be able to face Pete in his boxers without drooling.

Mind made up, Cassidy snatched up her car keys and headed for the front door. She shoved her feet into her sneakers, turned the knob, jerked the door open—and ran face-first into a brick wall.

At least, it felt like a brick wall. After recoiling and almost falling, she managed another look. No wall, but close. "Duke," she said stupidly while rubbing her bruised nose, "I'm sorry. Are you okay?"

Since Duke was built like a cement slab and thus considered himself invincible, he grinned. "I'm fine." He reached out and brushed some of her tumbled hair from her face. "Sorry about that."

"My fault entirely."

Next to Duke's six-foot-six, two-hundred-and-fifty-pound frame, her younger sister, Holly, looked like a delicate, disgruntled miniature. "Cassidy, what on earth are you doing?" She eyed the keys, Cassidy's sloppy clothes, then propped her hands on her hips. "If it was any woman but you, I wouldn't ask. Most women wouldn't be seen dead wearing what you have on. But knowing you don't care how you look, and considering you have your keys in your hand, I have to ask."

Please don't, Cassidy thought.

Her sister forged on, haughty in her accusation. "You *forgot* that you invited us over to dinner, didn't you?"

Invited them? It was more like she'd had her arm twisted. "Umm . . ." Lusting after Pete had warped her brain.

"Cassidy," her sister wailed, as if the world had started to descend into hell. "You promised."

Holly was set on getting her family to worship Duke as much as she did. Because their mom and dad wanted only the best for Holly, that wasn't likely to happen. But Holly was convinced that if she got Cassidy's blessing, their parents would fall into line. Like she had that much influence? Right. Just because she was the *sensible* one.

It was enough to make a red-blooded female howl.

Cro-Magnon man—otherwise known as Duke—ushered both women inside. For a football player, he was gentle enough. But in Cassidy's opinion, her sister was too young to concentrate on anything other than her college studies. She should be thinking about her career, about gaining her independence before she got tied at the hip to a gargantuan sports aficionado.

"Holly, calm down," Duke said. "Maybe Cassidy just had to run an errand."

Cassidy snatched at that excuse like a lifeline. "Exactly. I forgot dessert." *Thank you, Duke.* "I left steaks on the counter. With it ready to rain, I figured we'd just broil them inside. Why don't you two go ahead and get everything ready while I run to the bakery?"

Holly started to protest, but Duke squeezed her into his side and smiled. "No rush, Cassidy. We'll manage till you get back."

Cassidy looked at him from under her brows. Oh, she might be sensible, but she wasn't blind. She knew that heated look as well as any woman. Duke always looked that way when he was with Holly. Well, she *would* rush, damn him. It didn't matter that her sister was old enough to make her own decisions on intimacy. Cassidy didn't intend to aid and abet.

She went out the door in a trot, and even with family drama to occupy her mind, she couldn't help thinking of Pete. Had he already called another woman to come over? His car was in his driveway, but his condo windows were dark.

She wouldn't succumb like so many other women. Sure, succumbing would be sublime, but far too temporary. And after all, Cassidy *was* the sensible one.

What a curse.

Chapter Two

Pete couldn't take it. Somehow, Cassidy, with her contrary lack of interest, had him frothing at the mouth. He never frothed. Okay, so he'd had a few semi-serious crushes in his day, the most noticeable being toward Ariel. But that was before she became his brother's wife, even before she'd met Sam. Once she'd met him . . . well, everyone except Sam had noticed that Ariel was head over heels in love with him. Seeing that had cured Pete's crush real quick, and now he loved Ariel as a sister-in-law, but certainly nothing more.

Since then he'd just dated and enjoyed life and women and the fun of being single.

But there was nothing enjoyable about how he felt right now—sort of rejected and dejected and annoyed. Why didn't Cassidy want him?

Maybe he needed to clue her in, let her know he wouldn't be adverse to the idea of some cozy time in the sack. Hell, it'd be great. They were already friends. They knew each other, trusted each other, enjoyed each other . . . so why not enjoy each other a little bit more?

Pete pulled on a T-shirt and shorts, and barefoot, went out

the back to see if Cassidy was grilling yet. He'd sniff her steaks and she'd invite him to join her and he'd move from there. He'd be casual, relaxed—he'd sneak the idea of wild sex in on her. Anticipation had him semi-hard before he discovered that she wasn't in the back.

He was hot, but her grill was still cold.

Frowning in disappointment, Pete wondered if the weather had chased her inside. The sky had turned black and static filled the air. It would start storming soon, probably throughout the night. Perfect weather for making love.

Maybe they could skip dinner and go straight to the idea of sex. Feeling like a desperate voyeur, Pete peered in through her patio doors, but didn't see her. He considered his options, raised his hand to knock—and heard a noise in her bedroom. That window was open, too, and Pete stared at it, teased with the idea of Cassidy changing clothes, maybe getting in or out of the shower . . . The sound of a soft, hungry, vibrating moan resonated out to him.

Pete's heart, thoughts, and breath all stuttered to a standstill. Was that a moan of *sexual pleasure?* His reaction was swift and confusing: jealousy, possessiveness, and red-hot anger. He strained to hear more while everything masculine within him went on the alert.

Another moan reached him, then another, higher in pitch, each subsequent moan rising in excitement until they peaked—and Pete's hair damn near stood on end.

He felt betrayed!

She turned down a movie with him to have sex with someone else. Never mind that she didn't know he wanted to have sex with her.

Forcibly, Pete unglued his feet and stalked away in a temper, but even after he'd stepped into his own kitchen and slammed the door, the sound of her pleasure, sweet and deep, reverberated in his head, pounding against his skull.

Cassidy was involved sexually with someone—someone other than him. That sucked.

He'd only just decided that he wanted her, and he'd already lost his chance.

Dinner was a nightmare that had taken forever, but now it was over. The cake she'd bought was completely consumed, a pot of coffee polished off, and still Duke and Holly lingered.

Maybe she should have invited Pete over. She'd noticed his car still in the drive when she returned from fetching dessert. He could have served as a buffer, a guy for Conan the Barbarian to regale with football stories. For herself, Cassidy had heard enough about tackles, passes, and kicks to last a lifetime.

Pete was so good with people, he'd have found a way to steer the conversation, to keep it entertaining for one and all. He could have told more anecdotes about his cop brother, Sam, or his niece, Nicole. He could have discussed sport-induced injuries with Duke. He could have just been there, smiling and making everyone else smile.

Cassidy didn't realize that Duke had finished his story until she caught him grinning at her. Good grief, how long had she been sitting there with that stupid look on her face while she daydreamed about Pete?

With far too much perception, Duke asked, "Thinking of a guy?" When Cassidy just gaped at him, he said, "I hope we didn't interrupt your plans. You could have invited your boyfriend to dinner, too."

Cassidy's face burned. Her *boyfriend?* Pete was not a boyfriend. He was a miserable, sexy, forever-out-of-reach pal.

Holly started laughing. "Cassidy doesn't date!" She made

it sound like the most absurd thing imaginable. "She hasn't been involved with anyone since . . . gosh, when was it, Cass? Better than a year ago, I think."

Felt like ten years to Cassidy, but then, celibacy probably had that effect on many people.

Duke's smile turned sympathetic. "Now Holly, your sister is too pretty not to date."

Pretty? Well okay, she wasn't an ogre, but . . . Duke was probably just trying to score points. Still, Cassidy found herself tucking her disheveled hair behind her ears and twittering in the age-old way of women.

"I never said she wasn't pretty," Holly protested. "But as my folks are fond of saying, Cassidy is the levelheaded one. She doesn't waste her time on guys."

Uh-oh. Now Duke was sure to be insulted. After all, what male ego would like being called a waste of time?

But to Cassidy's surprise, Duke picked a different bone entirely. "Meaning you aren't levelheaded?"

Cassidy did a double take. She hadn't thought about it from that perspective. She knew her parents meant well, and she'd always taken the comments to mean Holly was the personable one, the one who got friends and compliments and dates easily. Cassidy thought they were throwing her a crumb, giving her the only credit they could. But the look on Holly's face assured her that Duke had read her sister right.

If Cassidy felt insulted for being called too responsible, how did the comments make Holly feel? Cassidy automatically reached out to her. "Holly, Mom and Dad didn't mean—"

Holly gave her brightest smile. "I bet you were wishing us gone so you could get to bed, huh?" And then to Duke, "Cassidy's an early bird. You'd think she was eighty-seven instead of twenty-seven, with the way she conks out so early."

Cassidy started to deny that accusation, but Holly's eyes

were pleading, so instead she fashioned a wide yawn. "Sorry. I did have a really busy week."

Duke pushed to his feet and gently hauled Holly up and into his side. He was a demonstrative man and he couldn't seem to keep his hands off her sister.

He was so attentive, no one could miss how he felt about Holly.

Teasing, Duke said, "I still think it was a guy. I've seen that look before."

Holly playfully swatted at him. "Not lately, you haven't."

"Not from anyone but you." He kissed Holly's nose. "It was really nice of you to have me over, Cassidy. Next time is my treat."

"Great idea, Duke." Holly hugged his arm while giving Cassidy a beseeching look. "Maybe you can talk Mom and Dad into joining us."

They acted like lovesick teenagers, Cassidy thought, and really, Duke was so very nice to Holly, would it be that bad if they were in love? "Sure, I'll see what I can do."

With a grateful squeal, Holly embraced her. "Thanks, Cass. I know this whole relationship thing is out of your league, but—"

Duke laughed, cutting Holly off. "She hasn't been living in a cave, Holly. Come on. Let's make a break for the car while the rain has slowed down."

Cassidy watched them go. The rain had been furious earlier, with lots of thunder and lightning, but now it seemed to have settled into a steady but gentle downpour. Duke made a point of holding his jacket over Holly's head. He opened her door for her, touched her cheek, and smiled at her with love and affection. Cassidy sighed. No one ever looked at her like that. She could see why Holly was smitten.

With food for thought and a final wave to her sister, Cassidy locked up. She turned out all the lights in her condo, took a quick shower, pulled on a tank top and panties, and climbed into bed. Her window was still open and the cooler breeze drifted over her face, her body. She'd probably end up chilled in the night, but for now she needed the fresh air.

She couldn't sleep. Thoughts of her sister in love tangled with thoughts of Pete. Why couldn't he dote on her the way Duke doted on Holly? She rolled to her back and answered her own question: because Holly was everything she wasn't— fun, beautiful, sexy.

Pete's last girlfriend had been the young executive type. She'd stopped in the center to pick him up, usually too early, which Cassidy could tell annoyed Pete. Not that he showed it, she just knew him really well. Maybe that's why things hadn't lasted with Ms. Corporate Exec.

Cassidy propped her arms behind her head and watched the shadows on her ceiling. Because she lived next door to Pete, she'd watched the women come and go. Usually a woman lasted about two weeks before Pete got bored. Any woman who set her sights on tying him down was bound for disappointment.

She certainly wouldn't expect anything lasting from him. Well, other than their friendship, which seemed pretty strong. But Pete liked women like her sister, polished to a soft glow, ultrafeminine, and very ladylike.

She didn't fall into any of those categories, so she didn't stand much of a chance at gaining his attention even on the short term. Not that she'd go out of her way anyhow. She had her pride.

But pride ran a cold second to kissing, touching, and being held. Maybe if she just gave Pete a nudge to let him know she was interested, he'd pick up from there. She couldn't be too obvious. For her entire life, she'd been *au naturel—*

what you saw was what you got. She wouldn't change who she was—not for Pete, not for anyone. But maybe she could just try a few small refinements.

Cassidy chewed her lip and considered her course of action.

A trim for her long hair was way past due; she'd just been too busy, and too unconcerned, to deal with it. But thinking of the too-curly mess it had become, she decided to set an appointment in the morning. And she could dab on a really subtle fragrance, something naturally earthy, like musk. While she was at the mall to get her hair trimmed, she'd also pick out a scent.

Pete had noticed her shorts, so she'd wear them again, maybe with a low-cut top. Her cleavage wasn't anything to crow about, but she wasn't flat-chested, either.

What did she have to lose?

Rolling to her side, Cassidy wondered if Pete would even notice the small changes. She would never be the type of woman he gravitated to, but they were friends, so maybe he wouldn't mind getting more intimate with her.

She'd put her plans into action tomorrow—and hope he didn't already have a date.

Pete was up with the sun. After hearing that disturbing moan—disturbing on too many levels—he'd tried turning in early. But sleep had been impossible and he'd spent hours tossing and turning, thinking of Cassidy over there with someone else while his muscles cramped and protested. He'd tried to block the awful images from his mind, but they remained, prodding at him like a sore tooth: Cassidy with some suit-wearing jerk; Cassidy getting excited; Cassidy twisting and moaning.

Cassidy climaxing.

He couldn't stand it.

By seven, he was showered, standing at his closet and staring at the lack of professional clothes. Oh, he had a suit, the one he'd worn for his brothers' marriages. Gil had fussed, trying to insist that he buy a new, more expensive one, but Pete refused. He hated the idea of shopping for the thing, trying them on, getting fitted. Then he'd have to pick out a shirt, and a tie, maybe cufflinks . . . He *hated* suits.

But Cassidy loved them.

Stiff and fuming, Pete jerked on khaki shorts and a navy pullover, then paced until it got late enough to go to her place. She generally slept in on Saturday mornings. He knew her schedule as well as he knew his own. Right now she'd be curled in bed, all warm and soft and . . . He couldn't wait a minute more.

He went out his back door and stomped across the rain-wet grass to her patio. He pressed his nose against the glass doors, but it was dark inside, silent. Daunted, Pete looked around, and discovered that her bedroom window was still open.

Shit. What if the guy was still in there? What if he'd spent the night? What if, right this very moment, he was spooned up against her soft backside?

A feral growl rose from Pete's throat, startling him with the viciousness of it. No woman had ever made him growl. He left that type of behavior to his brother, Sam, who was more animal than man.

Now Gil, he was the type of man Cassidy professed to want. A suit, serious, a mover and shaker. A great guy, his brother Gil. So what would Gil do?

He'd be noble for sure, Pete decided. Gil would wait and see if she did have company, and if so, he'd give them privacy.

That thought was so repugnant, Pete started shaking.

To hell with it. His fist rapped sharply on Cassidy's glass door.

A second later, her bedroom curtain moved and Cassidy peered out. "Pete?" she groused in a sleep-froggy voice. "What are you doing?"

"Open up." Pete tried to emulate Gil, to present himself in a calm, civilized manner. "You alone in there?" he snarled.

Her eyes were huge and round in the early morning light. "No, I have the Dallas Cowboys all tucked into my bed. It's a squeeze, but we're managing."

Pete sucked in a breath. *"Cassidy . . ."*

"Of course I'm alone, you idiot." Her frowning gaze darted around the yard in confusion. "What time is it?"

She was alone. The tension eased out of Pete, making his knees weak. "I dunno, seven or so." The chill morning air frosted his breath and prickled his skin into goose bumps. "Time to get up and keep your neighbor company."

"Seven!"

He took five steps and looked at her through the screen. She had a bad case of bedhead and her eyes were puffy, still vague with sleep. She looked tumbled and tired and his heart softened with a strange, deep thump. "Open up, Cassidy."

Still confused, not that he blamed her, she rubbed her eyes, pushed her hair out of her face. "Yeah, all right. Keep your pants on." She started to turn away.

"What fun will that be?"

Her head snapped back around. Seconds ticked by before she said, "Get away from my window, you perv. I have to get dressed."

The thump turned into a hard, steady pulse. "Don't bother on my account."

But she'd already walked away, so she missed his sentiments on the matter. Pete thought about peeking, knew he wouldn't and went back to the door to wait. Impatience hummed in his veins. He was a man on a mission, a man driven by testosterone and the ancient, savage need to stake a claim.

The fluorescent kitchen light flickered on and seconds later, her door slid open.

Assuming he'd come in without a greeting, Cassidy slunk away to the sink to start the coffee. Around an enormous yawn, she asked, "What's wrong? Why are you up so early?"

Pete soaked in the sight of her. Now seeing her with new eyes—new lusty eyes—he realized just how appealing she appeared with her long hair hanging in ropes around her shoulders and her skin flushed and warm. Plaid flannel pants hugged her behind and her black tank top molded to her breasts. Her feet were bare, her toes curled against the tile floor.

With the morning air so cool, her nipples had puckered.

Puckered nipples had never taken out his knees before, but now Pete groped for a chair so he wouldn't collapse into a horny heap in the middle of her kitchen. Like Pavlov's dog, his mouth started watering. He could just imagine pulling that skimpy top up and over her head, baring her breasts, taking a plump nipple into his mouth . . .

In between measuring out fragrant coffee grounds, Cassidy glanced up at him. "Pete?"

"I couldn't sleep," he mumbled, staring in awe at those breasts, mesmerized by the possibilities. He'd never really thought about her breasts before. But boy, she had them. Nice ones, too. Sort of small but perky, like the rest of her.

Someone had touched that lush little firm body just last night. Someone other than him. Pete hated that thought.

"So I don't get to sleep, either?" The coffeemaker started to hiss and spit. Cassidy pulled out a chair and slumped boneless in her seat, putting her head on her folded arms. Thick, curly hair went everywhere.

Pete didn't think about it—he just reached across the table

and drew his fingers across a long tendril, feeling the texture, the weight and warmth. He was close enough, so he leaned forward and brought it to his nose, breathing in the fragrance of her shampoo.

Cassidy froze. By small degrees, she tipped her face up until her eyes were visible above her forearm and she could lock gazes with him. He still had hold of her hair, still had it pressed to his nose.

She rose up a bit more. "Uh . . . Pete?"

Neither of them blinked. "Yeah?" He sounded hoarse, but damn, her hair was soft and sweet—as erogenous as her silky skin or a peek at that luscious behind. He imagined how her hair would feel slipping over his chest, his stomach, his thighs . . . He dropped his hand and sat back.

Cassidy continued to stare at him. As if moving away from a dangerous animal, she slowly pressed her spine into the back of her seat. Her breasts were soft and round under the clinging shirt, trembling with her fast breaths. Her tight little nipples jutted forward.

Pete tried, without much effort, to keep his attention on her face. It was futile.

Cassidy shoved back her chair. "I'll, ah, I'll be right back."

Pete stared up at her with a sense of *déjà vu.* "Where're you going?"

"I have to . . . brush my teeth and stuff." She ran off before he could stop her.

Pete got up and paced. He felt insane, a little lost, and a whole lot aroused. Once the coffee finished dripping, he poured two cups, doctoring Cassidy's the same way she always took it, with lots of sugar and cream. He even rummaged through her cabinet and found some prepackaged brownies, knowing she'd want one.

He was leaning against the sink, sipping his coffee and thinking of the deliciously depraved things he wanted to do to her, when she shyly came back into the kitchen. Pete stalled with the cup to his mouth.

She hadn't changed clothes, but she'd brushed out her hair and neatly braided it, leaving flirty little curls to tease her temples, her nape. Her face was pink, her lips shiny with clear gloss.

She'd fixed up for him?

Very slowly, Pete set his coffee aside. "I was thinking, Cassidy . . ."

She swallowed hard and charged into the room, grabbing her coffee with near desperation. After downing half of it, she wiped her mouth and in the process removed most of the gloss she'd just applied. Pete grinned. She was . . . adorable.

How come he'd never noticed that before? He remembered how, as soon as he knew Ariel wanted Sam, he stopped thinking of her sexually. She became family to him. Had he done that with Cassidy, relegating her to the category of friend and not allowing himself to think of her in any other way? He hadn't wanted to screw up with Ariel, to alienate her or his brother. And God knew he valued Cassidy's friendship too much to risk it.

Visibly bracing herself, Cassidy prompted him, saying, "Yeah? You were thinking?"

Usually they were comfortable with each other, but now she seemed edgy. Pete didn't like that, so he decided to ease into things.

"Are you dating anyone?" When she said yes, then Pete could suggest she date *him*, and they could move on from there.

But Cassidy shook her head. "You know I'm not."

Pete drew back, narrowing his eyes in thought. "You can tell me anything, you know. We're . . . friends."

"Sure." When Pete just waited, she said, "I don't have time to date."

Pete blinked. If she wasn't dating, then it had been what—a one-night stand? No. He shook his head. Cassidy wasn't into those any more than he was.

He decided to approach the idea of sex from a different angle. "You didn't come over to watch the movie with me last night."

She blushed. *Blushed.* What was that about?

"I know." She shifted her feet. "I had . . . other stuff to do."

Yeah, he knew what other stuff—like moaning out an orgasm. He locked his jaw and clenched his teeth. "Another guy to see?"

The blush gave way to frowning annoyance. "I just said no, didn't I?"

"But . . ." Why was she fudging the truth? "You're saying you didn't have a date last night?"

Exasperation sharpened her tone. "How many ways can I say it, Pete? I'm not dating anyone. I haven't had a date in a year. You see me every damned day, so I'd think you'd know it."

No date. Pete stood there for fifteen seconds before other ideas started squeezing past his confusion. Ho boy.

If she hadn't been with a guy, that meant she'd been *alone* when he heard that soft, excited, and sexual moan. And if she'd been alone and moaning like that, then she'd been . . .

His abdomen clenched with sexual images so vivid he thought he might collapse. Tenderness rolled over him, too. *She'd been alone.* All by herself. He stared at her, feeling both soft in the heart and hard in the crotch.

Bless her heart. He wanted to smile and hold her. He wanted to strip her naked and pull her down to the floor.

It was still up in the air exactly what he'd do, but he knew where to start. Throbbing with need, Pete took a small step toward her. "If I kissed you—"

Her eyes widened. "You're going to kiss me?"

Shock made her look almost comical. "If I did, what would you do?"

Her mouth opened twice before she whispered, "I don't know."

"Would you slap me?"

That had her frowning again. "No."

He took another step toward her. "Would you push me away?"

Cheeks flushed with warm color, she shook her head. "Of course not."

"Great." Pete moved closer still. He took her coffee cup and set it on the counter. "What would you do?"

She stared up at him, her blue-green eyes shining, her lips parted. "I'd kiss you back," she said on a breathless gasp, and then she attacked him.

Pete staggered back from her assault. And it was an assault. She had a death grip on his neck, her mouth plastered to his so hard his lips were smashed against his teeth. The small of his back landed with jarring impact against the sharp edge of the counter.

"Mmmrrrmm." Pete tried to speak, to tell her to slow down, but she wasn't exactly a weak woman and he didn't want to hurt her. When he tried to pull back, her fingers locked into his hair. Now that hurt.

Pete turned so she was the one nailed against the counter. He covered a breast with his hand.

That got her attention.

Got his, too. Boy, she felt good.

Cassidy freed his mouth and groaned, *"Pete."*

Her eyes were closed, her heartbeat hammering madly against his palm. He smiled and said, "Cassidy."

She tried to kiss him again, but Pete dodged her mouth.

"Take it easy, okay? How about you just stand there looking like you look, and let me do the kissing?"

"Was . . . was I bad?"

"Maybe just a little out of practice."

Her lashes lowered to hide her eyes. "Sorry. It's been over a year."

Shocked and appalled, Pete paused in his ascent toward her mouth. "A year since you've been kissed?"

"Yeah." And then, defensively, "I've been busy."

But not too busy to pleasure herself last night. Oh man, that was fodder for many fantasies to come. Had she been thinking of him? Now his toes were curling.

"Jesus, I'm glad I woke you up." He pried her fingers out of his hair.

"Me, too." She tried a grin. "So, uh, now what?"

A loaded question for sure. Pete caught her waist and hefted her up to the countertop. "That's up to you, but I'd say you have a year's worth of kissing to make up for."

Cassidy smiled. "Then let's get started."

Chapter Three

Cassidy had to fight against swooning. All it took was a braid in her hair, and Pete wanted her? Who knew?

Her hair was so long that braiding it was an awkward pain in the butt, a lesson in flexibility, but hey, if it turned Pete into a ravening animal, she'd braid it every single day.

With her fanny on the countertop, she was able to look down at him. But he didn't meet her gaze. No, he was staring at her chest. More specifically, her nipples, which even now were stiff against the thin material of her tank top.

It was a little embarrassing, definitely not something she was used to. She'd sort of figured on Pete being more a challenge.

Clearing her throat, Cassidy asked, "So did you come over here just for this?"

Distracted, he said, "Yeah." And then his hands covered her breasts and his eyes closed as he murmured, "Damn, you feel good."

She would have slid right off the counter except that Pete was there, standing between her knees, keeping her in place.

His thumbs brushed over her nipples and it felt so good,

so electric, Cassidy slumped back and banged her head on the wall. Now half reclining, she used her elbows to support herself and absorbed the wonderful sensation of being touched by Pete Watson.

He leaned forward, murmured something low, and then his mouth was at her breast, his lips plucking at her nipple through the material of the shirt. Cassidy groaned and said, "I was thinking about this last night."

"I know," he whispered in between taunting little nips with his teeth.

That momentarily stumped her. "What do you mean, you know?"

He paused, his hands stilling on the hem of her shirt. His dark brown eyes looked velvety and warm when they met hers, then he shrugged and tugged the shirt above her breasts, baring her to his gaze. He swallowed and color slashed his cheekbones. "I was thinking it, too," he admitted in husky tones. "Something happened between us yesterday, that's all I meant."

"Oh."

His mouth, scalding hot and damp, closed around her stiffened nipple.

"Oh." Cassidy arched her back, offering herself to him, amazed at the intensity of the feelings he gave her.

Pete sucked languidly. His tongue swirled around her, his teeth occasionally nipping before sucking softly again. "You taste good, Cassidy."

She was in the most awkward position, cramped against the wall beside her sink, her legs half-dangling off the counter at either side of his lean hips. She couldn't move much, couldn't really lie down or sit up. "Pete?"

He switched to the other nipple, latching on hungrily before slowing down, teasing with his tongue and teeth. "Hmmm?"

"Let's go to my bedroom."

His head lifted. His eyes were almost black now, heavy-lidded. He was breathing hard, his lips wet. "Yeah."

Before Cassidy could push off the counter, he put his arms around her hips and lifted, holding her tight to his chest, her legs around his waist as he made his way down the hall.

With one big hand splayed wide over her behind, Pete growled, "You know where this is headed, right?"

Hands braced on his shoulders, Cassidy gave him a blank look. The friction of his hard abdomen against the soft apex of her thighs was enough to leave her brainless. She nodded. "We're going to have sex. At least I hope we are."

Pete gave a rough laugh, surged into her room, and dumped her on her bed. He immediately followed her down, sprawling out over her, catching her hands and pinning them beside her head. "Damn right we are." His smile faded. "But I have to know you won't have regrets, Cassidy."

"Why would I?" she asked, when what she really wanted to say was, *Get on with it*.

"We're good friends." Slowly, Pete leaned down and touched his mouth to hers. A tender, almost loving kiss. Not sexual so much as emotional. It confused and elated her.

Between soft, small kisses to her lips, her chin, her throat, he whispered, "Very good friends. I value that. You're important to me. I don't want things to get . . . weird between us."

Meaning he didn't want her to start getting clingy. She understood that. To a freewheeler like Pete, she must seem like a complete stick-in-the-mud. The sensible part of her brain nagged at her, saying it wasn't too late to back out before she got hurt. But she'd been sensible all her life and damn it, she was lonely.

Eventually they'd part ways. In a year, two at the most, she'd have enough money saved, and enough experience, to open her own sports center. She couldn't see Pete working for her, so their friendship would likely wane. She hated that reality, even as she accepted it.

He was interested now. She was more than interested. For once she snuffed her sensible thoughts and went for broke.

Cupping his face, she held him back. Her fingers sank into the cool, silky thickness of his dark hair while her thumbs stroked his cheeks, luxuriating in the rasp of beard stubble, the lean hardness of his jaw. Cassidy smiled at him. It wasn't easy and her lips felt stiff, but she managed it. "I have long-term goals, Pete. You know that, just as you know how determined I am. I'm not going to throw all my plans into the wind just because we sleep together."

He looked far too serious and solemn. "Cassidy . . ."

"Shhh." She leaned up and took his mouth, loving his taste, even loving him a little. "I want you. I think you want me."

"You know I do."

She let out a breath. "We're both adults, both available, and as you said, we're friends. I trust you, more than any other guy I know. That's enough, isn't it?"

He ducked his head, and for one agonizing moment, Cassidy thought he was going to pull away. Then he moved to her side and put his hand on her belly. "I guess it'll have to be."

She had no idea what he meant by that, but his fingers were on her bare skin, teasing her abdomen before dipping under the waistband of her flannel pants. His baby finger tickled her navel, making her muscles pull tight in reaction.

Pete leaned over her and took her mouth, somehow making a mere kiss so much more—deeper, hotter, more intimate. She was still assimilating the wonder of that when his fingers pressed lower, into her panties, then tangled with her pubic hair.

Against her mouth, he said, "No, don't stiffen up." His fingers felt hot, callused. "I'm sorry if I'm rushing things, but I'm dying to touch you."

Dying to touch her. Cassidy sighed and parted her legs a bit. She wanted him to touch her. Everything about this felt magical: his delicious scent surrounding her, the heat of his muscled body pressed all along her side. The gentle, careful way his hands moved over her.

With his hand still cupping her mound, Pete rose on one elbow. "Look at me, Cass."

It was a struggle to get her heavy eyes open and focused on his face. Their labored breaths seemed to find a matching rhythm. Pete stared at her, his eyes smoldering, intense, and his fingers parted her, gently stroking, easing—he sank one finger deep inside her.

She didn't mean to, but Cassidy pressed her head back into the mattress, closing her eyes to hold in the sensations.

Pete went still. "Open your eyes, honey. Come on, look at me."

She panted, struggled to get control of herself, and finally, her bottom lip caught in her teeth, met his gaze.

"You're already wet." He looked at her mouth, smiled. "Don't bite your lip. Ease up. That's it. Now how does that feel?" He pressed in, pulled back.

There were no words, so Cassidy just nodded.

"Good?"

"Yes." She lifted her hips against him and groaned. "Very good. But not enough."

"Does this help?" He pushed a second finger into her. "Damn, you're tight."

"Oh God."

"Come on, Cassidy," he tempted softly. "Keep your eyes open. Let me watch you, let me see what you feel." He pulled his fingers out, slowly pressed them back in, out, back in. "You can move your hips with me."

Because she couldn't *not* move, she did.

Groaning, Pete said, "Yeah, like that." He ducked his head and captured her nipple, suckling, tonguing. Sucking hard.

Whenever Cassidy had thought about sex with Pete—and she'd thought of it a lot—it hadn't been like this, with them both dressed, him more so than her, and lying on her bed with him doing things to her. She'd imagined it being a reciprocal event, her touching him and kissing him and ogling him in the buff.

"Pete, please."

As if her words snapped him out of a daze, he sat up in a rush. "Let's get rid of this, okay?" He peeled her shirt completely off her, then his own.

Oh wow. Cassidy stared at his bare chest, lightly furred in dark hair, taut with muscle, wide and hard. If the sports center would change its policy about wearing polo shirts, they'd get more customers. Women would flock in to see Pete in nothing more than shorts, she was sure of it. When she got her own place, she'd talk him into letting her use him for a poster.

"Now these."

He reached for the waistband of her flannel pants and Cassidy was overcome with shyness. What would he think of her naked? Would he enjoy the sight of her body as much as she enjoyed his?

"Lift your hips."

She gulped down her nervousness and did as he asked and, just like that, she was naked. Pete sat back beside her, looking at her body in minute detail, taking his damn time.

She started to tremble. Despite his requests, she closed

her eyes and even turned her head to the side, waiting in an agony of suspense to see what he'd say. But he didn't say anything at all.

She felt his breath on her belly and jerked. "Pete?"

His lips moved over her skin; he nuzzled with his nose. "Pete!"

"You smell so damn good." He ended that statement with something of a growl and then his hands were on her upper thighs, pulling her legs open.

Shock kept Cassidy immobile. Surely he didn't think to— oh yeah, he did. Her head fell back again. *"Pete."*

After one hot kiss to her vulva, he slid off the side of the bed. "Keep talking to me, Cass. I like it."

Her eyes widened. Such an inane thing to say to her! Cassidy almost smiled, but she was too hot, too turned on, to find any real humor in the situation. And now that he'd requested it, she couldn't think of a single thing to say.

Pete kept kissing her inner thighs, easing them farther and farther apart with his forearms holding them there. When she was inelegantly sprawled, he stared down at her, his eyes half closed, his lips parted, his face flushed. His expression very intent, he moved closer, closer. Moaning, he sank his strong fingers into her tender thighs, and stroked his tongue into her.

For Cassidy, it was as much the idea of what he did, as the physical feel of it, that had her ready to explode. No one had ever kissed her there. The few dates she'd had that resulted in sex had been perfunctory and unsatisfactory. The men had rushed to get her naked, rushed to get inside, then rushed to leave.

Pete didn't seem to be in a rush at all. In fact, in that moment, he rumbled, "I could do this all night."

She didn't think she could take it all night.

"Talk to me, honey. Do you like this?" His tongue moved over her swollen lips, pressed deep inside.

"Yes."

"And this?" He stabbed with his tongue, short, quick strokes.

A quaking had started deep inside her, radiating out to her legs, making her lungs constrict, her heart thunder. She choked, "Yes."

"And how about . . . this." Very gently, he closed his mouth over her clitoris and flicked with his tongue and Cassidy knew she was lost.

"Yes, yes, *yes.*" The climax took her completely by surprise. She hadn't expected it. Not so easily. Her whole body went taut and hot, shaking uncontrollably, her hips lifting and twisting against his mouth, her hands gripping the sheets tight, trying to anchor herself.

"Oh God." It felt like she'd die, like she'd never be the same again. Even after the crushing pleasure faded, her body continued to pulse and shiver and she still couldn't get enough air into her lungs or any strength into her limp limbs.

Reality swam around her, not quite within reach. She felt good, alive and sated and weak. She knew Pete had moved, that he'd stood up, but she couldn't seem to gather her wits. Incredible aftershocks of sensation shimmered through her.

Then Pete was over her, his chest crushing her breasts, his hairy thighs wedging between hers. He held her face while speaking softly. "I should wait, I know it, but I can't." Something hard pressed against her sex. She was sensitive, still swollen, and she flinched. "Forgive me, Cassidy."

He thrust into her—heavy, thick, hot, and hard—and Cassidy melted in renewed pleasure. There was nothing tentative about the way Pete began moving, stroking steadily, already groaning, heat pouring off him.

"Ah . . . Christ," he said, and grabbed her face to hold her still for his voracious kiss. He was wild, his tongue in her mouth, his body smothering hers. The hair on his chest abraded her nipples, his abdomen rubbed against her belly, her thighs ached from the unfamiliar position, and Cassidy felt the swelling eruptions start again, building, overflowing.

She locked her ankles at the small of Pete's back, inadvertently sending him deeper, to a spot that was almost pain, the pleasure was so fierce. Sobbing, she tried to pull her mouth away enough to breathe, but he held her too tight, too close. He drove into her faster, harder, and when he stiffened, his hips jerking, Cassidy came with him, swallowing his groan and giving him her own.

Happiness, euphoria, cocooned her. Pete was still atop her body, their warmth sealing their damp flesh together. His breath had finally calmed in her ear and she felt him withdrawing as he lost his erection.

"Mmm." Lazily, she trailed her fingertips down his spine. His skin was sleek and hot, a little sweaty. "That tickles."

He didn't move. "What?"

"Your leaving me."

"Oh. Yeah, that happens when I get wrung out." Sluggishly, Pete forced himself up on stiffened arms. Their gazes met, hers a little timid, his triumphant. He smiled. "You're incredible."

Warmth flooded Cassidy's face. "Thank you. You, too."

His attention drifted from her eyes to her mouth. "Wanna do it again?"

Cassidy felt him growing hard once more. Her eyes widened. "But . . ."

Laughing, Pete rolled to the side of her. "In a little bit, I mean. Hell, I have to regain my strength." He reached over and absently patted her thigh. "I know the manly thing to do would be to hightail it into the bathroom to get rid of the rubber, but I'm not sure I'd make it. You got any tissues in here or anything?"

Cassidy stared at her ceiling, astounded by the turn of events. She, Cassidy McClannahan, the *sensible* one, was being queried by a gorgeous man on how to deal with a spent condom. She chuckled and forced herself upright with renewed energy. Pete was sprawled beside her, one hand on his chest, the other near her hip. His eyes were still heavy, a crooked smile still on his mouth.

"I guess I'm stronger than you." She swung her legs off the side of the bed and stood—then staggered.

Pete chuckled. "Yeah, right."

"Be right back."

As she headed into the hall, he said, "You're always saying that to me."

It didn't occur to Cassidy that she was naked until she stepped into the bright light of the bathroom and saw herself in the mirror. Gads. Her once-tidy braid now looked like a frayed rope. Little hairs stuck out everywhere. Cassidy jerked out the rubber band, brushed her hair, and decided against braiding it again. It'd take too long, especially considering she had a naked man in her bed.

She wet a washcloth, wrung it out, and headed back to Pete with the small bathroom trash can in hand. She could feel her hair feathering against the bare skin of her back, reminding her of her nakedness. Now that she'd thought about being naked, she felt more self-conscious. She peeked into the bedroom, saw Pete had pushed himself up against the headboard and knew there was no help for it. At least he was naked, too. A nice distraction, that. Trying not to look embarrassed, Cassidy waltzed in.

Pete leered at her. "I like your hair like that. Last night, I was thinking about all that hair sliding over me while we made out."

Cassidy drew to a stunned halt. "You were?"

"Yeah. What did you think about me?"

"Ummm . . ." To give herself time to formulate a safe answer, because after all, she couldn't tell him she'd been mooning over him forever, she came in and handed him the trash can and cloth. It was an amazing thing, watching Pete peel away a condom and use the washcloth as if having an audience of one very interested woman didn't affect him at all.

"Cassidy?" He dropped the cloth over the side of the bed and caught her hand, tumbling her onto his chest. "Snap out of it, woman."

She *had* been watching the process rather fixedly, she realized.

With no real assistance from her, Pete arranged her next to him, pulling one of her legs over his lap, her arm over his chest and tucking her face against his shoulder.

The position was so comforting, but so alien, Cassidy felt stiff. "This is new to me."

"Yeah?" His hand smoothed her hair, her shoulder. "Do tell."

Not in this lifetime. "I thought it was crass to talk about stuff like that."

"I don't want details." He shuddered at the thought. "But how come this is new to you? You're twenty-seven, right? Same as me?"

"Yeah." Disgruntled, she tangled her fingers in his chest hair and frowned up at him. "I didn't say I was a virgin. I just haven't done this much. And usually the guy didn't stick around asking stupid questions afterward."

Pete seemed to be chewing that over before coming to his

own conclusions. "So you've been with the wham-bam-thank-you-ma'am kind? That's pathetic."

She sighed and nestled closer. She could stay like this forever. "I know."

"Hey, I didn't mean you." He tugged on her hair to get her face tipped up to his. "I meant the jerk who walked. What an idiot."

"Idiots. Plural."

"So how many idiots have you been with?"

This time she gave his chest hair a tug. "That is none of your business and you know it. I haven't asked how many women you've been with."

"You can if you want to. Like I said, we're friends. I realized yesterday that we talk a lot. About everything."

Did he seriously think she wanted to tally up his conquests and converse about them? "No."

"I'm as comfortable with you as I am with the guys."

And that was supposed to reassure her? Cassidy thought about slugging him. She pulled her fist back, ready to poke him in the ribs.

"No guys ever kissed you between the legs before, huh?"

Oh God. Her arm fell to her side and she ducked her face against him. Maybe she could just sink into the bedding. Maybe she'd get lucky and disappear. No, Pete was still there. Still waiting.

"Cassidy?"

Beyond annoyed, she sat up and glared at him. "I may be new at this but I still don't think this is normal after-sex conversation, even between very good friends."

"I liked it." He grinned shamefully. "You taste good."

Cassidy thought her eyes might cross. He had no shame, no modesty, no understanding of the restrictions on polite conversation.

Giving up, she fell backward on the bed and pulled a pillow over her face. Her words muffled by goose down, she said, "You're outrageous. Will you please stop?"

"No." The bed dipped and shook as Pete moved. "In fact," he said, from somewhere near her knees, "I wouldn't mind doing it again. Right now."

Hot, moist breath touched her, obliterating all her objections—and someone knocked on her front door.

Chapter Four

Pete groaned at the intrusion. Where his palm rested on the inside of Cassidy's thigh, she was warm and firm and silky. "You expecting company?"

"No." Cassidy removed the pillow, twisted, and looked upside down at her alarm clock. "It's nine-thirty already." She flopped flat again and said to Pete with evident surprise, "I thought we'd only been in here a little while."

Grinning, Pete squeezed her leg. His fingertips were *that* close to her pubic hair. "Time flies when you're having fun." The knock sounded again and he sighed in disappointment. "Want me to get that?"

"Good God, no!"

She scrambled out of the bed, gloriously bereft of clothing. Her ass was round and soft, her waist trim, her legs sleek. That long hair swung around her, caressing her back, sides, shoulders. Pete lounged back and crossed his arms behind his head, enjoying the show.

"It could be my parents."

Right. June and Ward Cleaver. Pete made a face that she didn't see. "What do you want me to do?"

She jerked on a shirt and wrangled into her flannel pants. On her way out, she said, "Just be quiet." She closed the door behind her.

Pete was on his feet in a flash. He pulled the sheet off the bed and wrapped it around his hips. Carefully, not making a sound, he eased out of the room and followed Cassidy down the hall. He had just peeked around the corner when Cassidy unlocked her front door and pulled it open.

Gil stood there on her stoop with Sam beside him. "Morning, Cassidy. Did we wake you?"

Cassidy, poor girl, pressed a hand to her chest and stared. From Pete's vantage point, she seemed to be in shock. "Uh . . ."

Next to Gil, Sam stuck out his hand. "I'm Pete's brother, Sam. Gil thought you might know where he is."

Cassidy gave a very limp handshake and said again, "Uh . . ."

Both his brothers were here, looking for him? Pete stepped around the corner. "What is it? What's wrong?"

Her eyes so wide they looked ready to fall out of her head, Cassidy turned to face him. Gil gave him the once-over, making particular note of the sheet, and started fighting a grin. He cleared his throat, looked up at the ceiling, shifted his position.

Sam, who apparently saw nothing amiss, didn't so much as blink. "Everything's fine. We were just going to head out on Gil's boat and thought you might like to tag along. Sorry if we interrupted. Gil said you hang out here a lot."

It struck Pete then, exactly what he'd just given away. He looked at Cassidy, but she was beet-red and mute with incredulity. Damn it, he'd embarrassed her.

Gil cleared his throat again. "We can see you're otherwise engaged. Later."

He and Sam started to turn away, but Cassidy said, "No, wait." Using both hands, she shoved her hair out of her face. "We, ah, I had to go out now anyway."

Pete reached out and took her upper arms. "Cassidy . . ."

She wouldn't quite meet his gaze. "I need to go to the mall. And then I have to visit my parents and . . . you should go. Go with your brothers. Go on."

She actually shooed him.

Pete crossed his arms over his chest. "Can I get my shorts first?"

Poleaxed, she laughed too loud. "Yeah. Your shorts. I'll get them for you." And she practically ran out of the room.

Sam said, "Am I missing something?"

Gil grinned. "I believe the world just shifted."

"Ha ha." Pete walked to the front door and held it open. "If you two hooligans want to wait at my place, I'll be right there."

"What, and stand around outside? Your place is locked up." Gil started for the couch. "We'll just wait here."

"No."

"Yeah." Sam joined Gil, saying thoughtfully, "Do you remember a certain baby brother making our romantic lives hell?"

"I have a vague memory of that, yes."

Pete had tussled with his brothers many times. But not in a sheet. Odds were if he tried it now, he'd end up bare-assed and that just wouldn't do. He didn't wrestle with certain things flopping about unprotected. "Fine. But you're only embarrassing her, not me."

Sam, the only blue-eyed one of the brothers, stretched out his long legs in ragged jeans. "You mean like Ariel was embarrassed when you caught her in my boxers?"

"*That* was funny," Pete declared.

"Or when you tried to find out which websites featured Anabel on them?" Gil asked.

"I was curious." Then with disgust: "Come on, Gil. I was just teasing you then and you know it."

Sam settled in with a grin. "We'll be waiting."

With nothing else to do, Pete stormed into Cassidy's bedroom. She was perched on the edge of the bed, still pink but now dressed in jeans and a knit shirt. As if they could hear her, she whispered hopefully, "Are they gone?"

Pete threw the sheet aside. "Hell, no. They stuck their asses to your couch and they're not leaving until I leave with them." He grabbed up his boxers and yanked them on.

"I see." She licked her lips with her gaze glued south of his navel. "Maybe I'll just wait in here until then."

"Coward." Pete eyed her as he zipped up his shorts and grabbed for his shirt. "You don't have any reason to be embarrassed, you know."

"But I'm the sensible one. How sensible is this?"

Oh, now that stung. Eyes narrowed, he stalked to her and, as she hastily leaned back, caged her in with his fists on the mattress at either side of her hips. "What exactly does that mean, Cassidy?"

She swallowed hard. Braced on her elbows, her breath fast and shallow, she hissed, "You know what I mean."

Her hot breath brushed his mouth, and damn it, he wanted her again. "Explain it to me."

"You're a . . . a carouser." Once she said it, she warmed to the topic. "A hound dog, a hedonist. You're never going to settle down."

Pete went very still. He was . . . well, hell, he was hurt. And a little confused. Cautiously, he asked, "Did you want to settle down?"

"Yes! You know I do—someday." Her gaze was defiant. "I have my plans for the future, remember?"

"That's right." Plans that didn't include him. Pete straightened away. If he didn't put some distance between them, he'd be kissing her again and they both knew where that would lead. "You want a guy in a black tie, a corporate dude who's just like Daddy."

"Don't you dare be snide!" Temper shot her off the bed so she could glare up at him. "At least I have plans beyond getting laid!"

A tap sounded on her bedroom door and Cassidy nearly fell over.

Whipping around, Pete barked, *"What?"*

"We can hear you, and since it appears this argument won't be over any time soon, we're going to go ahead and mosey over to your place. Don't keep us waiting."

Eyes huge, her hand clutching his wrist, Cassidy whispered, "That was Sam?"

"Yeah." Pete ran his free hand over his face, far too frustrated for a guy who'd just had over-the-moon sex.

"He *heard* me." She freed her death grip on him to cover her mouth. "Ohmigod."

"Now don't faint." Amusement at her reaction took away some of the sting of her disapproval. "Sam's heard worse, believe me. And if I had to make a guess, they were cheering you on."

"But you're their brother."

"Exactly. It's no fun to pick on a girl, anyway."

"Woman," she clarified distractedly.

"What?"

"I'm a woman, not a girl." Then: "This is so embarrassing. I'll never be able to face them again."

Pete put his arm around her. "Sure you will. You're my

helper when I babysit, remember? And someday I'd like you to meet my sisters-in-law. They're terrific." He led her out of the room and to the couch that Sam and Gil had vacated. He felt safer getting away from the bed, where he could think clearer. Not much clearer, considering she looked well-loved, but at least this room wasn't scented by their love-making, too.

And it had been lovemaking, he realized. Not just sex. He'd had sex. Hell, he loved sex. But what he'd done with Cassidy was something . . . richer. Only she didn't seem to know it.

He frowned, trying to figure out what to say to her.

"You should go."

That pissed him off more. She did her best to rush him out the door. Talk about a wham-bam-thank-you . . . sir. "Look, Cassidy, we should probably get a few things straight."

"All right, but make it quick. I don't want your brothers to come back here."

His annoyance rose. Why had he never realized what a bossy, irritating woman Cassidy could be? "You want me to cut to the chase? Fine." He stood over her, forcing her to tilt her head back to see him. "I'm. Not. Done."

She scooted back on the couch. "Not done with what?"

"Not what, who. One time having you isn't near enough." Color flooded into her face until she looked sunburned. "Now don't start getting wide-eyed on me again. I don't intend to get in the way of your grand plans. I'm sure your suited Romeo will still be out there after we've finished exploring this . . . connection."

Her long hair hid her face from him. Her fingers twined together in her lap. Then she nodded. "Okay."

"Okay?"

She looked up, and she was smiling. "I want to explore it, too."

Well. That hadn't been as hard as he'd expected. "Great. So from now on, don't go shoving me out the door."

"Tell your brothers not to interrupt and I won't."

That made Pete smile. "If I told them that, they'd probably hang around as much as possible. It'll be better if I just don't say much about you at all."

Her wry expression told him just what she was thinking.

"Don't judge me by your own standards. I'm not embarrassed to be sleeping with you. I'm just trying to protect you from them."

"Why would they bother me?"

"Because I bothered them when they were—" Pete gulped. He'd almost said, *falling in love.* That'd really have her tossing him out the door. She didn't want anyone like him, not permanently anyway. She wanted a suit, a stuffed shirt.

Maybe he should meet her dad. Hmmm . . .

"What?" Cassidy gave him a funny look. "What are you thinking?"

"Oh, nothing." Shaking his head, Pete said, "We just like to rib each other, that's all."

"Okay then." She stood and started ushering him to the door. "Go and let them rib you so they won't embarrass me."

"Yes, ma'am." Pete pulled her into a hug first. "Cassidy? You were phenomenal."

Her grin was cheeky and fun. "Thanks. You, too."

Pete stepped outside and was just about to close the door behind him when Cassidy said, "Pete?"

Such a cautious voice. Turning back, he raised a brow.

Very softly, she said, "I'm not at all embarrassed to sleep with you."

"No?" That made him feel better although he wasn't sure he believed her.

"No." She pushed the door almost closed. "In fact," she said through the narrow opening, "I'm looking forward to sleeping with you again."

The door snapped shut and the lock clicked into place. Pete stood there, grinning like an idiot, oblivious to his brothers watching from the stoop next door—until Sam said, "Yeah, it's love. I recognize the signs."

"Most definitely," Gil agreed.

Pete jerked out of his daze. There wasn't anything he could do about his brothers ribbing him, not after the way he'd goaded them back during their courtships, but he could at least move it to someplace private to protect Cassidy. She was embarrassed enough already. Eventually she'd have to get used to his brothers . . . or would she?

"Eavesdropping?" Pete grouched. "Don't you two have anything better to do?" Fishing his keys out of his pocket, he strode to them and unlocked his front door.

Sam eyed him in the intimidating way only an older brother could. Given the older brother was a certified bad-ass, intimidation came easily. "You don't look too worried about being in love."

Gil bent to see Pete's face. "He's not blanching even a lit-tle."

Pete laughed. Yeah, he thought he just might be in love. What to do about it—that was the big question. He pushed his front door open with a flourish. "You might as well come on in."

Sam snorted. "As if you had a choice in that."

By rote, all three brothers headed for the kitchen. Didn't matter where they were, the kitchen was the official meeting place for anything important. Pete assumed this meant they considered his situation with Cassidy important, not just fodder for harassment.

He opened his fridge and tossed Sam a frosty can of Coke, then handed one to his quieter brother. Pete popped the tab on his own and started to drink, but Gil snatched it out of his hands.

"You two are such hillbillies." He turned to Sam, but Sam had that touch-my-drink-and-you're-in-trouble look. Sighing, Gil rinsed Pete's can under the tap and dried it. "Here. If you don't have enough breeding to use a glass, at least clean the thing."

So saying, Gil got down a glass and filled it with ice.

Sam had already guzzled half his Coke from the "dirty" can, and now he tipped it at Pete. "I'm more concerned as to whether or not you're using protection than if you get a few dust germs off your drink."

Pete took a long swallow before saying, "You know, Sam, when I was a teen—hell, even when I was in my early twenties—it was amusing the way you constantly reminded me about that. But in case you missed it, I'm grown now. And I'm as responsible as you or Gil."

Both brothers cracked up.

When Gil saw Pete's fuming face, he choked down his laughter. "Sorry. Okay, so maybe where birth control is concerned you're cautious enough."

"Thank you."

Sam was still snickering, which only drove home Cassidy's point that Pete wasn't a sensible choice for any wise woman to get involved with. Even his own brothers thought him reckless. That burned his butt big time.

Gil took a seat at the table. Sam hopped up on the counter. Pete lounged against the wall—and waited.

"So," Gil said. "Are you in love with her?"

"Maybe."

Sam eyed him. "You really don't seem too worried about it."

Shrugging, Pete admitted, "I'm more worried about what she thinks." It took the rest of his Coke and three deep breaths before he screwed up the nerve to spill his guts. "She thinks I'm irresponsible, too."

"Too?"

With a wry look, Pete pointed out, "Wasn't that you two just laughing your asses off at me?"

"Oh, now hey, we're you're brothers." Sam straightened with annoyance. "We're allowed to give you shit. You need it."

"Exactly," Gil agreed. "But if Cassidy really thinks that about you, then she just doesn't know you well enough."

"Don't get any ideas about clueing her in," Pete warned. "Our relationship is . . ."

"Delicate?"

"I guess."

Sam leveled him with a look. "Sex was good?"

"None of your damn business!"

Sam held up both hands, but he was grinning. "Such a reaction," he said to Pete, "means one of two things—either it was great and it has you floundering, or it was awful and you just wish it hadn't happened."

Thoughtfully, Gil shook his head. "No, I've gotten to know Cassidy. She's not awful at anything."

"An overachiever?" Sam asked.

"Something like that. She's one of those really organized women who knows what she wants and goes after it. She's got like a five-year plan and a ten-year plan. Hell, probably a twenty-year plan."

"Looked to me like she wanted Pete."

Gil shrugged and took another drink. "All things considered."

Pete really wished it was that easy. Sure, Cassidy had slept with him—then more or less told him he couldn't get in the way of her goals for a committed relationship. He rubbed the heels of his palms into his eye sockets, wishing he could figure her out. One thing was plain, though. "She's into guys in suits."

Gil rolled his eyes. "Yeah, so wear a suit."

Everything always seemed so cut-and-dried to Gil. He was one hell of a businessman, making plans and decisions with absolute certainty. Nothing ever threw him off course. He was more suited to Cassidy than Pete would ever be. Thank God Gil was already married. "I can't exactly wear suits to work out in the sports center, now can I?"

Slapping his hands onto his thighs, Gil said, "I have a solution."

Sam groaned. "Here we go."

"Shut up, Sam." Then to Pete: "Take a job with me. People love you. You'd be great at sales pitches, talking to the board, dealing with consumers . . ."

"But you'd have to wear a suit." Sam shuddered.

"That's the whole point, Sam. He said Cassidy likes suits."

"So why the hell isn't she wearing them? Did he ask her that?" Sam hopped off the counter. "The answer is not to do something you'd be miserable doing."

Gil stood, too. "Why would he be miserable working with me?"

His brothers were both nuts, Pete realized. And he loved them. "I wouldn't be miserable, but damn, Gil, you're so good at it I'd be trailing behind. And Sam's right, I can't change my life for her."

Sam slung a heavily muscled arm over Pete's shoulders. "I say stick with the great sex. It'll win her over for sure."

"Yeah," Gil conceded, "that just might do the trick."

All three brothers laughed. It didn't solve Pete's problem, but being with his brothers today was just the distraction he needed. "Are we going out on the boat or what?"

"We're going." Gil led the way out the front door. "It's too nice a day to stay inside. But Anabel and Ariel are planning a baby shower or something, so they couldn't go along."

"So I'm second choice, huh?"

Gil winked. "Over my wife? Always."

"I'm driving," Sam told them as he slipped on his mirrored sunglasses.

Gil snatched the keys out of his hand. "No, you're still shaking over the idea of Ariel being pregnant. I'd just as soon reach the boat alive, thank you very much."

Driving down the road with the setting sun in her face, Cassidy thought about all the time she'd spent at the mall. She'd done some shopping, and in the process, she'd ventured into a salon where she lost a good two inches of hair. The beautician had wanted to take off more than that, but Cassidy was too cowardly to do too much at once. She promised the woman she'd look at her hair when she got home, think about it, and maybe come back soon.

Now at least the ends were smooth instead of poofing out like dandelion fluff. She liked the softer look. To her, it made a huge difference, making her wonder if taking off a little more might be a good thing.

In the passenger seat of her car, a pretty pink bag rustled in the current from the open window. Inside that bag were her purchases of new underwear. Skimpy, sexy panties and two matching wisplike bras that she couldn't believe she'd bought, and doubted even more that she'd wear. They didn't look all that comfortable, but then, for the first time in her adult life, comfort wasn't the point.

On top of the bag rested a small box of positively sinful perfume. She'd loved the earthy, seductive scent the moment she dabbed it on her wrist. When she got home, she'd dab it in other places.

Having sex with Pete had turned her into a carnal-minded monster. All she could think about was seeing him again.

But for now, duty called.

Cassidy pulled into her parents' driveway, noting both cars. Good. She'd get this over with in one visit. Taking the walkway around to the side door, she entered the kitchen and caught her folks smooching. Some things, it seemed, never changed. In all the years they'd been married, her father continued to dote on her mother. As refined as he often seemed, he wasn't above cuddling.

Grinning, Cassidy said, "Knock-knock."

Dressed in a lightweight summer dress and matching sandals, her mother looked chic and flustered. Her father just laughed and came to Cassidy for a hug. "Cass. What are you doing here?"

He always smelled of the same familiar aftershave, even on the weekends. Unlike most men in movies, books, and the ones she knew in real life, her dad was predictable in everything he did. Every single day, without fail, he got up at six. He exercised, drank coffee, and read the paper. He was dressed, shaved, and had eaten his breakfast by eight. He didn't fret over losing his hair, but he did fret over his family.

Today he wore a natty, short-sleeved oxford shirt tucked into dark trousers. She had never seen her dad in shorts. Even when he golfed.

With typical fatherly affection, he hugged Cassidy right off her feet.

Avoiding his question for just a moment more, Cassidy went to her mom and embraced her as well. "Hey," she said to her blushing mom, "if a man and wife can't make out in their kitchen, then I don't want to ever be married."

Her mother laughed. "Oh, stop."

"We just finished dinner, honey. Want me to warm something back up?"

"No, thanks, Dad, but I'll take some tea." While her father poured three glasses of sweet tea, her mother sat with her at the table. Cassidy waited for the comments on her hair, for them to notice and ask her why she'd done it. She had her reply all planned out, and Pete wasn't a part of it. But neither one even mentioned her hair. A little disappointed by their lack of reaction, Cassidy said, "Holly came to see me last night."

Her father set the tea in front of her and took his own chair. "That's nice. You girls don't get to visit enough anymore with you working so much and Holly in school."

"She, ah, had Duke with her."

Her mother let out a breath. "She really is hung up on that boy."

Cassidy nodded. "They're in love, Mom."

With a sound of annoyance, her father said, "She's twenty-two, Cass. She doesn't know what love is yet."

"Actually, I think she does." Because that wasn't what her parents wanted to hear, Cassidy chose her words carefully. "You'd have to see the way she looks at him to know what I mean. She's never looked at any of her other boyfriends like that. And Duke is wonderful to her. I know he's not who you would have wanted for her . . ."

"He hopes to be a professional athlete. That's the equivalent of a young man who dreams of becoming a cowboy. *Most* outgrow that fantasy."

Cassidy shrugged. "From what Duke told me, he has a good shot at it. I bet if you see them together you'll realize that Duke is a really nice guy—" Albeit a bore. "—and that he loves Holly, too. Isn't that the most important thing?"

The doubting expressions on her parents' faces didn't look promising.

In for a penny, in for a pound. "Why don't we all get together?" Cassidy made the suggestion with a bright smile, trying to sound chipper about the idea. "You can get better acquainted with him."

"I want her to finish school."

Cassidy knew that stern tone only too well. "I know, Dad. And I think she will. But if you keep disparaging Duke, she might, *just might* do something stupid like marry him now."

Being a logical, levelheaded guy, her father reluctantly conceded. He turned to his wife. "Gina, what do you think?"

Her mother frowned in consideration. "We do have that benefit at the country club tomorrow."

"Perfect," her father exclaimed with a smile.

"No," Cassidy said at the same time. "I mean, that's a formal thing. I thought we could just get together at my place to grill out or something."

"But this would be the perfect opportunity to see Duke in a different setting. I've met the young man twice, not at length, but enough to know he might not have any great social skills off the field. Let's see if he'll do this for Holly," said her father.

Cassidy groaned. "But then that'll mean I have to dress up, too."

Her mother took her hand with a smile. "A painful prospect, for sure. I don't know why you shy away from dresses."

Because she looked and felt like a dolt in them.

Her mother wasn't above maternal bribery. "We need you there, Cassidy. Isn't that right, Frank?"

"Absolutely."

"You've always had such a good, sensible influence on Holly," her mother added.

Sensible. Right. What would they think if they knew she'd started a torrid affair with Pete? It might be worth telling them just to lose that hideous "sensible" label.

Cassidy pushed to her feet. "All right. I'll talk with Holly and set something up, then let you know." She kissed her mother's cheek, hugged her father again, and started out the door. But at the last second, she paused. "Mom, you know Holly is pretty smart. Just because she's beautiful doesn't mean she's lacking in brains."

Her dad laughed. "Honey, we know one asset doesn't rule out the other. Look at you." He winked. "Beautiful *and* smart."

Cassidy blinked at him.

"Holly's just young," her mother said. "We can't help but worry. About *both* of you."

Cassidy would have replied, but hearing herself referred to as "beautiful" put her in a stupor. She'd never thought of herself that way, and she wasn't sure she'd ever heard her father say it, either. Usually they harped on her brains, her common sense, and her determination.

She was still dazed when she stopped by the dorm to see Holly. Amazingly enough, her sister was in. Unusual for a Saturday night, but then Holly said they would be hooking up later.

Cassidy thought Holly would surely notice her hair, and again, she rehearsed how she'd explain the sudden attention to her appearance. But Holly just inquired as to why she was there, then started dancing in excitement at the idea of dressing up for a formal charity event. Holly, at least, loved the idea. But then Holly was a typical woman who adored spiffing up in her best duds.

Holly raced to the phone to call Duke, who agreed with no apparent hesitation at all, making Cassidy wonder if she was the only person on earth who detested formality.

Then she smiled. No, Pete hated it, too. And he suited her so much better than a businessman ever would.

Chapter Five

Cassidy assumed Pete was still out with his brothers when she got home. His car was in the drive, but his condo was dark and quiet. She hesitated, unwilling to look too desperate, then went next door and knocked.

No answer.

She was amazingly bummed by that, so much so that she gave herself a stern talking-to and marched her sorry butt into her own place. She had plenty to do before the evening anyway.

Oh God, what if he didn't come over that evening either? She'd only had sex with him once but was already suffering withdrawal. Her hands were shaking, for crying out loud. No, she wouldn't angst over it.

She threw her new undies into the wash on a delicate cycle. She always washed new clothes before wearing them, but especially underwear. These had to be line-dried instead of going into the dryer. What a pain. Pete was already affecting her life, making her too conscious of her sloppy appearance when it had never mattered to her before.

After the wash finished and she had the new items hung

up to dry, she jumped in the shower. Lingering under the spray, Cassidy forced herself not to rush, not to listen for the phone or door. But the second she got out, she checked her answering machine, which showed a great big, fat "0" calls. She stuck her head out the front door, trying to see if Pete was home yet. He wasn't, and she wanted to smack herself.

Wearing only an enormous navy nightshirt, Cassidy paced around her condo. Later, when the panties were dry, she'd put on a pair just in case Pete did show up. In the meantime, she was making herself nuts.

Two hours later, she was propped in front of the television with a snack, oblivious to the movie she'd turned on. A tap sounded on her kitchen door.

She jumped—actually jumped—from her seat. Forcing herself to slow, Cassidy smoothed her hair, wiped the bread crumbs from her cheese sandwich off her shirt, and walked into the kitchen.

Pete stood there at her patio door, his hair damp from a recent shower and with a little too much sun on his face. He had one long, muscled arm above his head on the doorframe, the other stretched out to the side of the frame. He grinned when he saw her and just like that, Cassidy went weak in the knees and hot in secret places. Boy, she had it bad.

Unlocking the door, she slid it open and said, "Why do you always come to this door—umpff."

Pete had his mouth all over her, as if he'd missed her just as much. One of his hands held the back of her head, his long fingers wrapped around her skull, while his tongue stroked into her mouth, tasting her deeply. His other hand was at the small of her back, going lower and lower until he cupped her bottom and squeezed her in close.

"Damn, I've thought about your mouth all day. That was the most boring boat trip I've ever taken."

Cassidy licked her tingling lips and struggled to get her eyes open. "Yeah?"

"My brothers had endless comments to make. The lake was choppy. And chicks in bikinis kept flirting with us."

Cassidy shoved back with a frown. "Oh, and I just know you hated that."

Pete's grin widened. "You sound so snide." He caught her and pulled her close again. "With Gil and Sam both hitched, it was up to me to send the girls off with smiles."

"But you sent them all off?"

He chuckled outright. "Snide and suspicious. Of course I did. Now if you were in a bikini . . ."

"Right. I wouldn't be caught dead . . ."

"Did you do something to your hair?" He frowned, lifted a lock and ran his fingers down to the end. "It looks different. Shorter."

Ohhhh. He noticed. Cassidy felt her heart turn over in her chest at the same time she started blushing. No one had noticed—but Pete had. "I just got it trimmed," she mumbled.

"You lopped a lot off."

"Just a couple of inches."

Pete didn't comment, just kept examining it. Then the hand on her bottom shifted and he growled, "Are you wearing panties?"

Oops. She'd forgotten. Before Cassidy could stop herself, she glanced into the laundry room off her kitchen where the new underwear hung across a line. "I—"

Pete followed her gaze and his eyes darkened. "Well, what have we here?"

"Pete." She grabbed the waistband of his shorts when he started that way, and ended up dragged across the linoleum floor. "You leave my laundry alone."

Of course, he ignored that order. Cassidy went from embarrassed to mortified when Pete fingered the panties, examining the lace and silk. Then his gaze swung around to her lower body.

"You naked under that shirt, Cass?"

She backed up. The big-bad-wolf look on his face had her giggling nervously. "Maybe."

"I think you are." He released her underwear to stalk her. "Much as I'd like to see your sweet ass in those little bits of nothing, I think I'd just as soon see it bare."

She clutched the material of her nightshirt tight around her thighs. "Is that right?"

"Come here, Cass."

"No." She shook her head and giggled some more.

"You want me to chase you?" His gaze brightened. "I'm up to a few games if you are."

"No! I didn't mean—"

"Better run," he suggested. *"Now."*

His expression was so hot and intent, Cassidy didn't question him further. She just whipped around and fled. She felt Pete behind her, heard his big feet pounding on her floor, and her heart shot into her throat. She ran as fast as she could, and all the while she kept giggling hysterically like a ninny of a schoolgirl.

She darted behind the couch, squealed when Pete went over it, and dashed down the hall. He was toying with her, she realized, when his fingers brushed her bottom again and again but he didn't bother snagging her. Her open bedroom door offered the only escape, so she flew inside and tried to slam it shut, but Pete didn't give her a chance. She screamed in surprise when he surged in right behind her.

Backing up, breathing hard, Cassidy watched him.

Pete's wicked grin was full of promise. "Nowhere else to go, Cass. Now be a good girl and lift the shirt and let me see if you've got on underwear."

It was impossible to wipe the smile off her face. But at the same time, her heart beat so fast she thought she might faint. "You know I don't."

"Let me see."

The back of her knees hit the mattress, bringing her to a jarring halt. Slowly, feeling like a tease, she caught the hem of her shirt—then flashed it up and back down again.

Pete laughed. "That was too fast."

"It's all you get."

"Not even close." He advanced and Cassidy caught her breath. Slowly, he took the bottom of her shirt and pulled it up, up, until it rested above her naked breasts. Somehow she felt more bared than she would have without the shirt. "Hold it there."

Feeling light-headed again, Cassidy did as she was told.

Until Pete went down on one knee.

She whimpered. *Whimpered*. She wasn't even the whimpering type, but she'd heard the ridiculous sound come out of her throat . . . his fingers parted her, stifling all coherent thought.

A gasp, another whimper, then a soft groan. *"Pete."*

"I kept wondering," he said huskily, "if you really tasted as good as I remembered." With his fingertips still holding her open, he looked up at her. "You do."

And he must have meant it, given how much tasting he did for the next ten minutes. Cassidy's knees were shaking, her legs like noodles, when she finally called a halt. "I have to sit down."

"How about lying down instead?" Pete stood, tugged her shirt the rest of the way off, and began stripping his own clothes away. "I should see to you first," he said, while staring at her breasts, "because the way I'm feeling, this won't last long."

"I don't care." Cassidy couldn't wait a second more and

went to work on his fly. She had his shorts off in a heartbeat. He was fully erect. Breath held, she cupped him in her hands and stroked the length of him, reveling in the velvet texture over tensile steel. She glanced at Pete's face, saw his eyes were closed, his jaw locked, and felt more powerful than she ever had in her life. "I want to taste you, too."

He ground his teeth a moment, then swallowed. Locking his dark gaze with hers, he murmured, "Be my guest."

It was Cassidy's turn to kneel, and she took her time, feeling him, playing with him. His thighs were rock hard, his big feet braced apart, his hands fisted at his sides.

She'd never done this, but she'd certainly read about it. Curling her fingers tight around the base of his erection, she brought him to her mouth and licked—slow, soft, wet.

Pete dropped his head back and groaned.

He was a little salty, very warm, and she liked it. A lot. Opening her mouth, Cassidy drew him in, moving her tongue, teasing, then sucking just a bit.

In a rough, hoarse voice, Pete said, "You're something of a tease, aren't you?"

"Mmmm." If it meant doing more of this, she thought she could be.

"Oh, hell," Pete complained around a broken laugh. "That's it. That's enough." He caught her shoulders and pulled her up. "It's been too long and my control is obliterated."

Cassidy felt herself hauled upright and said with some surprise, "But it was only this morning—"

"In the bed you go."

He was moving at Mach speed, not giving her time to think. "What about you?"

"I need to fetch the raincoat first. Trust me, I'll be right with you." Pete snatched up his shorts and dug through the pocket for his wallet. Waving one condom at her, he said,

"After this, I'll head next door for reinforcements." He tore the package open and rolled the rubber on with ease, proving just how much experience he had at this sort of thing.

Cassidy didn't care. He was wonderful, a fabulous lover, and he'd noticed her haircut. She opened her arms to him.

There were few preliminaries this time. Pete settled between her legs and kissed her hungrily while cupping her breasts, teasing her nipples. Unlike the first time, he didn't drag out the foreplay. Within minutes he used his fingertips to open her. Cassidy felt the broad head of his penis pressing inside.

"Hold on to me, Cass," he told her. "This is going to be a rough ride."

Just hearing him say it thrilled her, and she wrapped her arms tight around him seconds before he lifted her hips and drove forward. They both gasped.

Around a groan, Pete said, "You feel so fucking good. Too good."

The power of his thrusts rocked the bed and had the springs squeaking rhythmically. Cassidy put her legs around him, gripped his shoulders, and gave herself over to the incredible sensations of physical pleasure and emotional fulfillment. God, she knew she loved Pete. Nothing else could explain why she both wanted to weep and laugh with joy. She did neither. As her climax approached, she tightened, moaned, cried out—and felt Pete join her with a resounding, husky groan.

Yep, she loved him.

Now what?

Pete didn't exactly mean to fall asleep with her. Staying over with a woman wasn't something he ever took for granted. It wasn't something he normally did, because it signified advancement in the relationship and there'd been only a few times he'd felt comfortable with that level of commitment. But after running back to his place to grab a box of rubbers, he'd returned to Cassidy and cajoled her into modeling her new underwear.

She was such a turn-on, blushing while wearing something so sexy, laughing at him while her eyes glowed with the same powerful lust he felt. He loved watching her come. He loved holding her. He just plain loved being with her.

All through the night, while she slept soundly in his arms, he was aware of her. He'd slept little, but then, he had a soft, naked woman beside him, and everything about her fascinated him.

He hated it that she'd cut her hair. What if it had been his teasing comment that prompted her to do it? Her hair was a big turn-on for Pete. Not styled, totally natural, totally female. Like Cassidy.

Sometime during her third screaming orgasm, Pete realized he loved her because of her naturalness. Strange, when usually the really polished women appealed to him. But his relationships with them had always been polished, too. Tidy, shiny, and very surface. He'd never harassed any of them or had them laugh at him. He'd never just been himself with them.

Cassidy murmured in her sleep and her fingers tightened in his chest hair. She'd kept a death grip on him all night. Pete liked that. It gave him hope that she felt just a modicum of the desperate need he experienced.

Carefully prying her hold loose, he lifted her hand and kissed her fingers. She stirred, but didn't quite awaken. He examined her small hand with the short and clean, unpainted nails. She wore no jewelry. Because she was asleep and wouldn't know, he rubbed her fingertips over his lips, his chin. They were a little callused, yet he thought Cassidy McClannahan was about the most feminine woman he'd ever known.

He brought her palm up and pressed it to his mouth.

"Pete?"

Her slumberous eyes were sexy as hell. Enticing. "I love touching you," he said before he could censor that L-word out. Then he decided, what the hell. "I love the way you feel and how you smell. And how you taste." He drew her finger into his mouth and curled his tongue around her, sucking lazily.

Eyes smoldering, Cassidy stared at his mouth while hers opened to accommodate her accelerated breaths. She pressed closer, her breasts flattening against his side, her thigh sliding across his boner with tantalizing effect.

Pete closed his eyes and licked his tongue down to the seam of her fingers, probing gently. Cassidy said, *"Pete,"* with unmistakable yearning—and her phone rang.

At first, they both ignored it. Then a young woman's voice sang into the answering machine, "Hey, Cass. I wanted you to know that Duke and I are coming by your place tonight before the benefit. We figured we'd ride together so you won't be able to forget us. Again." She giggled, said something muffled to someone. "Duke said you should invite your mysterious boyfriend. It'll round out the night and give Mom and Dad someone to focus on besides him."

Jolted into frenzied motion, Cassidy shoved herself away from Pete and dove out of the bed. She stood there looking at him, the fingers he'd licked curled protectively against her naked chest. In a horrified whisper, she said, "That's my sister."

Thinking of strangling her, Pete narrowed his eyes. "She can't see us, Cass, and she can't hear you."

"I don't care." She turned her back on him, affording Pete a fine rear view. "I'm still embarrassed."

"Why?" Pete heard the phone disconnect and pushed himself up against the headboard, settling in for a confrontation. "Because you lied to me about your boyfriend?"

She whipped around so fast, her tangled hair flew out and her breasts jiggled. "I do not lie, damn you, and you owe me an apology."

Confusion swamped Pete. "Then what was your sister talking about?"

Cassidy scrubbed both hands over her face. "Duke and Holly came over the other day. Duke's an athlete and boring beyond belief, especially when he starts gabbing on about football, but Holly worships the ground he walks on. At one point I zoned out and Duke is hell-bent on believing I was mooning over a guy."

"Were you?"

She frowned and blushed at the same time. "Yeah, but he's not a . . . a boyfriend."

"Who is it?" Knowing she'd mooned over some guy put Pete in a killing mood.

The way she crossed her arms under her breasts plumped them up like an offering. She thrust her chin up, adding to Pete's suspicions. Then, taking the wind right out of him, she said, "You."

"Me?"

"I told you he wasn't a boyfriend." She paced away, came back. "Remember you said we were both thinking about sex? Well, I was. I suppose Duke knows the look and he wanted to tease me."

A queer little feeling settled into Pete's stomach. *She'd been thinking about him.* He really did need to get this all sorted out. "So Friday night, when you didn't ask me to dinner even though you had enough beef for four, and you didn't come over to watch the movie with me, it was because your sister and Duke were visiting?"

"The steaks were for them, yeah." She rolled one shoulder. "But I wouldn't have watched the movie with you anyway."

"Why not?"

Her look told him that should have been obvious. "Because I was already . . . well, lusting after you. I didn't want to put myself through that."

His damn heart ached. "I'm sorry."

She waited two seconds, then shrugged and scampered back into bed. "Trust me. You've made up for all my suffering."

Pete pulled her up to sit on his lap, arranging her so she faced him, her legs folded at either side of his hips. Holding her thighs, he asked, "Your sister insinuated that you'd forgotten about them?"

Wiggling her bottom, Cassidy grinned. "You sure you want to keep talking about this? I can think of better things—"

"Cass."

Rolling her eyes, she sighed. "After all your teasing, I totally forgot about them coming over. I was on my way out the door when they showed up. I was going to go to the theater and see a cheesy movie and eat popcorn until I was sick, but I lied and told them I was going for dessert."

"Aha." Pete smiled widely. "I thought you didn't lie."

"I don't." She smoothed both hands over his chest, leaned down and kissed his nose. "Not to you."

She started to sit up again, but Pete pulled her back for a longer, more satisfying kiss, then allowed her to settle against him. The position was nice, with her knees drawn up by his hips, her belly flush against his. He smoothed his hands over her bottom, offered up so nicely. "So they were here alone in your place?"

"Yeah, why?"

Should he admit it? He grunted at himself. He wanted her to always be truthful with him, so he had to be truthful, too. "I think I heard them making whoopee."

Cassidy started in surprise, but Pete held her secure. "That's insane. Not in my home!"

"Afraid so. I heard a lot of sexy moaning."

"Oh, God." She covered her face.

"I assumed it was you."

Her head jerked up. "That's why you kept asking me who I was seeing?"

"Yep." Pete grinned, tightened his hold, and said, "But when you insisted you weren't seeing anyone, I assumed you were playing solitaire."

"Who moans over solitaire?"

His grin widened. "You misunderstand. I heard those moans, Cass. I thought you were . . . alone."

She still looked confused.

Sighing, Pete said, "I thought you were flying solo. Taking care of business. All alone."

In slow progression, confusion gave way to understanding and her eyes flared. "You thought—!"

"Yeah."

It was probably the toothy grin that got to her. She punched him. Hard. Groaning, Pete grabbed his ribs, then had to grab her to keep from getting another shot.

"Jerk!"

When he laughed, she tried to scamper away. Pete wrestled her down, making a point to let her come close to slipping away, again and again. He liked wrestling with Cassidy. The match finally ended when he got her flat on her back, used his knee to open her legs, and thrust inside her.

They both went still, breathing hard. Cassidy struggled to get her hands free, only to wrap them around his neck. "You win," she told him huskily.

Pete pressed his face into her shoulder. He wasn't wearing a rubber and no way in hell would he do that to her. "Promise me you won't move."

"But I want to move. I want you to move."

"I'm not wearing anything."

"Oh." She nudged his shoulder. "Well, go get something."

"In a second." Pete smoothed her beautiful hair away from her face. "So?"

"So what?"

Watching her expression, Pete pressed in a little tighter, making Cassidy inhale sharply. He knew he was playing with fire but he was willing to use whatever coercion he could.

"Can your mysterious boyfriend accompany you to the benefit?" Though the question sounded light, Pete's apprehension was so great, his lungs hurt. He couldn't recall anything mattering quite so much to him.

Cassidy froze. "It'll be boring."

"Maybe I'll liven it up a little." Shit. She probably didn't want that. He frowned and started to retract that statement when she smiled.

"That's what I was thinking the other night when Duke accused me of daydreaming about a guy. I kept thinking if you were there, it wouldn't be so bad."

Ah damn, now she had him feeling all mushy inside. Softly, he urged, "Then let me be there."

"It won't just be Duke and Holly tonight." She stared at his chin while chewing her bottom lip. "Mom and Dad are going to the benefit, too."

Every muscle in Pete's body drew so tight, he felt brittle. He wasn't good enough for June and Ward? "You're afraid I'll embarrass you."

"No!" She rushed to reassure him, then scowled. "How could you even think such a stupid thing?" Just as quickly, she softened. "Mom and Dad are great and I'm sure they'll like you."

"Then?"

She let out a long, grievous sigh. "It's a dressy thing. A formal event at the country club. Dad will probably break out his tux."

"I promise not to wear shorts." How he'd find something appropriate on such short notice, he didn't know. Gil would probably have a variety of tuxes in his wardrobe, though, and they were about the same size . . .

Cassidy was laughing. "I wish we could both wear shorts. I'd sure be more comfortable in them." She sighed, then said, "If I invite you along tonight, will you please *get a damn condom?*"

At least she wanted him sexually. As Sam and Gil had assured him, he could work from there. And he'd start right now. He'd take her five ways to Sunday, make her scream, beg. He'd devastate her with pleasure. "Yes, ma'am. Be right back."

But as Pete finished rolling on the condom, Cassidy said, "I have, you know."

He turned to face her. She was sprawled in the bed, sleekly muscled, strong in ways that only a woman could be. Damn, he adored her. "Have what?"

"Thought of you."

"Yeah?" He stretched out next to her.

"While flying solo, I mean."

Pete's heart all but stopped. Well, hell. He looked at her, knew he was lost, and fell on her like a starving man. Later. He'd devastate her later. For now, he just had to have her.

Chapter Six

She still couldn't believe Pete wanted a date with her and her family. Didn't that signify . . . something?

Since he left early that afternoon, she used the remainder of the day to buy new pantyhose—a chore that made her grimace—and while she was out, she decided to have her hair trimmed a little more. Not just because Pete noticed, she assured herself, but because she'd like it.

By the time the beautician finished, her once witchy, waist-length hair now hung to just below her shoulder blades. Still long, but much tidier and more manageable.

Cassidy located her one and only black dress at the back of her closet. She removed the dry cleaning bag and tugged it on over her head. It was a simple dress with sleeves, a high, round neckline, and a straight fit that fell to just below her knees.

It was . . . *comfortable.*

Seeing herself in the mirror was almost depressing. Give her a scythe and a hood and she'd pass for Death. Cassidy groaned and dug out her black heeled pumps. They didn't help. Now she looked like a cross-dressing Death.

To make matters worse, Pete knocked on her door before she had time to consider any alternatives. Not that she had any, owning only that one black dress. It'd have to do. She hoped Pete wouldn't turn tail and run when he saw what a formal misfit she was.

For once, he came to her front door, and when Cassidy opened it, she almost fell over.

Pete wore a tux.

Her gaze traveled all over him and still she couldn't take it in. All spiffed up, he didn't even look like Pete. He looked good, no two ways around that. Just . . . different, not *her* Pete anymore.

And she'd once thought she wanted a guy who wore suits? How stupid.

He was busy fiddling with a black tie. "I'm lousy at this crap. Never done it enough, I guess. Can you help?" He looked up then and got caught. A frown pulled down his brows and Cassidy waited for him to question her choice of dress.

"You cut your hair again?"

Whoa. No mention of her black tent? She cleared her throat. "Technically, the beautician did."

He forgot all about his tie. Releasing the tie so it fell to his chest, he propped his hands on his hips and glared. "Why the hell do you keep cutting it?"

Beyond Pete, Cassidy saw her mother and father pull up to the curb, and behind them, Duke and Holly. Oh boy. Let the fun begin.

Oblivious to their audience, Pete caught her shoulders to regain her attention, then moved her back so he could step in. "I like it long, Cassidy."

"It's still long." Nervously, Cassidy watched as her family plus Duke approached, all of them very attentive. Her parents had expected to deal with one nonconforming boyfriend. Now they were faced with two.

"Not as long as it used to be." Pete looked bedeviled, then blurted, "Was it something I said? Because if it was, forget it. I love your hair."

"No." Cassidy tried to quickly explain that her parents were right behind him. "Uh, Pete . . ."

He wrapped his hands in her hair, crushing fists full as if savoring it. "I don't want you changing on me, Cass. I adore you just as you are."

Her mouth fell open.

Pete stepped closer. "I adore you enough to get into this damn monkey suit to impress Ward and June—though God knows I have no idea about this stupid tie, so you're going to have to help me with it."

From behind Pete, Duke said, "I can do that if you like."

Pete turned, saw the crowd, and gave a sheepish grin. Both Duke and her father wore tuxes, and to Cassidy's surprise, Duke looked very comfortable in his.

"Let me see," Pete said. "You must be Duke, because you're definitely not Ward."

"Right in one." The two men shared a hardy handshake.

"And this has to be Cassidy's pretty little sister, Holly."

Holly twittered a laugh. "That's me," she said, then realized she'd just complimented herself and blushed.

Pete cleared his throat and faced her father. "And you must be—"

Fighting a grin, her father stuck out his hand. "Not Ward."

Pete winced. "Sorry. I was just, uh . . ."

"Going by Cassidy's description? She's told me that before, too. Where she sees a resemblance, I'll never know."

Relaxing at the easy banter, Pete accepted his hand. "It's nice to meet you, Mr. McClannahan."

"Anyone who adores my daughter has to call me Frank. And this is my wife, Gina."

The obligatory greetings were performed without Cassidy's help. She sank back against the wall and closed her eyes. Pete said he adored her and everyone had heard. He'd noticed her hair again when no one else did. And he didn't notice her hideous dress, even though both her mother and Holly were there, providing awesome comparisons.

Her mother said, "Cassidy, he's right. You've done something to your hair."

"Twice," Pete pointed out.

"It looks lovely," Gina said, earning a frown from Pete, and when Holly agreed, he looked ready to fume.

Duke stretched out his massive arms to include everyone and herded them inside. "Why don't we move this indoors? We have a little time before the benefit starts."

Cassidy remembered the purpose of this blighted soiree and launched into compliments aimed at Duke. He kept Holly at his side while reciprocating. "I usually only dress up for weddings and funerals. But considering how much time I spend in sweaty jerseys, I like to trade up every now and then."

Near Cassidy's ear, Pete murmured, "This feels like the latter."

She shushed him. "Mom, Duke has the record for touchdowns at his college. Isn't that impressive?"

"Very," Gina said.

Duke pulled Pete around and began knotting his tie. "Thanks. I was pretty pleased about it."

Holly beamed at everyone. "He also made the dean's list."

Frank gave his attention. "Excellent. What's your major?"

With the tie finished, Duke threw his arm around Pete's shoulder, nearly knocking him off balance. "Business. If I don't make it in football, I'd like to open my own sporting goods store. Maybe build up to a chain."

"Good plan," Pete said, then scowled when he noticed Cassidy was staring at Duke.

The differences in the two men hit Cassidy. Both were big and strong, but next to Duke, Pete looked leaner, more refined. Definitely more handsome—but then, that was just Cassidy's opinion. Holly, apparently, felt just the opposite.

Because Pete kept giving her odd looks, Cassidy said, "I'll put on a pot of coffee." She ducked out of the room, anxious for a moment to herself. Pete had said he adored her. It wasn't love, but it was better than a quick fling. Maybe she could build on that.

She had her back to the kitchen entrance, waiting for the coffee to finish, when warm male hands slid around her waist. Pete's scent enveloped her, so warm and familiar. Curse the stupid benefit—she'd rather lose their clothes and cuddle in bed.

Next to her ear, Pete rasped, "Why the hell do you keep staring at Duke?"

Did he sound jealous? No, that was absurd. Because she wasn't about to tell Pete that she'd been comparing them, she shrugged. "He looks different in a suit. Nice." She twisted around to face him. "My parents will be pleased."

"He doesn't normally wear a suit."

"What an understatement. Duke is a jock through and through. But that business degree surprised my parents." She smiled. "I think old Duke is full of surprises."

"You like him?"

She realized she did. How could she not like Duke when he was so good to her sister? "You know, I really do. He's not flighty like I thought. He's got a plan, and a backup plan. And he's going after what he wants."

Pete groaned, then tucked his face against her neck. "You know, Cassidy," he murmured, and she could feel his lips on her skin, "I was thinking there were a few things—just small things—that you could possibly change about yourself. What do you think?"

Heat rushed into her face. "The dress is awful, I know."

Pete straightened. "What?"

Holding out the sides of the hideous tent, she repeated, "This dress. But it's the only black thing I own."

Confused, Pete shook his head. "I like you better in shorts, sure, but you look great no matter what you wear." He smoothed his hands up and down her sides. "You're such a goal-oriented person."

What that had to do with her dress, Cassidy didn't know. "Sensible Cassidy, that's me."

"Sleeping with me wasn't all that sensible. You told me so yourself."

"I've changed my mind on that. Sleeping with you is one of the best decisions I've ever made."

"Yeah?" He started to grin.

From behind them, her father said, "Well, I think we can segue right into good-byes."

Cassidy gasped, Pete turned, and they both saw that it wasn't just her father standing there. Her mother, Holly, and Duke were all within earshot. Well, hell. Couldn't they have made a little noise? Cleared a throat? Whistled?

Without missing a beat, Pete asked, "Is it time to go already?"

Frank stepped into the kitchen. "For us, yes. But my daughter looks tortured at the moment, so perhaps she'd like to skip it."

All eyes turned to Cassidy. She wanted to shrink in on herself. "Uh, no. I'm all right. Really. I can—"

Duke smiled. "We're getting along fine, Cassidy. You

don't need to run interference, though Holly and I both appreciate the effort."

Gina hooked her arm through Frank's. "It's not that we don't want your company, but I think Pete has a few more things to say." Gina turned to Pete. "Cassidy has always been an overachieving tomboy. Put her in a dress and she's miserable. She'll be happier staying here and, ah, working things out with you."

Cassidy groaned. Her mother's attempts at matchmaking weren't all that subtle.

Her father sent her a fond look. "My sensible Cassidy. She'll have things squared away in no time."

Just what was she supposed to square away? Pete?

Pete left the ball in her court. "Whatever you want to do is okay by me, Cass."

No way did she want to go, but she'd feel guilty if she didn't. "You've already rented the tux . . ."

"Naw. I borrowed from Gil." Pete flashed her a grin.

"Then it's all settled," her mother said before Cassidy could reply. Behind Pete's back, Gina gave Cassidy the thumbs-up. "We can see ourselves out. Have a nice night, kids."

Her family managed a mass exodus in record time, leaving a heavy silence behind.

Pete zeroed in on Cassidy. "About that dress."

He looked so intent, she started to fidget. "Horrible, huh?"

"Let's get it off you."

So he wanted to head straight to bed? Did he intend to just skip past everything else that had been said? Would he now ignore his statement about adoring her? "In a hurry, are you?"

Pete nodded. "If you strip, I can, too."

Relief sent a grin across her face. Slowly, she pulled the

knot from his tie and opened the top button of his dress shirt. "Poor baby. You're really uncomfortable in this suit." Almost as uncomfortable as she was in the dress. Of course, Pete looked delicious, while she didn't.

"Yeah, but for the right incentive I can suffer through anything." The way he said that left no confusion: he considered her the right incentive.

Using the tie like a leash, Cassidy led him down the hall to her bedroom. Her heart beat fast in anticipation. "Then by all means, let's get you out of it."

He followed along willingly enough, but as Cassidy closed her bedroom door, he said, "About those changes I mentioned . . ."

Did he have to keep harping on that? To distract him she pushed the coat off his shoulders and finished unbuttoning his shirt. "Let's get this off you."

"But I wanted to talk."

"We'll talk in bed." She reached for his belt, and Pete gave up with a groan. The dress pants came off easier than his stiff jeans, and in no time, Cassidy had him buck naked. He looked so gorgeous, and for the moment, he was hers.

Remembering how he'd teased her earlier, chasing her and wrestling with her, Cassidy decided to get back a little of her own. She picked up the length of black tie and beckoned Pete into bed.

His dark eyes glittered. "What are you going to do?"

"Just have a little fun." She patted the mattress. "Put your sexy self right here while I lose my dress."

"Now, there's an idea." With no sign of modesty, Pete stretched out on her bed, his arms folded behind his head, one leg bent. "Go ahead. I'm ready."

Man, he looked good on her sheets. Sighing, Cassidy said, "No you aren't. Not yet." She went to the bed and looped the tie once, twice around his erection. "Leave that right there for a moment."

Eyes wide, Pete stared down at his decorated penis. "Uh, Cass . . ."

After kicking off her pumps, she reached beneath her dress and stripped off the strangling pantyhose. Forgetting the tie, Pete gave her his undivided attention.

Cassidy smiled, pulled her dress up, over her head, and tossed it aside. Now that it was gone, she felt better. She'd burn that thing before she wore it again. Now she stood in front of Pete in her new underwear, and judging by his expression, he liked what he saw.

Striking a pose, Cassidy asked, "Is this the kind of change you mean?"

Pete's gaze was glued to her belly. "What?"

"You want me to change. Does the sexier underwear help?"

As if someone had doused him in ice water, Pete shot upright on the bed. Furious, he growled, "I do *not* want you to change!" Then almost as an afterthought, he said with less heat, "I like the panties, though."

Cassidy propped her hands on her hips. "You said I could change a few things."

He groused and grumbled his way out of the bed to tower over her. The tie remained looped around his penis, the long ends dangling down. Cassidy pursed her mouth to keep from snickering.

Pete didn't even seem to notice. "Not your hair or your clothes." His vehemence made the tie shiver. "Not anything that's *you*."

Cassidy stepped closer and smiled up at him. "That doesn't make any sense, Pete."

He ran a hand over his head, drew a huge breath, and blurted, "I love you, Cassidy McClannahan."

That statement, sort of falling out of nowhere, rendered them both mute. Pete scrutinized her, waiting. All Cassidy could do was stare. She tried to reply, but nothing would come out of her throat. He loved her. Tears threatened.

Seeing that, Pete groaned. "Ah, damn it, Cass, please don't cry."

No, she wouldn't. She sniffed, took several necessary breaths, and licked her very dry lips. "So . . . you love me?"

"I do."

He sounded almost wrecked about it. Here he was, the most gorgeous, wonderful, impossible man she knew, in *her* bedroom, wearing a most unconventional black tie, declaring himself and looking morose about it. Cassidy covered her mouth but she couldn't stifle her euphoric giggle.

Pete's eyes narrowed. "You aren't going to cry now?"

She shook her head. "No." And she smiled.

Clearing his throat, Pete said, "Good." He propped his hands on his hips and took an arrogant stance as if he didn't have a black tie embracing his manhood. "So do you think you could change your mind about wanting a guy in a suit?"

She wanted him. "Maybe. What do you have in mind?"

Pete rubbed the back of his neck. "I did some thinking today. I'm going to get my teaching degree. I only need a few credits—"

Excitement shot through her and Cassidy threw herself into his arms. "Pete! That's wonderful. I've always known you'd make a great teacher."

Pete held her away. "A gym teacher, Cass. No suits."

"Yeah, so?"

Exasperated, Pete shook her. "You want a black tie kinda guy. You told me so, remember?"

Feeling very impish, Cassidy pointed out, "You're wearing a black tie right now."

His expression was comical. He looked down and said, "Damn. I forgot." He reached for the tie but Cassidy caught his hands.

"I love you, too, Pete. Just the way you are. I can be myself with you. If you were a guy like my dad, then I'd need to be a woman like my mom, and I'm not."

"You're beautiful."

Oh, see, how could she not love him? Ready to swoon, she said, "I'm glad you think so."

Pete bent his head and kissed her, long, deep, and the next thing Cassidy knew, they were on the bed. With a little maneuvering, Pete got between her thighs and then she felt the head of his erection pressing in. "I need you, Cass."

"Yes."

He pushed her hair away from her face. "I don't have anything with me."

"Will you marry me?"

He grinned. "That was my next question to you."

"Yes."

"Good." He pressed in, the friction incredible, the pleasure complete. They both groaned. "Do you want a big wedding?"

"My mother will insist."

Pete quickened his strokes. "All right." His arms tightened, holding her closer. "I guess I can borrow Gil's tux again."

"Whatever."

"You want kids?"

"Sure." She barely knew what she was saying, but she knew she loved him and didn't want him to pull away. Not now. Not ever.

"Me, too."

"Pete?"

"Yeah?"

She wrapped her legs around him and arched her back. On a gasp, she said, "Shut up."

"Yeah." Pete slid his hands down her back to her hips and lifted. The position pressed his chest closer to her breasts, abrading her already stiffened nipples. Cassidy cried out at the onset of release.

"I love you," Pete told her again, and that did it. She came, squeezing him tight, moaning and shivering. And just as the wild contractions ended, Pete went taut over her, grinding out his own orgasm. Cassidy knew she could end up pregnant, but it didn't worry her. She was twenty-seven, on track with her career, and now ahead of the game with love.

Pete slumped against her, boneless and breathing fast and hard, giving her all his weight. But she didn't mind. Not at all. In fact . . . "Pete?"

He grunted.

Hugging him, Cassidy said, "I love you in your jeans. And you're pretty loveable naked."

He puckered up enough to press a kiss to her shoulder, then went limp again.

Cassidy caressed the long length of his strong back. "But Pete," she whispered, still a little in awe and more than willing to tease, "the way you wear a black tie is phenomenal."

Two seconds passed before Pete stiffened and shoved himself off her. "Oh, hell." He stared down at his lap where the mangled black tie was crushed. "I think it's ruined."

Cassidy started laughing and couldn't stop. "You *think*?"

He tugged it loose and dropped it over the side of the bed. "I'm going to have to buy Gil a new one."

"Maybe we'll buy ten."

"Ten? Why?"

So happy she was ready to burst with it, Cassidy said, "I've decided I like the effect black ties have on you."

Slowly, Pete grinned. "Fine by me. As long as I don't have to wear the suit with it."

Read on for a taste of Lori Foster's

TOO MUCH TEMPTATION,

coming this August!

Noah Harper stood frozen in the carpeted hallway of his fiancée's house while his skin prickled with some vague, unsettling emotion. It wasn't really anger or grief. It sure as hell wasn't jealousy.

If Noah hadn't known better, he might have sworn it was . . . relief. He shook his head at the thought. No, he'd wanted to marry Kara. He'd accepted it as his fate and even viewed it as part of a grand plan for the future. Not really *his* grand plan, but then, he didn't think in grand terms. His grandmother did.

Noah liked Kara, respected her and her parents, and his grandmother adored her. Almost from the time he'd met Kara, everyone had assumed they'd eventually marry. In one month, they would have.

But now . . .

Without a conscious decision, Noah moved toward the obvious sounds of soft moans, low encouragement, and rustling sheets. He wasn't in any particular hurry, because he already knew what he'd find.

He was wrong. *Very, very wrong.*

Oh, Kara was in bed all right, doing exactly what he'd suspected she was doing: having very passionate sex, when all he ever got from her was perfunctory attendance. It was her partner who was so unexpected.

Not that it really mattered.

Noah's eyes narrowed as Kara gave a particularly ardent moan and bowed her slender body in a violent climax. He watched, unmoved.

Faced with such a bizarre circumstance, Noah pondered what to do, and settled on propping one shoulder on the door frame, crossing his arms, and waiting. Surely he'd be noticed soon enough, and at the moment, his territorial nature rejected the idea of offering them privacy. After all, Kara was his fiancée—or rather, she had been.

That had all changed now.

Her skin dewy from exertion, her eyes dazed and soft in a way Noah had never experienced, Kara leaned back and sighed. "Oh God, that was incredible."

"Mmm," came the husky, satisfied reply. "I can give you more."

Looking scandalized and anxious, Kara purred, "Yes?" and came up on one elbow to smile at her lover.

That's when she noticed Noah.

Kara's beautiful face paled and her kiss-swollen lips opened in a shocked, horrified *oh*. Her lover, with his dark eyes glittering and bold, lounged back in antagonistic silence.

Amazingly enough, Kara snatched up the sheet to conceal her body . . . from Noah.

Noah shook his head in disgust—most of it self-directed. He'd been a royal fool. He'd treated her gently, with deference, with patience. And she'd cheated on him.

"Don't faint, Kara. I'm not going to cause a scene." Noah didn't even bother to glance at the other man—there was no challenge there.

Instead, Noah lent all his attention to the woman he'd expected to be his wife. "Under the circumstances, I'm sure you'll agree the wedding is off."

Kara gasped in panic. Having said his piece, Noah turned on his heel to stalk away. He was aware of the race of his pulse, the pounding of determination that surged in his blood. It wouldn't be pleasant, ending elaborate plans already in progress. The upper society of Gillespe, Kentucky, was about to be rocked by a bit of a surprise.

Kara's parents, Hillary and Jorge, had gone all out on preparations for the celebration. They'd rented an enormous hall and purchased a wedding gown that had cost more than many houses. Guests were invited from around the country, and all of Gillespe was aware of the impending nuptials.

His grandmother . . . God, Noah didn't even want to think about Agatha's reaction. She fancied herself a leader of the community, and she was tight with Hillary and Jorge, treating them like relatives as well as her dearest friends. In many ways, she already thought of Kara as her own.

Noah bounded down the spiraling carpeted stairs two at a time, anxious to get away from the house so his mind could quit churning and settle on a course of action. He'd learned at an early age, while being shuffled from one foster home to another, to make cool, calculated decisions and then to analyze the repercussions so that nothing could ever again take him by surprise.

This time, he had few choices, so his decisions were easy. He wouldn't marry Kara now, but at the same time, he hated to disappoint his grandmother.

He'd just started to pull the front door open when a small hand grabbed his upper arm. "Noah!"

Damn. He'd really hoped to avoid this confrontation. He sighed and turned.

Kara stared up at him with wet eyes and a trembling mouth. Her fair skin blanched whiter than usual, with none of the rosy glow he'd grown used to. She wore only a hastily tied robe that emphasized the swells and hollows of her body—a body he'd once thought very sexy. Her short golden brown hair was becomingly tousled and as Noah watched, she released him and ran a shaking hand over her forehead, pushing her wispy bangs aside.

Her shoulders slumped and she looked down at her bare feet. "I'm sorry."

A cynical smile curled Noah's mouth. He could just imagine how sorry Kara felt right now. How could he ever have considered making her his wife? "Sorry you were caught?"

She clasped her hands together. "There's more than just our wedding at stake, Noah, you know that. My parents . . ." She shuddered. "Oh God, I can't imagine how they'll react. Everyone has been planning for us to marry for so long."

Noah snorted. "Your folks accepted me, Kara, mostly out of respect for my grandmother. I doubt they'll be broken-hearted not to have me in the family. There're plenty of other guys they'd rather you marry and we both know it."

"They love Agatha." Kara looked at him, her expression fierce. "*I* love Agatha."

At least that much was true, Noah decided. "Yeah, my grandmother loves you, too." *Much more than she'll ever care about me.* "You're the daughter she never had, the grand-daughter she wants, the female relative to fill all the slots. She dotes on you, and I doubt that'll change."

Kara swallowed hard. "This will kill her."

The laugh took him by surprise. "Kill Agatha? She'll out-live us all."

"Noah, please, don't do this."

"This?"

Big tears ran down her cheeks and she quivered all over, truly beside herself, pleading. Why the hell did women always resort to tears to get their way?

"Please don't ruin me. Don't ruin my family. I can't bear the thought of everyone—"

Realization dawned, and with it, a heavy dose of disgust. Didn't Kara know him at all?

Noah looked at her sad, panicked eyes and accepted that no, she didn't. She'd have married him, but she didn't really know him.

Just as she'd never really wanted him.

He said, "Hey," very softly, and watched her try to gather herself. Any second now he'd have a hysterical woman on his hands.

Looking at it from her perspective, now knowing what she expected of him, Noah could understand why.

Feeling a surge of compassion, Noah took her delicate hands in his. "Listen to me, Kara. The wedding is off; there's no changing that. But why we ended it is no one's business but our own, all right?"

Her mouth opened and she gulped air. She wiped her eyes on her shoulder, sniffed loudly. "You mean that? You really mean that?"

Hell, he was used to worse hardships than censure. Kara had led a pampered life protected from ugliness, never forced to face the harsh realities life often dealt

Noah had learned to survive almost as a toddler. He could shoulder the heat much more easily than she. "Yeah, why not?" Then he added, "I'll break the news to everyone if you want."

She pulled her hands free and searched in her pocket for a tissue. "I don't believe you." A shaky laugh trickled out. "You're too damn good, Noah Harper."

Now there was a joke. "No, I just don't relish being humiliated either."

Rather than make her laugh, she covered her face and sobbed. "I'm so, so sorry. I didn't mean for this to happen."

"We were obviously never meant to marry, babe, you

know that." It was Noah's turn to glance up the stairs, but her lover wisely stayed out of his sight. Noah shook his head, still bemused by her choice. "Your secret is safe with me."

She threw herself into his arms, leaving him to awkwardly deal with her gratitude. Noah wanted only to escape. Even at the best of times, he'd never totally felt at ease with Kara. She was too refined, too polished and proper—the opposite of him.

Noah set her aside and said, "Maybe you should think about a quick trip, until you have time to figure out what you want to say. I'll wait to tell Agatha until tomorrow, to give you time to get away."

She managed a pathetic smile. "Thank you, Noah. Really."

Kara had just saved him from making a horrible mistake. Though he felt like thanking her right back, Noah merely nodded and walked out. For more than the obvious reason waiting upstairs, tying himself to Kara would have been a disaster.

For one thing, he didn't love her. If he had, he wouldn't be so easy right now. He should have realized that sooner.

As he went down the walk, he felt the sun on his face, the chill of a late spring breeze, the freshness of the day—but he didn't feel hurt or heartsick. He felt no real sense of loss.

For another thing, sex with Kara had offered no more than base physical release. She'd never blown his mind, never burned him up. During their engagement, he'd been faithful, and he'd made do with the few quick, passionless screws he'd gotten from her.

But God, he missed the burning satisfaction of hot, sweaty, grinding sex. He missed the bite of a woman's nails, her teeth, when she felt too much pleasure to be gentle. He missed the clasp of sleek thighs wrapped around his waist and the softer, hungrier clasp of a woman's body on his cock. He missed the throaty, raw groans during a woman's climax.

**Don't miss Lori's Christmas anthology,
YULE BE MINE,
in stores now.**

*Sparkling days, crackling fires, long steamy nights . . .
Christmas is all about making memories. In three delicious
tales of seduction and romance,* New York Times *bestselling
author Lori Foster brings you all the pleasures of the sea-
son—and then some . . .*

Officer Parker Ross hates Christmas, while Lily Donald-
son lives for it. But he's willing to be converted, especially
when Lily is the one doing the persuading.

Sergeant Osbourne Decker suspects pet psychic Marci
Churchill is barking mad, but she's also a knockout. And
when she's accused of stealing a donkey from the local na-
tivity scene, he can't stop thinking about frisking her.

Furious at her cheating fiancé, Beth Monroe decides to
enjoy a payback tryst with his gorgeous best friend, and
finds that revenge is best served hot and sweet . . .

**Read on for a special preview from each of her three
stories in this book!**

"Parker . . ." Lily fidgeted with her hair. "May I ask you something?"

Mesmerized, he watched her delicate fingers as she teased that long, loose curl hanging over her shoulder, twining it around and around. He asked, "What?" and was appalled at how hoarse he sounded.

"It's kind of personal."

His gaze shot back to her face. She looked far too serious and alarm bells went off in his beleaguered brain. "This might not be the best time . . ."

"Why don't you like me?"

Damn it. Her blurted words hung in the air. She looked anxious and young, and Parker wanted to reassure her—then ravage her for about a day and a half.

"Don't be ridiculous." Unable to meet her gaze, he stared down at his plate of food. "Of course I like you."

"But you've never asked me out."

Trying to appear blasé instead of edgy, Parker forked up another big bite of ham. "We're neighbors, Lily. Friends."

She folded both arms onto the table and leaned toward him, giving him a clear shot of her cleavage. His tongue stuck to the roof of his mouth. Lust churned in his belly. Heat rose.

"I'd like us to be more."

A man didn't get to be his age without meeting plenty of women. He'd liked some, he'd lusted after others. A few he'd really cared about.

But none of them had ever looked at him the way Lily did. None of them had ever sent a jolt to his system that obliterated all thought. More times than he cared to admit, he'd gone to sleep thinking of her, and awakened in the middle of explicit dreams.

"I've tried," she pointed out, as if he might not have noticed all the ways she deliberately provoked him. "But you don't even see me as a woman."

Parker did a double take, and sputtered. "That's just plain stupid."

"Is it?"

Gaze dipping to her breasts, then darting away, Parker snorted. "Trust me, Lily. Your . . . *femaleness*, is not something I'd miss."

"Then you must find me unattractive."

He rolled his eyes. She deliberately put him on the spot, but Parker couldn't stop himself from reassuring her. "You have mirrors. You know what you look like." When she remained quiet, just waiting, he huffed out a long breath. "You're beautiful. Okay?"

Pleasure brought color to her cheeks. "Thank you."

"You're welcome."

"So if you like me and find me attractive, why haven't you asked me out?"

A full frontal attack. And at a time when his defenses were down. Stalling for time, he took another bite of ham. Hell, he was too hungry *not* to eat. He swallowed, then eyed her with cynicism. "What's this all about?"

Lily pushed out of her seat and began to pace.

Parker again noted her bare feet. She really did have cute, sexy toes.

Turning to face him, she folded her arms under her breasts and drew a deep breath. "I want you."

A Christmas Present

Why oh why couldn't this be a normal storm? Instead of soft, pretty snowflakes dotting her windshield, wet snow clumps froze as soon as they hit, rending the wipers inadequate to keep the windshield clear. Even with the defroster on high, blasting hot air that threatened to choke her, the snow accumulated.

Refusing to stop and refusing to acknowledge the headlights behind her, Beth Monroe kept her hands tight on the wheel. Let him freeze to death. Let him follow her all the way to Gillespe, Kentucky.

She'd still ignore him.

She'd ignore everything that had happened between them, and everything she felt, everything he'd made her feel.

Oh God, she was so embarrassed. If only she could have a do-over, an opportunity to change the past, to correct mistakes and undo bad plans. That'd be the most perfect Christmas present ever.

A simple do-over.

But of course, there was no such thing, not even with the magic of Christmas. And there was nothing simple about the current mess of her life, or the complicated way that Levi Masterson made her feel.

Finally, after hours that seemed an eternity, her stepbrother's hotel came into view. Beth breathed a sigh of relief. Now if she could just park and get inside before Levi shanghaied her. Ben knew of her imminent arrival. She could count on him to send Levi packing.

Not that she wanted Levi hurt . . . or Ben for that matter.

Fool, fool, fool.

Tires sliding on the frozen parking lot, Beth maneuvered her Ford into an empty spot. After shutting off the engine, she grabbed up her purse, a tote bag loaded with presents, and her overnight bag. Arms laden, she charged from the vehicle.

Three steps in, her feet slipped out from under her. The stuffed overnight bag threw her off balance and she went flying in the air to land flat on her back. Her bag spilled. Wind rushed from her lungs. Icy cold seeped in to her spine and tush.

For only a moment, Beth lay there, aching from head to toe, stunned and bemused. Then she heard Levi's hasty approach.

"Beth, damn it—"

Determination got her back on her feet. She gathered her belongings with haste and then, slipping and sliding, wincing with each step, she shouted into the wind, *"Go away, Levi."*

Harsh with determination, he yelled back, "You know I won't."

Daring a quick glance over her shoulder, Beth saw him ten feet behind her. He hadn't even parked! His truck sat crossways in the middle of the lot to block hers in, idling, the exhaust sending plumes of heated air to mingle in the frozen wind.

Good God, he looked furious!

Beth lunged forward and reached the door of the diner attached to Ben's hotel. She yanked it open and sped into the warm interior. The tote bag of presents fell out of her hands, scattering small gifts across the floor. Her overnight bag dropped from her numb fingers.

Several people looked up—all of them family.

Oh hell.

Why couldn't there have been crowds of non-filial faces? An unbiased crowd, that's what she sought. Instead she found Noah and Ben in close conversation at a table. Their wives, Grace and Sierra, sat at a booth wrapping gifts. And her father and stepmother paused in their efforts to festoon a large fir tree situated in the corner.

Upon seeing her, her father's face lit up. He started to greet her—and then Levi shoved through the door, radiating fury, crowding in behind Beth so that she jolted forward with a startled yelp to keep from touching him.

In a voice deep and resolute, vibrating with command, he ordered, "Not another step, Beth. I mean it."

She winced, and peeked open one eye to view her audience.

Not good.

Levi obviously had no idea of the challenge he'd just issued, or the uproar he'd cause by using that tone with her in front of her family.

And now it was too late.

She hadn't wanted this. She wanted only time to think, to hide from her mortifying and aberrant behavior, to . . . She didn't know what she wanted, damn it, and it wasn't fair that Levi refused to give her a chance to figure it out.

Muttering to herself, she dropped to her knees to gather the now damp and disheveled gifts one more time. As she did so, she said, "Hello, Dad. Hello . . . everyone else." She tried to sound jovial rather than frustrated and anxious and at the end of her rope.

She failed miserably.

With a protectiveness that still amazed Beth, her stepbrothers moved as one. Noah's expression didn't bode well, and Ben appeared equally ready to declare war. Even her calm, reasonable father stalked forward with blood in his eyes.

Plopping her belongings on a nearby booth, Beth held up both hands. "Wait!"

No one did. From one second to the next, Levi had her behind him . . . as if to *protect* her? From her *family*?

Unfortunately, even that simple touch from him, in no way affectionate or seductive, had Beth's tummy fluttering and her skin warming.

She quickly shrugged off her coat.

Levi took it from her, then asked, "Did you hurt yourself when you fell?"

"No. You can leave with a clear conscience. I'm fine." She reached for her coat.

He held it out of her reach. "I'm not going anywhere, so you can quit trying to get rid of me."

The men drew up short. Her father barked, "Who the hell are you?"

Levi turned to face their audience. Positive that she didn't want him to answer that himself, Beth yelled from behind him, "He's a friend." And she tried to ease backward away from him.

"A whole lot more than a friend," Levi corrected, and he stepped back to close the distance she'd just gained.

"Where's her fiancé," Noah asked.

"Busy," Beth said.

"Gone," Levi answered in a bark. He reached back and caught Beth's wrist. His thumb moved over her skin, a gentle contrast to the iron in his tone. "For good."

Confused, Ben asked, "You mean dead?"

"Far as Beth is concerned, yes."

Oh for crying out loud. Knowing she couldn't let this continue, Beth yanked her wrist free and, without quite touching any part of Levi's big, hard body, went on tiptoe to see beyond him.

The masculine expressions facing her didn't bode well.

She summoned a smile that felt sickly. "Hello, Dad. Brandon is fine, but we're not engaged anymore."

Kent Monroe brought his brows down. "Since when?"

"Since she's with me now instead," Levi told them.

"No," Beth corrected sweetly, "I'm not."

Levi half-turned to face her. "Wanna bet?"

His challenge got everyone moving again.

Oh God, she had to do something. "Dad," Beth begged, "I don't want him hurt."

Her father stopped in his tracks. Noah and Ben did not.

But her lovely sisters-in-law took control.

"Noah," Grace called from across the room. "You heard her."

Frowning, Noah paused about three feet from Levi. "I also heard him."

Sierra, a little more outgoing than Grace, raced up to Ben's side and thumped his shoulder. "Knock off the King Kong impersonation, Ben. You're embarrassing me."

"You'll survive." Keeping his eyes on Levi, Ben crossed his arms over his chest and waited.

For reasons that Beth couldn't begin to fathom, Levi stood there as if he'd take all three of them on at once. Idiot.

Determined to gain control, she chanced touching him long enough to give him a good pinch.

"They're my *family*, Levi."

He nodded—but didn't relax.

Fed up, Beth moved around him. "I'm sorry for the dramatic entrance, everyone. Levi is a friend—"

"Damn it, Beth, we left friendship behind days ago."

Beth let her eyes sink shut. She'd kill him. She'd never speak to him again. She'd—

His hand caught her shoulder and he turned her to face him. As if they stood alone, as if he had no concept of privacy or manners, Levi lowered his nose to almost touch hers.

In a voice that carried to every ear in the room, he ground out, "I've had enough, Beth. I mean it. We're both adults, both healthy, and finally we're both single. It's ridiculous for you to be embarrassed just because—"

"Don't!"

But her warning came too late, and Levi had already said too much. Silence reigned as everyone absorbed his meaning.

Then she felt it, the smiles, the amusement, the awful comprehension.

It took three breaths before Beth could speak.

Eyes narrowed, she nodded at Levi, turned to face her family, and announced, "I've changed my mind. Hurt him all you want."

And with that, she literally ran away.

Noah and Ben kept Levi from following.

Do You Hear What I Hear?

Osbourne Decker had no sooner pulled his truck into the frozen, snow-covered parking lot to start his shift than his pager went off. Typical SWAT biz—a barricade with three subjects holding two hostages. He'd grabbed his gear, ran into the station to change so he could respond directly to the scene, and from that point on, the night had been nonstop. Being SWAT meant when the pager went off, so did the team.

After a lot of hours in the blustery cold that stretched his patience thin, they resolved the hostage situation without a single casualty. And just in time for his shift to end. He couldn't wait to get home and grab some sleep.

He'd just changed back into his jeans, T-shirt, and flannel when Lucius Ryder, a friend and sergeant with the team, strolled up to him. Osbourne saw the way Lucius eyed him, like a lamb for the slaughter, and he wanted to groan.

He fastened his duty firearm in a concealed holster, attached his pager and Nextel, grabbed his coat and tried to slip away.

Lucius stopped him. "Got a minute, Ozzie?"

Shit, shit, *shit*. He already knew what was coming. Lucius would be on vacation for ten days—the longest vacation he'd ever taken. He'd be back in time for Christmas, but laying low until then, soaking up some private time with his new wife in Gatlinburg. But the wife was concerned about her loony-toons twin sister.

And that's where Lucius wanted to involve him.

"Actually," Ozzie said, hoping to escape, "I was just about to—"

"This won't take long."

Ozzie thought about making a run for it, but Lucius

would probably just chase him down, so he gave up. He dropped his duffel bag and propped a shoulder on the wall. "Okay. Shoot."

"You think Marci is hot?"

Ozzie gave him a double take. "Is that a trick question?"

"No, I'm serious."

Serious, and apparently not thinking straight. Marci and Lucius's wife, Bethany, were identical twins. No way in hell would Ozzie comment on her appearance. Hell, if he admitted he thought Marci was beyond hot to the point of scorching, well, that'd be like admitting that Lucius's wife was scorching, and his friend sure as hell wouldn't like that.

If he said no, it'd be a direct cut to Bethany, Marci's twin.

"She's a replica of your wife, Lucius, all the way down to her toes." Ozzie shook his head. "You really want to know what I think of her?"

Struck by that observance, Lucius said, "*No*. Hell no." He glared at Ozzie in accusation, then slashed a hand in the air. "Forget I asked. I already know you're attracted to her because you went out with her a few times."

"No way, Lucius."

Lucius warmed to his subject. "I thought you two had something going on for a while there."

"No."

"You were chasing her pretty hot and heavy—"

Ozzie forgot discretion. "She's a fruitcake. Totally nuts. Hell, Lucius, she stops to talk to every squirrel in the trees."

"She does not." But Lucius didn't look certain.

"She even chats with birds." Ozzie nodded his head to convince Lucius of what he'd seen. "She gives greetings to dogs as if they greet her back."

"She's not that bad," Lucius denied, but without much conviction.

"Not that bad? I've heard her carry on complete conversations with your dog!"

Lucius shook his head. "It's not like that. Hero doesn't talk back to her. She just . . . she's an animal nut, okay? She's real empathetic to them, so she likes chatting with them."

"No shit. But she doesn't chat the way most of us do. She chats as if she knows exactly what they're saying, when anyone sane knows that they're not saying a damn thing."

Lucius paced away, but came right back. "It's an endearing trait, that's all."

Because Ozzie loved animals, he might have been inclined to agree. But crazy women turned into insane bitches when things didn't go their way, and he'd had enough of that to last him a lifetime. There was nothing more malicious, or more determined on destruction, than a woman who refused logic. "No thanks."

"Okay, look, I'm not asking you to marry the girl."

"I'm not marrying anyone!" Just the sound of the "M" word struck terror in Ozzie's heart.

"That's what I said, damn it, and keep your voice down."

Ozzie glanced around and saw that the others were watching them, their ears perked with interest. Dicks. Oh yeah, they all wanted to know more about Marci. None of them would hesitate to go chasing after her. In the three months that they'd all known her, more than one guy on the team had tried to get with her.

'Course, none of them had yet discovered her whacky eccentricities. Then again, maybe none of them would mind.

In a more subdued tone, now infused with annoyance, Ozzie said, "Any one of them would be thrilled to do . . . whatever it is you want me to do."

"Bullshit. This is my sister-in-law we're talking about. Any of *them* would be working hard to get in her pants."

True. And it pissed Ozzie off big-time, but rather than say

so, he pointed out the obvious. "And you think I wouldn't be?"

Lucius's eyes narrowed. "Not if you know what's good for you."

Ozzie threw up his hands. "Great. Just friggin' great. So what the hell am I supposed to do with her, if not enjoy her?"

Disgruntled, Lucius growled, "You talk about her like she's a pinball machine."

"Right." Ozzie rolled his eyes. "With a few lights missing."

Lucius drew a deep breath to regain his aplomb.

Ozzie watched him. He really didn't want to get on his buddy's bad side. Lucius stood six-four, and though he was a good friend with a sense of style that leaned toward raunchy T-shirts, he also took anything that had anything to do with his wife very seriously.

"Nice shirt," Ozzie commented, hoping to help Lucius along in his efforts to be calm. The shirt read: WORLD'S GREATEST and beneath that sat a proud rooster.

"Forget the shirt." Lucius glanced at his watch. "I need to get going. Bethany's waiting for me. So do we have a deal or what?"

He had to be kidding.

On an exhalation, Lucius barked, "I only want you to keep an eye on her. There've been a few strange things happening—"

"Like her talking to turtles or something?"

"Your sarcasm isn't helping," Lucius warned him. "I meant something more threatening. Marci feels like someone's been following her. She's not a woman given to melodrama—"

"That's a joke, right?"

"—so her concerns also concern me," Lucius finished through gritted teeth. "And they concern my wife, who won't be able to enjoy our belated honeymoon unless we both know someone is keeping an eye on Marci. Someone I can trust not to hurt her."

"I don't hurt women."

"Exactly." Lucius glanced away. "But I was talking about her feelings, actually."

Seeing no way out, Ozzie crossed his arms over his chest and conceded. "So what's in it for me?"

"What do you want?"

"I very recently inherited a farmhouse from my granny. It needs some work—"

"Done." Lucius stuck out his hand.

Whoa. That was way too easy. "Understand, Lucius. This is an old house. I don't want to just slap up drywall and cheap paint. I want to maintain the original design and—"

"Shake on it, damn it, so I can go."

Ozzie shook, and he had to admit, anticipation stirred within him. So he'd be seeing Marci again. Huh. He had very mixed feelings about that, but mostly he felt—

Rather than release his hand, Lucius tugged him closer to whisper, "Put on your coat. You're advertising a stiffy. And you know, I think maybe you should be wearing my shirt." Then the bastard walked away laughing.

Ozzie glanced down at the rise in his jeans. Cursing his overactive libido, especially where it concerned Marci Churchill, he turned his back so no one else in the room would notice.

He didn't have a full boner, but rather a semi-boner. Though for a man of his endowments, it showed about the same.

And just because they'd discussed Marci.

How the hell was he supposed to watch over her, be close to her, and *not* touch her?

More by Bestselling Author

Lori Foster

Available Wherever Books Are Sold!

Check out our website at **www.kensingtonbooks.com**

Books by Bestselling Author
Fern Michaels

___The Jury	0-8217-7878-1	$6.99US/$9.99CAN
___Sweet Revenge	0-8217-7879-X	$6.99US/$9.99CAN
___Lethal Justice	0-8217-7880-3	$6.99US/$9.99CAN
___Free Fall	0-8217-7881-1	$6.99US/$9.99CAN
___Fool Me Once	0-8217-8071-9	$7.99US/$10.99CAN
___Vegas Rich	0-8217-8112-X	$7.99US/$10.99CAN
___Hide and Seek	1-4201-0184-6	$6.99US/$9.99CAN
___Hokus Pokus	1-4201-0185-4	$6.99US/$9.99CAN
___Fast Track	1-4201-0186-2	$6.99US/$9.99CAN
___Collateral Damage	1-4201-0187-0	$6.99US/$9.99CAN
___Final Justice	1-4201-0188-9	$6.99US/$9.99CAN
___Up Close and Personal	0-8217-7956-7	$7.99US/$9.99CAN
___Under the Radar	1-4201-0683-X	$6.99US/$9.99CAN
___Razor Sharp	1-4201-0684-8	$7.99US/$10.99CAN
___Yesterday	1-4201-1494-8	$5.99US/$6.99CAN
___Vanishing Act	1-4201-0685-6	$7.99US/$10.99CAN
___Sara's Song	1-4201-1493-X	$5.99US/$6.99CAN
___Deadly Deals	1-4201-0686-4	$7.99US/$10.99CAN
___Game Over	1-4201-0687-2	$7.99US/$10.99CAN
___Sins of Omission	1-4201-1153-1	$7.99US/$10.99CAN
___Sins of the Flesh	1-4201-1154-X	$7.99US/$10.99CAN
___Cross Roads	1-4201-1192-2	$7.99US/$10.99CAN

Available Wherever Books Are Sold!
Check out our website at www.kensingtonbooks.com

Romantic Suspense from
Lisa Jackson

Absolute Fear	0-8217-7936-2	$7.99US/$9.99CAN
Afraid to Die	1-4201-1850-1	$7.99US/$9.99CAN
Almost Dead	0-8217-7579-0	$7.99US/$10.99CAN
Born to Die	1-4201-0278-8	$7.99US/$9.99CAN
Chosen to Die	1-4201-0277-X	$7.99US/$10.99CAN
Cold Blooded	1-4201-2581-8	$7.99US/$8.99CAN
Deep Freeze	0-8217-7296-1	$7.99US/$10.99CAN
Devious	1-4201-0275-3	$7.99US/$9.99CAN
Fatal Burn	0-8217-7577-4	$7.99US/$10.99CAN
Final Scream	0-8217-7712-2	$7.99US/$10.99CAN
Hot Blooded	1-4201-0678-3	$7.99US/$9.49CAN
If She Only Knew	1-4201-3241-5	$7.99US/$9.99CAN
Left to Die	1-4201-0276-1	$7.99US/$10.99CAN
Lost Souls	0-8217-7938-9	$7.99US/$10.99CAN
Malice	0-8217-7940-0	$7.99US/$10.99CAN
The Morning After	1-4201-3370-5	$7.99US/$9.99CAN
The Night Before	1-4201-3371-3	$7.99US/$9.99CAN
Ready to Die	1-4201-1851-X	$7.99US/$9.99CAN
Running Scared	1-4201-0182-X	$7.99US/$10.99CAN
See How She Dies	1-4201-2584-2	$7.99US/$8.99CAN
Shiver	0-8217-7578-2	$7.99US/$10.99CAN
Tell Me	1-4201-1854-4	$7.99US/$9.99CAN
Twice Kissed	0-8217-7944-3	$7.99US/$9.99CAN
Unspoken	1-4201-0093-9	$7.99US/$9.99CAN
Whispers	1-4201-5158-4	$7.99US/$9.99CAN
Wicked Game	1-4201-0338-5	$7.99US/$9.99CAN
Wicked Lies	1-4201-0339-3	$7.99US/$9.99CAN
Without Mercy	1-4201-0274-5	$7.99US/$10.99CAN
You Don't Want to Know	1-4201-1853-6	$7.99US/$9.99CAN

Available Wherever Books Are Sold!
Visit our website at **www.kensingtonbooks.com**

More by Bestselling Author
Hannah Howell

__Highland Angel	978-1-4201-0864-4	$6.99US/$8.99CAN
__If He's Sinful	978-1-4201-0461-5	$6.99US/$8.99CAN
__Wild Conquest	978-1-4201-0464-6	$6.99US/$8.99CAN
__If He's Wicked	978-1-4201-0460-8	$6.99US/$8.49CAN
__My Lady Captor	978-0-8217-7430-4	$6.99US/$8.49CAN
__Highland Sinner	978-0-8217-8001-5	$6.99US/$8.49CAN
__Highland Captive	978-0-8217-8003-9	$6.99US/$8.49CAN
__Nature of the Beast	978-1-4201-0435-6	$6.99US/$8.49CAN
__Highland Fire	978-0-8217-7429-8	$6.99US/$8.49CAN
__Silver Flame	978-1-4201-0107-2	$6.99US/$8.49CAN
__Highland Wolf	978-0-8217-8000-8	$6.99US/$9.99CAN
__Highland Wedding	978-0-8217-8002-2	$4.99US/$6.99CAN
__Highland Destiny	978-1-4201-0259-8	$4.99US/$6.99CAN
__Only for You	978-0-8217-8151-7	$6.99US/$8.99CAN
__Highland Promise	978-1-4201-0261-1	$4.99US/$6.99CAN
__Highland Vow	978-1-4201-0260-4	$4.99US/$6.99CAN
__Highland Savage	978-0-8217-7999-6	$6.99US/$9.99CAN
__Beauty and the Beast	978-0-8217-8004-6	$4.99US/$6.99CAN
__Unconquered	978-0-8217-8088-6	$4.99US/$6.99CAN
__Highland Barbarian	978-0-8217-7998-9	$6.99US/$9.99CAN
__Highland Conqueror	978-0-8217-8148-7	$6.99US/$9.
__Conqueror's Kiss	978-0-8217-8005-3	$4.99US/$6.
__A Stockingful of Joy	978-1-4201-0018-1	$4.99US/$6.
__Highland Bride	978-0-8217-7995-8	$4.99US/$6.
__Highland Lover	978-0-8217-7759-6	$6.99US/$9.

Available Wherever Books Are Sold

Check out our website at
http://www.kensingtonbooks.com